LIZ COSTANZO

FLASHBACK

Until Next Time
Book Two

Blurb

Senior Jack Vander Zee seems to be living the dream. He made the All Iowa Football Team, he's the star of his own YouTube show, and it looks like he's getting a full ride to college. Jack's dreams, however, are more like memories…memories of a soldier from the Vietnam War and a girl named Christine.

Ivy Drake moves to Newton, Iowa, for her senior year in high school. Moving senior year is hard, and it's even harder when Ivy starts dreaming about stuff from 1969. The dreams feel more like memories of a girl named Christine and her boyfriend Johnny.

Jack and Ivy meet, and Jack knocks Ivy off her feet, literally, onto the high school track in front of…well, pretty much everyone. Jack and Ivy have an immediate connection that grows stronger as they discover their dreams may actually be memories of another couple from the past. Jack and Ivy try to reconnect in the twenty first century while dealing with frenemies, a potential murderer, and senior year.

Fireborn Publishing Copyright Statement

PUBLISHER

Dedication

To those who served during the Vietnam War, with a special remembrance to the soldiers who fought at the Battle of Fire Support Base Ripcord.

Chapter 1

Ivy

The cornfield dream kept replaying over and over in my mind.

My heart was racing as I fled through the field of corn. Corn stalks seemed to reach out and grab my arms and legs, slowing me down as I ran. I knew I had to escape from someone or something. I just didn't know who or what it was. I glanced over my shoulder looking for the threat. *Damn.* I tripped then started to fall…

Remembering the dream caused my pulse to quicken. How weird was that? Obviously my angst—*angst*, great word—over the move to Iowa was causing the nightmares. Maybe when we actually arrived in Newton, the dreams would end. Endings… Today was definitely about endings.

The lyrics to "Leaving on a Jet Plane"—one of my dad's favorite songs—played in my head. Ironic, or a coincidence, the song was featured last week on *Flashback 1969.* The song was super appropriate for today. It would be even better if the song was "Leaving in a Minivan".

Hmm…just doesn't sound as cool.

Plane or van…didn't matter. Saying goodbye totally sucked. Taking a deep breath, I walked slowly down the driveway. Alex, Erica, Claire, and Audrey were leaning against Alex's car.

"Thanks for coming," I said softly as I tried really hard not to cry. Claire ran up the remainder of the drive and hugged me so tightly that it was hard to breathe. We clung to each other as we walked to Alex's car.

Audrey wrapped her arms tightly around my waist. "I'm

going to miss you so much." She smelled liked cotton candy, super-sweet Audrey.

"Hey, my turn." Alex gently pushed Audrey out of the way. "Ivy and I have been friends the longest. We went to pre-school together."

Then Erica came up and hugged me and Alex at the same time.

"Okay, no more hugging," Audrey said. "We have a present for you."

Alex pulled a large package from the trunk of her car and placed it in my arms.

I tore the wrapping from the package and carefully examined the poster. It was pictures of us. Once again I fought the tears. "This is savage. I love it. I really, really love it."

"Look at this. It's from kindergarten. We were so cute." Erica pointed to the picture.

Glancing at my friends then looking at the photographs documenting our lives together caused a lump to form in my throat. Losing my dad, leaving my friends, moving to Iowa… A girl can only take so much. My eyes started to sting, and I knew I was going to cry…again.

"I think you're missing the most important point," Claire said, pointing to the captions under each picture. "It's to help you review for the vocab on the college entrance exam. We know you love big words."

I wiped my eyes and read the caption under the photograph of our first day of kindergarten. "Oh my God," I said as I started to laugh.

"No, really." I then read the caption aloud: "Alex, Erica, Claire,   Ivy,   and   Audrey   suffer   from hippopotomonstrosesquippedaliophobia   as   they   enter kindergarten."

Alex was sniffing, struggling not to cry as she laughed. "Do you see the irony? We're standing under the word wall. Look. The biggest word is *and*." Alex pointed at the photograph. "I guess when you're five, *and* seems like a big word."

"I did the tie-dye background," Erica said. "We have your two obsessions, big words and the 1960s, with your favorite people…us."

"Hi, girls," Mom called from the top of the driveway. "They have cell phones and wireless Internet in Iowa. I know. It's really quite shocking, but true." She was shaking her head and laughing as she walked toward us. It was great to hear her laugh.

"Come on, ladies. Give me a hug," she said as she embraced each of the girls. "You have been great friends. You know you are always welcome to visit us at our new home. It's only a five-hour drive."

"Look at the poster we made for Ivy, Mrs Drake," Audrey said as she turned it to Mom.

"This is great," Mom said with a smile. "It will be perfect in Ivy's new room. Nice use of multisyllabic words." She paused. "Way to support her addiction."

"Ivy, we need to go. I'll back out the van, and you can give your friends one more hug."

Mom drove the minivan to the street. I opened the back door and put the poster inside. "Bye," I said as I got into the car.

"Wait," Claire shouted waving frantically. "I forgot to give you your reading material." She handed me the latest issue of *Seventeen*. "It's got everything you need to know to start the school year right."

I looked at our house for the last time, then waved at the girls until they were out of sight. Tears rolled slowly down my cheeks as I stared out the window, seeing nothing.

"Well, that was hard," Mom said to the windshield. She reached over, grabbed my hand, then gave it a squeeze.

"Mom, why don't you tell me a little about Newton? I Googled it, but didn't find out much."

"What did you learn?"

"Um, it was on *60 Minutes* in a show called "Anger in the Heartland". I watched the video. It was kind of depressing. The town looked cute, but it looked kind of—I don't know—barren. I also checked out the high school website. I'm really glad you forced me to submit a video for cheerleading tryouts. The captain friended me online, and now I'm friends with the entire squad." I stared out the window for a moment. "Mom, why didn't we visit Newton when Daddy was alive?"

"It's complicated." She looked out the side-view mirror, passed a car, then continued, "You know I have an older sister—or *had* an older sister. Anyway, she disappeared or left town in the early 1970s around the time I was born. My parents would never leave town because they were waiting for her to come home. When I graduated from high school, I was determined to force my parents to leave Newton, even for only a few days at a time. Christine hadn't contacted them in seventeen years. I don't know why they thought she was going to show up at the house one day, seriously." Mom sounded kind of mad. She was apparently a little bitter over the whole thing. *My aunt's name was Christine. Who knew?*

"Anyway, at first, Grandma and Grandpa refused to visit me at college. My sophomore year at Iowa State, my dad started visiting me when he realized I was not coming back. I refused to go home for holidays. Summer? It was pretty miserable. Finally, after you were born, they started traveling together to see you. So, we just never had a reason to go there, because my mom and dad came to our house for the holidays." She paused and took a deep breath, "I know this move is difficult for you. It seemed like the right thing to do. Everything about St. Louis reminds me of your dad. I just couldn't stay. I'm sorry, honey. I wanted to make it work until you graduated, but it was too hard, even hard to breathe. For some reason, Newton was the only place I wanted to live. I actually loved growing up in a small town. I don't think you are going to hate it."

Not hate it. Well, I guessed that was something to look forward to—not hating it. "Well, that's interesting. What do you think happened to Aunt Christine? You've never talked about her before. I don't think I even knew her name."

"I don't know. It was the early '70s. Maybe she hitchhiked to California and joined the peace movement or something. My parents never talked about her, but her pictures were displayed all over the house." Mom stopped talking for a moment. "I named you in honor of her, the sister I never knew. Maybe I thought my parents would stop worrying about my sister Christine if they had another one in the family."

"My middle name is Christina." My mom named me after a sister she didn't know but obviously resented? *Weird.*

"I added the *A* on the end because your dad liked how it sounded. Ivy Christina Drake." Mom turned on the radio. She was done talking.

I was moving to Newton, Iowa.

Maybe it wouldn't be horrible. The girls I'd met online seemed nice, and the pictures of their friends and parties looked like ours. Okay, maybe the picture of people at a party in a barn—a real barn with real farm equipment surrounded by a cornfield—wasn't the same. But different could be okay.

"I love John Mellencamp. I love this song," Mom said, interrupting my musings.

I listened for a moment. "Mom, 'Small Town', really?" I turned up the volume.

"Oh, the irony," she said with a laugh as she play-punched me on the shoulder. We sang…really loud and really badly.

Chapter 2

Jack

"Jack! Jack! Get up here now."

The woman did not respect my work. I shoved my chair away from the desk and carefully placed *Abbey Road* in the cube next to the turntable.

"Jack!"

Damn. Mom was loud, and she had the patience of a friggin' flea.

Taking the stairs two at a time, I made my way to the kitchen. "Mom, you have the patience of flea."

"Take a seat." She pointed to one of the chairs at the kitchen table. "Son, I just got off the phone with Dr Marx. She said you were supposed to discuss your condition with your dad and me."

"Which dad are you talking about, Mom? My real dad? The one who left, who moved to California a couple years ago, or the one you married, whom I refer to as Stan?"

Mom shook her head then closed her eyes. I'd hurt her feelings again. Sometimes I was a real ass. It was easy to play the dad card when I wanted to end a conversation.

"Sorry, Mom. Stan's a good guy. He's just not my dad."

"Okay, Jack. We are not having the 'why your father left us discussion' today. We need to talk about your visit to the doctor." She tilted her head then placed her hands on her hips. "And I know you do the whole *dad* thing when you want to avoid having a conversation. It's not working today, buddy."

"I left the notes on the counter. Didn't you read 'em?" Resorting to sullen and angry seemed like a good strategy as I stood to leave the kitchen. Talking about my diagnosis was a topic I preferred to avoid.

"Sit down, Jack," she said as she pulled the paperwork out of the junk drawer. "I read the notes. Then I looked up Dissociative Identity Disorder on my phone. I still don't understand the diagnosis." She fidgeted with her wedding ring. Fidgeting with her wedding ring was a clear indicator she was upset.

"Dr Marx is not exactly sure why I have memories from the Vietnam War or why I have an apparent fixation on the years 1969 and 1970. She doesn't know how come I suffer experiences of Post-Traumatic Stress Disorder, either. She actually has an opinion on PTSD. The doc thinks that's connected to the Vietnam War memories that I couldn't possibly have."

Stan walked into the kitchen then joined me at the table. "She doesn't seem to know much about anything."

"You got that right," I said to Stan, sharing a nod of mutual understanding. He really was a good guy, but I wasn't ever gonna call him dad.

"Her best guess was Dissociative Identity Disorder. It used to be called Multiple Personality Disorder," I explained.

"And?" my mom said as I paused trying to figure out how to explain DID.

"Basically, Dr Marx believes I had a traumatic event occur during my life that I can't deal with. So, I revert to my 1969 personality and act totally different from myself, like a dude from the 1960s." I waited a moment for their response.

"That doesn't make sense," Mom said as she carefully studied the report that was with the notes. "You always are you. You just have really bad nightmares and sometimes you totally zone out, but you never have a"—she read directly from the report—"'second personality with its own posture, gestures, and ways of talking.'" She looked up from the paper and glanced from Stan to me. "You guys were right. Dr Marx is a waste of time and money. I'm sorry, Jack. I really wanted to help you." Her voice cracked. *Damn.* She was gonna cry. I hated it when she cried.

"Mom, I'm okay," Getting out of my chair, I walked to where she was standing next to the fridge. Wrapping my arms around her, I gave her a hug. Her hug back was so tight that I thought she wanted to squeeze the breath out of me.

"When did you get to be so big, Jack?" she asked, somewhere into my mid-chest. She stepped back and looked up at my face, "Wow, my little boy isn't so little."

I stepped out of Mom's embrace then lifted her out of the way of the fridge.

"And you're strong too," she said as she swatted me with the report she was still holding.

They needed to know I really wasn't okay. Something was wrong with me. I didn't think I had multiple personalities or Dissociative Identity Disorder, but something was not right. "Some of the symptoms," I said as I opened the refrigerator door to grab the carton of milk, "are similar to what I experience."

"Like"—she pointed to something on the paper—"headache, amnesia, time loss."

"Nah, I was thinking more about the drug and alcohol abuse listed in column two," I replied with a grin.

"Jack, you are *not* funny." Mom handed me a box of cereal to go with the milk, shaking her head in disgust as she tried to hide her smile.

"I think the flashback thing is what stands out to me," I continued, ignoring the remark about my comedic talent. "The dreams, or whatever, are phantasmagorical. I wonder if Dr

Marx could hypnotize me to figure out what's really going on?"

Stan looked up from his paper and smiled. "Nice use of the word *phantasmagorical*."

Mom lifted a brow—a sure sign she wanted the definition.

"Probably the best definition connected to what Jack experiences is a constantly shifting complex succession of things seen or imagined. Jack, would you agree?" Stan asked.

I nodded in response to the question.

"Hypnosis might be a good idea," Stan said. "It could also uncover any traumatic events that you might be subconsciously hiding." Mom and Stan shared a look, not sure what that was about. Maybe they thought I actually had had some kind of past traumatic event.

"I guess if I were hiding something subconsciously, I wouldn't know it, hence the subconscious hiding." I didn't say anything for a few minutes. Mom and Stan patiently waited for my reply to the actual question.

"I think I'm up for hypnosis. Can you schedule it for, umm, November?"

"Jack…" Mom said in exasperation.

"Football starts tomorrow. I don't want anyone messing with my head until the season is over." Mom looked at Stan. Maybe she was hoping for support or something.

"This is Jack's decision. If he is comfortable waiting, then we should be too. You sure you're okay waiting? The nightmares seem to be getting worse." Stan studied my face carefully as he waited for my reply.

"Nah, I'm sure. I know you guys think they're getting worse. I kinda think they're getting better."

I didn't believe they were getting better, as in, there weren't less than before. It was the content that was a whole lot better. Lately, the dreams had been about an incredibly beautiful girl who seemed to be as into me as I was into her. Damn. *Into…* That was the 1960s talking for sure. No need to share that with the adults in the room.

"Are we good?" I asked. "If we are, I'm taking the milk and the box of cereal and returning to the basement to finish my weekly show." I paused at the top of the stairs to look back at Stan and Mom, "I make big bucks doing the show. Not sure why, but *Flashback 1969* has some serious Internet crowd appeal."

"Don't spill anything," Mom called as I walked down the steps, back to my basement studio.

I put the cereal and milk on a table away from the electronics. Mom might not want me to spill on the carpet, but I didn't want to spill on my stuff.

My head was pounding again. I leaned back in my chair and closed my eyes. The headaches increased in intensity after I started dreaming about the girl. Now, not only was I messed up with the Vietnam stuff, but the empty feeling in the pit of my stomach grew. It was like I'd forgotten something or someone really important. She seemed to be the key. The strange thing was—okay, seriously, this is *all* strange—she looked familiar. Not like familiar as in "I see her in my dreams of the 1960s and I remember her," but familiar like I've seen her recently.

Shaking my head, I cleared my thoughts. My online show really was making money. I was going to be able to pay for college if I didn't get enough in scholarships. Well, that was if I wanted to go to college. Ironically, I was kind of thinking about the military. I stared at the turntable, contemplating life and music. The music? Well, the music from 1969 seemed to soothe my soul.

I wouldn't be going anywhere if I didn't get my show up

and running. I rummaged through my album collection. *Who should be the featured artist today?* I grabbed the Foundations.

I flipped over the album and read the list of songs. "Build Me Up Buttercup". I checked my list of. There it was, number nine.

Huh? Why hadn't I played this one of the top one hundred from that year before?

I looked up the band on the Internet. My viewers would like the story. The group was from the UK and it was composed of dudes from the West Indies, the UK, and Sri Lanka. *Nice.* I quickly typed up my notes, then found some pics and video to add to the show.

"Hey, Jack's back with your Sunday night edition of *Flashback 1969*. Tonight's featured artist, the Foundations." Talking into the camera, I shared their brief history, adding the video footage and pictures of the band as I talked. The pit in my stomach was gnawing, and I was feeling pretty lightheaded. I just needed to make it through the show. I pulled the album out of the cover and placed it on the turntable. "Tonight we're listening to the Foundations' number nine hit from 1969, 'Build Me Up Buttercup'. To all of you listening, let me know what you think at Flash1969 hashtag buttercup. That's right, hashtag buttercup. Or just leave me a message on the channel. Peace, love, and rock 'n roll." I flashed a peace sign, turned on the turntable, then placed the needle on the album. The song blasted out of the speakers. My head felt like it was going to explode...

*****

Summer, 1969

"How can you not love this song? Come on, Johnny,"

she said as she turned up the volume on the radio in my new Camaro. "I think it's groovy."

"I think *you're* groovy." I reached across the console to pull her into my arms.

Looping her arms around my neck, she smiled and whispered, "It's a great make-out song." She pulled my head down to hers.

"You're right," I replied with my lips nearly touching hers. "I love this song."

"Now, call me 'Buttercup'."

We laughed as she pressed her lips to mine.

*****

Present day

The sound of the needle signaling the end of the album pulled me out of my trance. *Damn.* I gently removed the needle off the album, hoping my album and needles weren't damaged. I carefully examined the album then the needle. It was all good.

I watched the show, made a few edits, then posted it to my channel. I put the album back on the turntable then played the song again. God, it was so elusive. She was so elusive. I knew I knew her. I just couldn't place her. Maybe I should do the hypnosis thing now, before football.

"Jack," Stan yelled from the top of the stairs, "we're going to the Mexican place for dinner. You ready?"

"I'm coming," I replied as I placed the album back in its cover. The gnawing feeling was back. Since I hadn't eaten the cereal, maybe I was just hungry.

Chapter 3

Ivy—Summer, 1969

"Build Me Up Buttercup" played on the radio as I kissed Johnny. I love how he makes me feel when we make out in his Camaro. Actually, I love how he makes me feel when we make out anywhere.

His hands edged up to the bottom of my top. I should say no but I wanted to say yes. I thought all the time about him touching me. I really wanted to let him make it to second base. I really did. On the other hand, I didn't want him to think I was easy.

I unwrapped my arms from around his neck and gently placed my hands on his to stop their upward progression.

"Christine," he murmured against my mouth, "you blow my mind."

*****

Present day

"Ivy. Ivy. Ivy Christina. Ivy Christina Drake. Wake Up. We're almost there." Mom gently pushed on my shoulder.

I peered out the window just as we passed a sign indicating Newton was the next exit. I stretched my legs, my arms, and moved my head back and forth, trying to get comfortable. I picked up my phone and saw a ton of messages.

"Don't start responding now. We need to take in the moment. Absorb the scenery. Pick out the landmarks."

Shaking my head in acknowledgement, I kind of laughed as I surreptitiously looked at the messages.

Surreptitiously? Well, that's a good word for being sneaky. I sent a text to Claire, sharing my thoughts.

"Ivy," Mom said in a slightly disgusted voice. I tossed the phone into my backpack and dutifully looked out the window at the...well, fields and cows. "The scenery looks pretty much like the scenery I was staring at around the time I fell asleep."

"What were you dreaming about, anyway?" Mom asked. "You were smiling in your sleep."

"Hmm, I don't remember. Maybe I got a good score on my ACT." Then I did...I remembered. My dream was not about my score on a college entrance exam. My dream was way more interesting. I was making out with a boy named Johnny in an old car—a vintage car with a boy with a vintage name, kind of funny. Maybe I'd find the boy of my dreams in Newton. I closed my eyes and pressed my forehead against the glass. The boy reminded me of someone.

"Hey, it's the Newton exit. So, look to your left. You'll see the NASCAR race track. Isn't it totally amazing? A NASCAR track in Newton, Iowa. Grandpa said I should be sure to point it out and tell you they are considering powering it with solar energy.

"Mom"—I laughed at her forced enthusiasm—"I love that Newton might be saving the planet with solar, but I want to know when I became a NASCAR fan?"

"Oh, don't be a spoil sport," she said with a smile. "You can Tweet about it to your friends."

I reached for my phone in my backpack.

"Not now. You need to take in the ambiance." She gently grabbed my hand to keep me from grabbing my phone.

"Ambiance? Really?" I shook my head and laughed.

We drove past a Walmart and a few other stores.

"Now"—the pause was almost reverent—"we are going down First Avenue. It's like the main street in Newton. We would drive around First Avenue when I was in high school."

"Drive around?"

Mom glanced at me like I was crazy. "Drive around. How can a daughter of mine not know the definition of *drive around*? Oh, wait, *drive around* is not in the top one-hundred words for the ACT. No wonder you are confused. Well, we would get in cars and drive around town. It was a fun thing to do."

"Oh my God," I whispered, "people drive around for fun. Seriously?"

"Maybe they don't do it anymore. I mean, I'm sure there are lots more exciting things to do since I graduated from high school.

"This is the Newton square," she said proudly. "I worked in a clothing store called Leonard's with some of my friends. Hmm, it's gone now. Lots of the stores are gone. But it looks like they added new stuff, like a coffee shop. Oh," she said, gesturing to a little restaurant with floor-to-ceiling plate glass windows, "that's the Maid-Rite where we would go for cherry Cokes and French fries. I wonder if they're still as good." She sounded kind of wistful.

"Mom," I asked softly, "are you happy to be back?"

"I really am. This was the right choice." She wiped the corner of her eyes then squeezed my hand. "Let's see. Your Grandma and Grandpa's house is"—she turned on her blinker, and we pulled into the driveway of a big white house—"here."

Mom put the car in Park and stared silently at the house. Tears rolled down her cheeks. To my surprise, she placed her head on the steering wheel and started to sob.

This is crazy. My mom is stoic. She never cries.

"It's okay, Mom." I patted her back awkwardly. Stoic: *definitely a word to know for the ACT. Jeez, what kind of daughter am I? My mom is losing it and I'm thinking about the vocabulary section of an entrance exam.*

She pulled herself together then wiped her eyes and nose on the bottom of her T-shirt. She grinned, though her eyes were still teary. "Kind of gross, right?"

"I don't know, Mom. Gross seems a little tame. I was thinking abhorrent, repulsive, or just plain nasty."

"Ha ha."

Well, at least she wasn't crying.

Grandpa and Grandma stepped onto the porch. I waved from the car then grabbed my backpack from the floor.

"Come on, Ivy," Mom said. "Let's do this."

I got out of the car. I stood on the driveway, staring at the Victorian-style house that was going to be my new home.

Home. This place felt like home.

I continued to stare at the house. I had never been to this house but I *knew* this house.

I knew this house…

*****

Summer, 1969

"Come on, Johnny," I whispered. "If we are very quiet, I'll be able to convince the parents we fell asleep on the porch swing. Watch out for the second step," I said, just as Johnny stepped down hard. The creak was so loud that it sounded like a clap of thunder. The porch lights came on in an instant. "It squeaks," I whispered loudly and glanced at Johnny with a grin. He rolled his eyes in response. He's such a hunk.

"Christine," Dad said, "you are thirty minutes late."

"Johnny's just leaving." I reached up and gave Johnny a kiss on the cheek. "You better split."

"You're as fine as wine." Johnny waved, then jumped off the stairs. I watched him race to his car, which was spotlighted by the street light. He leaned against his Camaro, waiting for me to go inside.

"Christine," Mom said, in her angry voice.

"Coming," I called. Opening the door, I turned, then blew Johnny a kiss. He reached up, grabbed the kiss from the air, then pressed the hand that had caught it to his mouth. I'm glad he was parked under the street light or I would've missed the whole show.

*****

Present day

"Ivy, come on, honey."

What just happened? Did I have an awake-dream about the Johnny from the car dream? It was kind of phantasmagorical, a phantasmagorical scene from the 1960s or something.

I waved at Grandma and Grandpa. "We're here," I called as I walked toward the steps. Nothing like stating the obvious.

Grandma stretched out her arms like she was a zombie or something. "Christine," she whispered. "Oh my God," she cried out. "Christine is home. Dave"—she turned to Grandpa—"Christine is home."

Grandpa stood, unmoving, on the top step, as if he were frozen in place. I rushed forward with my arms outstretched as Grandma began to collapse. Mom was faster. She caught her before Grandma tumbled to the ground.

Must call 9-1-1. I snatched the phone out of my backpack and punched in 9-1-1. "Hello," I said to the dispatcher, "my grandma just collapsed. She's breathing and everything, but she's unconscious."

Grandpa grabbed the phone from my hand with an apologetic nod. "My wife experienced a shock. She has probably just fainted, but I'm concerned it could be a stroke." He paused, then nodded. "We live at 115 First Avenue. Thank you."

Grandpa handed me back my phone which I then put it in my pocket. The sound of an ambulance siren pierced my ears.

"Wow, that was fast," I said to no one in particular.

Was this an omen? If it was an omen, it did not bode well for our move to Newton. We're here for like…a minute, and Grandma passed out. That can't be good. *Bode… That is such a great word. Stop with the words. Jeez.*

"The firehouse is just a few blocks away," Mom said as she rubbed Grandma's hand.

The ambulance and fire truck pulled up to the house. The paramedics jumped out of their vehicle and ran across the lawn. They checked Grandma's vital signs.

"Christine. Christine," Grandma mumbled. "Christine is home. Praise Jesus, Christine is home."

I gave Mom a look. She shrugged her shoulders. My mom's name was Suzie, not Christine. Apparently Grandma had my mom confused with her older sister.

"We're going to take her to the hospital," one of the paramedics said. "It doesn't appear she suffered a stroke, but we need to be certain."

Once the paramedics finished asking what seemed like a million questions they gently lifted Grandma onto the stretcher, fastened her on, then rolled her to the ambulance.

"We'll meet you there," Grandpa said to the paramedic as he climbed into the passenger side of Mom's minivan. I climbed into the back as Mom started the car.

"Your mother thought Ivy was Christine," Grandpa said as we drove quickly to the hospital. "We noticed the resemblance at the funeral, but that was over a year ago. Ivy looks just like Christine." Grandpa glanced at me in the rearview mirror and smiled. "Don't worry, Ivy. You look like you, too. The way the sun hit you as you walked across the lawn made the resemblance uncanny."

"I hope Grandma's okay," I managed to whisper. How strange was that? I'd had a trance-like moment about a girl named Christine just as my grandma, and apparently my grandpa, thought I was their daughter Christine? *Weird...definitely weird.*

I've been in Newton less than an hour—so far, not boring.

Mom dropped Grandpa at the emergency room entrance then parked the car. The parking lot was full, so it took a little searching to find a spot. Then we walked in silence to the ER. "Maybe coming back wasn't such a great idea." Mom reached down, then clasped my hand in hers.

"Mom, Grandma is going to be fine. She just had a moment."

Grandma and Grandpa were waiting for us in the ER. "I'm fine," Grandma said. "I just fainted. I'm so sorry, Ivy. For a moment, you looked just like Christine did around the time she disappeared. I'm so sorry."

I nodded in acknowledgment as I reached down to hug Grandma. "That's okay, Grams," I replied. "I'm glad you're okay."

"I'll get the car and be right back," Mom said as she walked toward the exit.

"I am so sorry, Ivy," Grandma said again.

"Seriously, Grandma, you don't need to apologize."

We waited in silence until Mom pulled the minivan in front of the ER doors. I walked next to Grandma as Grandpa rolled her in a wheelchair to the car.

Grandma seemed to be in much better spirits as we approached the house. "Suzie, we put you in your old bedroom. It now has a queen bed. We didn't think you'd appreciate sleeping on a twin." Grandma laughed. "I boxed all of your things and stored them in the basement. When you and Christine—I mean Ivy—move into your new home, you can sort through them then.

"Ivy," Grandma continued, "we made up a bedroom for you in the attic. We hope you like it. If not, we can change it to whatever your heart desires." She took a deep breath. "Grandpa and I are so happy you have come back to town. You know you can stay with us as long as you like, as long as you need to."

"Thanks, Mom," Mom said to Grandma. "Ivy and I really appreciate it."

We pulled in front of the house. The sense of déjà vu was overwhelming. "Mom, have I been here before?" I didn't think so, but still…

"No," she replied. "Why?"

"I don't know," I said. "It just seems so familiar, yet not familiar."

We grabbed a couple of suitcases from the back of the van. I walked up the stairs then into the house, filled with feelings of—I don't know—nostalgia, maybe? Feeling nostalgic made absolutely no sense. I mean, you can only feel nostalgic if you were remembering something.

There was nothing here for me to remember…

Yet, I did. I knew this house. Inside the front door was a sitting room with a baby grand piano. A staircase led to the second floor. The kitchen was in the back of the house. In the kitchen pantry, there would be a cookie jar full of chocolate chip cookies or maybe pecan icebox cookies too. The upstairs had four bedrooms.

I looked at the steps leading to the second floor. Several of the steps would creak. You had to be careful if you were going to sneak out. *Whoa. Where did that come from?* How did I know about the house? I must have been here before. Maybe I came to visit Grandma and Grandpa, and Mom just forgot. Maybe Mom told me stories about her old house and now I remembered.

"You don't think I should sleep on the second floor?" I asked as I started to climb the staircase with my two suitcases.

"You're going to love your room," Grandma said with a smile. "We even added your own bathroom for you."

"Awesome," I said as I climbed to the top of the stairs. Three of the doors were opened. The door at the end of the hall near the steps to the attic was closed. I glanced in each room as I walked down the hall. I wondered why the last door was closed. I placed my suitcases on the floor and turned the handle. The door was locked.

*****

Summer, 1969

"Hurry up," Johnny shouted from the bottom of the stairs.

Boys were not allowed on the second floor of my

parents' house. I laughed to myself. Mom was so square. Didn't she realize we could do whatever she thought we might do upstairs pretty much anywhere? *Oh well.* I closed the door to my bedroom.

"Hold your horses, Johnny," I said as I walked down the stairs. "It's not even dark yet. Drive-in movies don't start until it's dark."

"Wow." Johnny seemed to like what he saw.

"You look pretty groovy yourself," I replied as I admired Johnny. He was boss. I loved everything about him— his black hair, his blue eyes, his really broad shoulders.

"You kids be good at the passion pit," Dad said with a laugh, as he and Mom walked us out to the porch. He tried so hard to be hip, using our lingo.

"Dave," Mom said as she squeezed his arm, "don't call it that. You might give them ideas."

"Goodnight, Mr and Mrs Van den Berg. I'll have her home by curfew. I promise," Johnny said as he opened the car door for me.

"Nice ride," Dad called as he and Mom stood on the porch, watching us leave. "You're going to need to take me for a spin. I bet that Camaro has a bit more under the hood than my old station wagon."

"Sure, Mr V," Johnny replied. "I might even let you drive her."

"Bye, Dad." I waved as we pulled away. Johnny put his arm around me and pulled me as close as he could. The car was out of this world, but it had a console.

Passion pit? Dad was probably right. I shrugged as I snuggled the best I could into Johnny's side. *Who goes to the drive-in to watch the movie, anyway?*

*****

Present day

I sat down on the step with a thump. *What is wrong with me?* I was obsessed with the Johnny from my dreams. He reminded me of someone…I just couldn't place him.

I stood. Then trying not to bang my bags on the steps, I trudged up the stairs to my attic room.

Wow! The room was perfect. I stuck my head out the door then yelled, "I love it!"

"That's great, Ivy Godivy," Grandpa called back.

I took out my phone, took pictures of my new room then sent a group text with the photos to my girls in St. Louis. I re-read my text:

IVY: *Aesthetically pleasing.*

Claire was the first to respond

CLAIRE: *Love the room. Nice use of the Top 100*

ALEX: *Room is great. Top 100*

ERICA: *ACT vocab… Love it!*

I think she meant the room, not the word.

IVY: *Love you girls*

CLAIRE: Flashback 1969 *comes on in 5. You*

love to watch the first post. You don't love us that much.

IVY: Ttyl8r

Claire knew I would hate missing a new segment of *Flashback 1969*. How was I going to survive with my best friends so far away?

I glanced at my phone…four minutes until the new video posted. Sure, I could watch it whenever, but I liked to watch the show when it was first put up. I turned on my tablet. *Shoot.* I needed the Wi-Fi code. *Crap.* My grandparents probably didn't have Wi-Fi. I ran down the steps and into the kitchen. I went to the cookie jar stored in the pantry next to the fridge. "Grams," I said, "hope you don't mind that I grabbed a few cookies. I love these rectangular ones, the icebox cookies. Mmm. Do you have a Wi-Fi code?" I asked, with my mouth full of cookie.

"Yes, we do," Grandpa said, handing me a piece of paper. Grandma was staring at me. I guessed I must have looked like Christine again or something.

"Thanks!" I said as I dashed up the stairs. I quickly typed in the code.

Yes, connected, and I just made it. The familiar *Flashback 1969* logo appeared on the screen.

"Hey, Jack's back with your Sunday night edition of *Flashback 1969*. Tonight's featured artist, the Foundations." I stared at the boy on the screen. That explained it. Jack from *Flashback 1969* looked almost identical to Johnny the dream boy.

Apparently I had a very big crush on a boy I will never meet. *Great.*

Oh well. I turned up the volume. I love "Build Me Up Buttercup". Actually, I was kind of obsessed with pretty much everything from the 1960s, particularly 1969. Obviously Flashback Jack's show was part of my obsession.

I finished my cookies while listening to the song.

In my head I heard myself say, "Now, you can call me 'buttercup'." Where did that come from? I wouldn't want anyone calling me a buttercup.

I took a selfie looking sad then sent a group text.

IVY: *When are you coming to Iowa?*

Chapter 4

Jack—Summer, 1970

"Damn," I shouted at Mike. "Those Huey crews are saving our butts." Wiping the sweat from my face, I watched another Huey fly through a wall of anti-aircraft tracers.

"Is the tear gas theirs or ours?" Mike yelled.

"Not sure," I shouted back. "I think it's theirs. It's probably blinding our pilots 'cause it's sure as shit burning my eyes."

"The napalm is definitely ours," Mike was still shouting as we fired our M60s down the hill through the smoke into what we believed was the advancing North Vietnamese Army I glanced up and watched our jets sweeping low for a napalm run.

I looked down the row of soldiers protecting the perimeter. Maybe twenty of us were still guarding the mountain as we waited to be extracted from Ripcord.

"Holy shit," Mike or one of the other guys shouted. We watched in stunned fascination as fire licked up the 155mm ammunition. When it blew—and it was gonna blow—it was going to be massive.

The ammunition exploded. The noise was deafening. As I took in the situation, I realized we'd lost our defensive position.

"Move out, soldiers," our commanding officer ordered.

"Where in the hell are we supposed to go?" Mike shouted back.

The smoke shifted. "Shit, the NVA are moving up the hill. Man, they look like a swarm of ants," I said to Mike as we moved with the remaining men to create a security perimeter. My M60 machine gun was slung low as I fired from the hip, trying to keep the NVA back so we could board a helicopter and get the hell out of Dodge.

I felt a stinging and burning in my shoulder. "What the…" I murmured as I reached up to check it. Warm, sticky blood seemed to be pumping out. I realized it wasn't my shoulder that had been hit. It must have been my neck.

"Mike"—I groaned—"I've been hit."

"Oh crap," Mike said as he studied my wound, still firing his weapon at the advancing NVA. "We gotta stop the flow, man."

Holy shit…I'm gonna die on this friggin' mountain. I let myself slip to the ground as I continued to shoot at the incoming enemy. Another Huey landed. Mike tried to pull me to the front of the line. We were too far away. The Huey took off before we could reach it. Another quickly approached the landing pad. Only a few of us remained. This one was our ticket out of there.

Mike, the other guys, and I continued firing at the enemy. The smoke cleared for a moment, and we could see the NVA. They looked like they were maybe a hundred yards away.

A hundred yards… That's like one football field. The thought of football triggered a picture of Christine in my head. She was such a babe in her Pacesetter uniform.

"Johnny." Mike was talking to me. I could hear him, but he sounded far away. "Johnny, damn it, do not die. Did you hear me, man? Do *not* die."

*****

Present day

"Jack," Mom said, shaking my shoulder. "Wake up. Come on, Jack. Snap out of it."

I was covered in sweat. I was shaking. There was no doubt about it. I was experiencing PTSD. "Thanks, Mom," I said softly. "It was that dream again."

She walked to the window then opened the blinds. The early morning August sunshine was blinding. "Mom, you're killing me." I pulled the pillow over my head, blocking out the brightness.

"Are you sure you don't want to do the hypnotist thing sooner than November?" Mom asked as she picked up one of my shirts from the floor.

"I'm good, Mom, really. Thanks for waking me up."

"No problem, honey," she said. "Get moving. You don't want to be late on the first day of football." She picked up some socks from the floor. "I heard there's a cute new girl on the cheer squad. Maybe she'll elicit your concupiscence."

"Mom, seriously, you want my lust elicited for some new girl? You're my mother!" I threw a pillow at her retreating back.

"Stan!" I shouted, "Stop teaching her new words. It's embarrassing." I mumbled the last of it. That woman was always trying to hook me up with someone. I pulled on some shorts and grabbed a T-shirt. *Concupiscence.* I smiled, seriously?

Opening my door, I walked into the hallway and right into the twins, who were sitting patiently on the floor.

"Jack, Jack," Stella and Stevie said in unison, "carry us."

"Come here Thing 1 and Thing 2." I scooped them up, holding them under my arms like a couple of sacks of potatoes. If something good had come from the divorce, I considered as I lugged the giggling kids to the kitchen, it was the twins. I was glad Mom and Stan had decided to have kids. Stevie looked kinda like me, and Stella was just plain adorable.

I gently dropped the twins in a wriggling pile on the kitchen linoleum. "Hey, Mom," I said with a laugh, "here are your children." I grabbed a bagel and chugged milk from the carton.

"Jack, that is disgusting. You will not impress girls with manners like that."

"Bye, Mom," I said, giving her a hug. "Bye, brats." I smacked them gently on their butts, resulting in lots of giggles from the heap on the floor.

I got into my truck, backed out of the driveway—avoiding a bunch of kid's toys—then drove down First Avenue. I cut down the side street, taking the shortcut to the high school. *Maybe tomorrow I'll run to practice. The more I run, the better I sleep.*

The team meeting in the gym lobby before the first practice was a Newton High tradition. I guess Coach thought the trophies of football teams past would be an inspiration or something.

I wasn't so much interested in the inspirational speech. I was interested in the grueling practice that was to follow. Like a good run, a grueling practice would drive the dreams out of my head.

"Hey, Jack!" Trey shouted from across the parking lot as he jogged over to catch up. "Are you ready to kick some serious butt this season?"

"You know it," I replied as we entered the lobby.

"This is our last 'ghosts of seasons past' speech. I'm feeling a little choked up," Collin said as he joined Trey and me at the front of the group already formed outside the gym. "As the team captains, we need to see and be seen," Collin said with a laugh.

"Well, boys," Coach said as he walked out of the gym,

"welcome to Newton football. I hope you all are ready for some grueling two-a-days. By the end of two weeks, I can guarantee if you are not men, you will not be playing ball for this organization."

My head started to pound…

*****

Spring, 1970

"Hello, Ladies," Sergeant greeted us with a sneer as we stood at attention in the weak January sun. "Welcome to Fort Campbell. I'm not sure how it happened, but you girls are here to become members of Charlie Company, 2nd Brigade, 506th Infantry of 101st Airborne—next stop Vietnam. Look at you little ladies," he continued as he walked down the row, inspecting our ranks. "After we're done with you girls, you're going to think your time at Fort Bragg in sunny North Carolina was a vacation at a damned five-star resort."

*****

Present day

Trey jabbed me in the stomach with his elbow, abruptly bringing me back to the present. *Maybe I should do the hypnosis thing now instead of later?* I refocused on Coach and the team.

"What's with you?" Trey whispered. "Coach is gonna be pissed if you aren't paying attention to the speech on the great tradition that is Newton High football."

I stood up straight and crossed my arms, "Who says I

wasn't paying attention?" I asked softly. "I was contemplating the heroes of the game."

"Right. *Contemplating…* Seriously, dude, I can't wait till we take that damn test," Trey whispered back as he jabbed me again.

"Now, let's hear from our Captains." Coach gestured to Trey, Collin, and me. "These gentlemen have a few words to share."

We moved to stand next to Coach. Collin and I flanked Trey as he spoke to the team, "You all heard Coach. We walk in the footsteps of giants, and you stand in the shadow of giants." He gestured at me and Collin. "Jack Vander Zee and Collin Clark, captains and two of the three 3A players on the Des Moines Sunday Register All-Iowa Football Team. Who is the third player and your other captain? It's me, Trey Smith. We stand before you, not as individuals, but as part of this great team and part of a great tradition that is Newton Cardinal Football."

"Bring it in, boys," Coach shouted.

The chant started softly, "Huh, huh, huh, huh, huh," as we moved to make a circle in the middle of the foyer. The chant crested as Trey shouted, "Who do you play for?"

"Cardinals! Cardinals! Cardinals!" erupted among the guys.

"Move out," shouted Coach. Trey joined Coach at the front of the line to lead the guys in the traditional run from the high school to HA Lynn Field. Collin and I jogged in place, waiting to bring up the rear.

Collin was jogging in front of the trophy case. He swung his arms back and forth in a crisscross motion, loosening up for the run.

I nudged Collin with my shoulder to get him moving. I

glanced at the case. I stared in stunned disbelief at an old photo peeking out from one of the victory cups. It was her, the girl from my 1969 fantasies. *Well, hell, that explains it.* I'd probably looked at the photo hundreds of times and never really noticed it. So, the girl wasn't someone I knew. She was just a photograph imprinted on my subconscious. She was probably older than my mom. That was just sick.

I shook my head and kinda laughed. "C'mon, Collin. Let's get moving."

We left the gym then ran to the street. It was a pretty decent jog to the football field. As my foot hit the pavement, my head began to pound. I thought about the girl in the photograph...

*****

Fall, 1968

"Johnny, let's split," Christine said with a smile as she grabbed my hand and tugged me away from my seat at the table surrounded by all the seniors on the team.

The guys hooted and hollered as I followed Christine out of the restaurant. It was kinda chilly, so I slid out of my letterman's jacket and placed it around her shoulders.

"Thanks," she said as I pulled her against me then wrapped my arm around her. "You guys played so good tonight," she offered as we walked past the cinema toward my car. "My throat hurts a little from all the cheering."

I grinned as I rested my chin on top of her head. "I was a little distracted by this one Pacesetter who was dancing at halftime," I said. "She really knew how to shake her pom-poms. And those high kicks..."

"Johnny," she said as she tugged my arm tighter around her, "just whose pom-poms were you admiring?"

I gently pushed her against the truck and caged her in with my arms. "Oh baby, you know whose pom-poms I like," I said as I leaned down to kiss her.

*****

Present day

Collin grabbed my arm, pulling me from the street to the sidewalk with a fast jerk. "Damn, Jack," Collin said as we waited for a couple cars to pass before crossing, "you could have been killed, dumb ass." Collin started to sprint. I quickly caught up then passed him.

"Hey, I heard there was a new girl on the cheerleading squad. You know, the one the girls were pissed about 'cause she made the squad with a tryout video. She's friends with Bri online. I saw her picture… Pretty hot."

I ignored Collin. What was it with everyone? Why were they always trying to get me interested in some new chick? *Damn… Chick?* Seriously. I gotta get my brain out of the 1960s. Maybe I do have that disorder the doctor was talking about.

Collin and I sprinted past the boys who were slightly in front of us—the super slow dudes, for sure. "Come on," I yelled at the guys we were passing. "Run."

When we reached the field, I bent over to catch my breath near the concession stand. Collin was also breathing real hard. He leaned over next to me.

My hands were braced on my knees as I watched the other guys pass through the gate. They definitely needed more training. I lowered my head and inhaled deeply…

*****

Spring, 1970

"That wasn't so bad," said the guy bent over next to me, catching his breath from our six-mile foot march. "I'm Mike."

I glanced up from my hunched-over position. "I'm Johnny. Nice to meet you."

"Attention," Sergeant shouted. We picked up our packs and moved into a couple of straight lines. "The six-hour foot hike was nothin', fellas. Now I'm gonna inspect your packs."

I stared straight ahead, hoping I'd included everything on the list. If I was going to be in the Army, I wanted to be part of the 101st.

*****

Present day

"Jack, come on. You're hardly even winded."

I stood up and grinned at Collin. *What the hell. I'll just embrace the insanity.*

"Just wanted to give you plenty of time to recover, old man," I said as we walked into the equipment room that was located underneath the bleachers.

Chapter 5

Ivy

"Bye, Mom," I said as I got out of the car in front of the entrance to the football field. "Practice ends at eleven." I waved as I turned away from the car.

Weird. This football field seemed oddly familiar, yet not, like my grandparents' house. Mom must have brought me here at some point in my life, and she just didn't remember. I stared at the street side of the white-painted concrete bleachers. I felt a little dizzy. I reached out and placed my palm on the wall for support…

*****

Fall, 1968

"I love our uniforms," Cindy said as she rubbed her glove-covered hands down her red velvet dress. "The elbow-length gloves, the knee-high boots, the short red dress… They're so much cuter than the cheerleaders' uniforms."

I agreed with Cindy, but I didn't say anything because I didn't want to be disloyal to my friends on the cheer squad. Johnny loved the uniform too. Actually, I corrected myself, he loved the uniform on me. He thought I looked like a go-go dancer.

We stood by the entrance to the stadium, ready to perform our very first routine during the halftime show. I was disappointed that we'd had to miss the first half of the game, but our dance team sponsor wanted us to make a dramatic entrance.

"Line up, girls," one of the seniors said to the group. We

made two lines as we prepared to strut in perfect formation from the entry gates onto the field. The buzzer sounded. It was halftime. The team came off the field. Cindy grabbed my hand and squeezed.

"Ladies and gentlemen, it's my pleasure to welcome the Newton High School Pacesetters to the HA Lynn Field for their inaugural performance."

*****

Present day

"Hey," said a girl in red shorts and a white Newton High Cheer T-shirt from behind me, startling me out of my trance, "you must be Ivy."

"Yes, and you're Bri. You look just like your profile picture." We walked into the stadium and onto the track, I shook off the awake-dream thing and asked, "So, are we conditioning today or starting to practice cheers and stuff?"

"We'll do both. We practice at the far end of the field," she said, gesturing to the goal post where I could see a bunch of girls stretching out. "The Pacesetters, our dance team, doesn't practice now because they need the field and the band for their routines. The football team practices now, too. I scheduled our cheer practices so they end when football ends. My boyfriend, Collin, usually drives me home. Today the guys started practice at the high school, so I'll be giving him a ride back to school."

"Sounds good." I wasn't sure what response she was hoping for. Maybe she was trying to let me know Collin was taken, or Collin played football, or she had a car? Who knew? Did she say something about the Pacesetters? That was the name of the dancers in my dream thing. *Weird.*

We walked on the track then stopped when we reached the other girls. "Hey, girls," Bri said in a loud, attention-grabbing voice, "this is Ivy."

A chorus of "Hi, Ivy," came from the girls sitting on the ground. I sat down and started stretching.

"Here come the boys," said one of the girls seated near me. "I'm hoping Jack will notice me this year," she continued as she pulled her shirt down so her V-neck exposed more boobage.

"Katie isn't after Jack for his mind," Bri said with a laugh. "Katie, you've known Jack since kindergarten. I don't think this year is going to be any different than last year."

"Or the year before that," said another girl seated near us. "I'm Chloe, by the way. If you can tumble like you did on the video, we definitely have a chance of winning State."

Bri stood up and studied the guys running onto the field. She waved in the general direction of the players and one of them waved back. That must be Collin.

"Personally"—another girl stood up and walked over to Bri—"Jack is going to be my guy this semester. He hasn't been with anyone. It's about time for him to get a girlfriend—or at least get *some*," she said with a laugh as she emphasized the "some".

"I guess Jack must be kind of hot?" I asked from my spot on the ground.

"Oh my God," Katie said, "he is *so* hot. He just keeps getting hotter."

Jack was probably a stuck-up tool. But, if these girls thought that was hot? Well, good for them. I'd be super happy if I met my Flashback Jack, but I'm guessing he lived in LA or NYC or some hella cool city.

"Did you leave a guy back home?" Bri asked.

"No. I've known most of the guys at my old school since

we were little kids. I had a lot of great guy friends, though."

"They probably thought you were stuck up or something." A girl I hadn't met added to the conversation.

"Do I seem stuck up to you?" I asked, totally surprised by her comment. I didn't think anyone thought I was stuck up. *What would* Seventeen *suggest for this situation? Awkward.*

"Well, you're really pretty and you have a great body. Of course people think you are stuck up. Oh, and your hair... You must have extensions or something. Who has hair like that?" the girl asked.

I touched my pony tail, wondering why she thought I had extensions. My hair was just long. "I'm sorry," I said, changing the subject, "what did you say your name was?"

"My name is Alexis. You're the reason my best friend is no longer on the squad, and I doubt you can do half of the stuff that's on the video." Her words were filled with disdain.

"I'm sorry about your friend," I responded sincerely.

"You know," Alexis continued, "lots of us think that was not you. I mean, seriously... You tumbled like you were doing a floor exercise routine at the friggin' Olympics."

I looked at Bri. "You girls think I sent a fake video?"

"Well..." Bri replied, looking at her feet rather than at me.

"Come on, Bri," Katie chimed in. "You said you didn't think anyone in high school could tumble like that."

Wow. I looked at the girls seated around me. I'd certainly made a mistake thinking these girls were like my friends at home. The only word I could think of to describe them was...well, mean. "All righty then," I said as I stood up then did a bridge to stretch out my muscles. "Give me a minute to warm up, then I'll do a tumbling pass for you."

I jumped up and down on the track as I tried to get the

feel of the surface. The football players and coaches were all on the field, leaving the track clear. I stretched to the left then the right as I put the tumbling pass together in my head. I had about forty yards from where I was standing to the fifty-yard line. *I'm thinking round off, handspring, full, round off, a couple more handsprings and a double. Fun.*

I glanced behind me. The entire squad was standing in a semi-circle with their arms crossed, waiting for me to fail. *Silly girls.* I shook my head and focused on the pass. Taking off at full speed, I hit the round-off with power. It was just me and a lot of track.

A shrill whistle broke my concentration as I was heading into the double. *Holy crap. I'm going to hit a big white wall.*

Chapter 6

Jack

"Jack," Coach said, walking toward me while I was stretching a little and trying to get the feel for the pads, "let the kid over there throw you some passes before we get the warm-up going. We're waiting for a few more guys to get their gear on."

"Sure, Coach," I said. "You looking for a backup for Trey?"

"Just looking for potential," he said with a grin, then slapped me hard on the pads.

"Hey," I yelled to the freshman standing by a butt-load of footballs, "Coach wants me to try out your arm."

The kid looked around, trying to figure out who I was talking to. Shaking my head, "You. I'm talking to you." *Dumb ass.* The kid was a dumb ass. I decided not to call him one though. He was just a freshman. It would probably intimidate him or something.

He threw the first pass. "Not bad," I shouted as I caught it. Not spectacular though.

"I'm going long," I yelled, then started down the field.

The kid threw the pass. "Damn," I said as I followed its trajectory. The ball was heading for the cheerleader tumbling down the track. I ran for it with every bit of strength I had. It was like everything was moving in slow motion. I could see what was going to happen. The girl was going to be nailed by the ball, and it wasn't going to be pretty. I leaped over the bench and stretched, knocking the ball out of the way.

I turned just as she was coming down from her last flip thing. *Umph.* She nailed me in the chest. I wrapped my arms around her, tucking her head under my chin. I was a football player. I knew how to land after a hit. I hoped my pads would absorb the impact.

We hit the track hard. The impact sort of reverberated through my entire body. We came to an abrupt stop. I laid my head on the ground, staring up at the sky. My body felt all…I don't know. It tingled where the girl's body rested against mine. I didn't think it was a medical condition, like I was paralyzed or something.

She didn't lift her head, but I could feel her breathing. I could feel her heart racing.

Chaos erupted around us.

"Is Jack okay?" a voice asked.

"Who's the girl?" another voice wondered.

"Is she okay?"

The questions were coming from all sides. For some reason, I didn't want to move.

"I want you to tell me no one is standing in a circle staring at us," she said softly. "It is okay if you prevaricate."

I didn't know how to respond, so I didn't say anything. I thought she'd just used *prevaricate* in a sentence. *Impressive.*

"Oh my God," the girl said, trying to loosen my grip. "You're unconscious, and I've just been lying here like a piece of dead wood."

"I'm fine," I whispered. "I just didn't want to prevaricate about the gawkers. I never lie."

"Jack, Jack," Collin shouted in my ear. "Dude, are you okay?"

"Yeah," I replied. "We're just trying to catch our breath here. I'm also working on regaining my hearing. Dude, you're friggin' loud."

"You can loosen up the grip on my head now," the girl

said.

I slowly removed my hand from where it held her head against my chest. It was kind of painful. Not physically painful, but emotionally painful, whatever the hell that meant. "I think it was fortuitous I was in your path. Otherwise you would have been nailed by the football." Damn, I had just said *fortuitous*. *Now she's going think I'm a tool.*

"Fortuitous..." she repeated softly. "It certainly was fortuitous," she said as she pushed herself up against my chest, kind a like she was doing a push up and my body was the exercise mat. My hands held onto her hips loosely, not wanting to let her go. Though people were shouting and talking around us, it felt like we were in a bubble, just me and the girl.

She leaned down and I looked into her face for the first time. I couldn't breathe. I was looking into sparkling green eyes, into the face of the most beautiful girl I had ever seen. It was her, the girl from my dreams. Damn, she looked like the girl in the old photograph too. This girl, however, was definitely not older than my mother, I considered, remembering how the picture had sort of freaked me out.

The girl stared at me, not saying a word. Then she kind of whispered, "Oh my God, it's you. It's really you."

I reached up and pulled her head down to mine and I kissed her. It was crazy. It was like a first kiss, because it was. It was also the kind you gave to someone who'd been away a long time, and you were reuniting. Whatever the kiss was, I decided it was not going to end anytime soon.

"Jack, Jack Vander Zee," a voice shouted. "Dude, you don't start making out with a girl on the track in front of the entire football team and the cheer squad. Get up, dumb ass. Do you even know who she is?"

The voice was Trey's. *Right now Trey is the voice of*

reason? Trey was *never* the voice of reason. Something must really be wrong here. I kissed the girl of—or from—my dreams one last time, to hell with the spectators. She looked a little dazed as I rolled over and pulled her to her feet.

"Hi, I'm Jack Vander Zee, the dumb ass who did not mean to embarrass you in front of"—I kind of gestured with my hand—"all these people."

She looked up at me and grinned, even as a blush stained her cheeks. She was truly the most beautiful flesh-and-blood person I had ever seen. Her dark brown hair was coming out of her ponytail, and I wanted to kiss her again.

"I'm Ivy," she said, extending her hand like she wanted to shake hands or something, "I'm so sorry I tumbled into you. I hope I didn't hurt you." I clasped her hand in mine so she couldn't walk away.

"Jack," Coach yelled, "if you aren't injured, get your butt on the field. Nice job saving the girl from the errant football, by the way. I guess the kid's going to need a little more practice."

"You got that right, Coach," I replied.

"Ivy," I said, "can I give you a ride home from practice?"

She studied me for a moment. "Sounds good. Thanks again for your fortuitous actions saving me from the football." The word *fortuitous* rolled off her tongue. It was friggin' sexy. *Damn.* I was feeling pretty concupiscent. Mom had actually picked the perfect word.

"My pleasure," I replied as I reluctantly let go of her hand. I turned to walk away, but I couldn't leave her. I closed the space between us. "I've got to kiss you again."

I pulled her against me and kissed her softly at first. Then I licked her lips with my tongue before slipping it into her mouth. Her tongue rubbed against mine. *Damn.* That girl could kiss.

A football knocked me in the back of the head.

"See you after practice," I said as I rubbed my head and jogged back on the field, trying not to trip over my own feet. I glanced at her again. One thing was for sure…I didn't want to let her go.

*****

Late Winter, 1970

The bus pulled to a halt in front of the station. I stood with several other recruits as we waited to board the bus that would take us to basic training. I had my arms wrapped tightly around Christine.

"Let's go, soldier," the recruiting officer said, indicating I should let go of Christine. I bent down and kissed her.

The door to the bus opened. This was it, and this was goodbye. I turned to walk away, but I couldn't move. I closed the space between us. "I've got to kiss you again," I said as I pulled her against me. I didn't want to let her go.

*****

Present day

Collin pounded me on the back, "Smooth move with the new girl. As far as pick-up strategies go, that, my friend, was sick. Dude, I can't believe you laid one on her in front of Coach and everyone. Shoot, even Wild Willie"—Collin gestured to the school's handyman, who was working on the announcer's booth—"saw the public demonstration of affection."

I grinned at Collin then knocked him hard on his pads. Turning, I glanced at the stands, waving at Willie, who was standing near the announcer's booth. I shoved Collin with my shoulder. It seemed like a bad idea to jump and yell, *yes*. Instead of making a bigger ass out of myself than I already had, I jogged over to where Coach had gathered the team to start practice.

"Are you ready to focus, Vander Zee?" Coach asked. He looked like he was trying not to laugh.

"Yes, sir," I replied. The whistle blew. It was time for some mind-numbing exercise. I dropped to the ground to complete my first series of up-downs. A tough practice might not keep the Vietnam stuff out of my head, but Ivy? She could.

Chapter 7

Ivy

Hmm. Shaking my head in bewilderment, I walked away from Jack Vander Zee. For a moment I imagined he was Johnny from my dreams. My head was still ringing from the impact, or maybe it was ringing because a guy I'd just met kissed the breath out of me. Still feeling a little breathless, I inhaled deeply as I walked toward the squad. He was a great kisser, used the word *fortuitous*, and knew the meaning of *prevaricate*. That was so hot. I considered the idea I might actually be sapiosexual. Maybe I was attracted to him for his intellect. Then I recalled his blue eyes, dimples, and the feel of his rock solid abs... Maybe I was more than sapiosexual.

Tumbling into Jack was not going to win me any friends. Well, he had actually kissed me. *Stop trying to justify it. You kissed him back.*

"Well," Katie huffed, "you certainly know how to make an impression. Thanks a lot for ruining my chances with Jack this year."

"Seriously," said the girl who wanted to give "some" to Jack. "I wouldn't have shared my plan if I'd thought you would put it into action right here at practice. I hope you enjoyed your walk of shame from the fifty-yard line."

Well, welcome to Newton. These girls were certainly rancorous. *Rancorous* sounds so much better than bitchy.

"Listen, girls," Bri said.

This ought to be good. My new best friend was surely going to say something I'm going to wish she hadn't.

"First, we challenged Ivy to do a tumbling pass, which, I might add, was pretty amazing. We are *so* going to win State."

Bri clapped her hands with excitement. "Second, as much as I admire a girl who uses unorthodox strategies to get a guy, Ivy had no intention of knocking Jack on his butt. From where I was standing, Jack was the one who initiated the kiss, not Ivy. And, I have it all recorded on my phone. Yay me! I can't believe Jack Vander Zee kissed you in front of…well, everyone. He is so not like that. I can't wait to talk to Collin about it."

Bri just couldn't stop talking.

"So, girls, get over yourselves, leave Ivy alone, and let's work on being the most epic cheer team Newton has ever seen."

"Thanks," I said to Bri, I was so shocked she'd defended me.

"I'm sorry," she said. "We were pretty upset about Becca not making the team. Sorry I doubted your mad tumbling skills. Ladies," Bri shouted, taking charge of practice, "two lines. Shorter girls need to be in the front and taller girls in the back. We're going to run through chants first, then work through the cheers."

Bri looked at me, "Just follow along. I'm sure you'll catch on quickly."

Chant followed chant, cheer followed cheer. Luckily, many of the chants and cheers were the same as my old school's with just a few changes. I needed to concentrate, but all I seemed to be able to think about was Jack and our kiss. Not glancing at the football team was pretty hard.

"Break, ladies," Bri shouted after we finished a pretty complicated stunt. I tried not to be obvious when I glanced at the players while taking a drink from my water bottle. I pulled up my T-shirt and wiped the sweat from my face on the bottom of my shirt.

"Focus, Vander Zee," I heard someone shout from the field. I looked up just as a football hit Jack in the back. I guess he was trying not to watch me just like I was trying not to watch him.

"Jack never loses focus," said one of the girls—I think her name was Chloe—with a grin. "That must have been some kiss."

"Okay, ladies"—Bri called us back together—"I need to go over the practice schedule, uniform distribution, and a bunch of other stuff. Let's go to the shade."

We grabbed our bags and water bottles and walked into the shade on the side of the bleachers. The boys were leaving the field and heading into the showers, I guessed. *They must have a locker room under the bleachers. That's kind of cool.*

I glanced at my phone. Only five more minutes of practice. What was I going to talk about on the way home with a boy I'd just met? Butterflies fluttered in my stomach. Luckily it was a short drive.

"Okay," Bri said, "that's it. See you girls tomorrow."

Somehow I'd missed the entire info session. That was bad for a new girl. I put the paperwork into my cheer bag. I would read it later.

Shoot. I grabbed my phone to text my mom. I'd forgotten to tell her not to pick me up from practice. Sending the text, I glanced around the field, trying to take it all in. The football field was pretty amazing for a small town. The home bleachers were white concrete, which was kind of interesting. *Hmm.* A man was in the announcer's booth as the top of the bleachers. I guess the announcer's booth had to be prepared for the season too. The Cardinal head in the middle of the field looked like something from a college. *Football must be big in Newton. Damn.* The dizzy feeling started again…

*****

49

Fall, 1968

Standing outside the gate with Cindy, I waited patiently for Johnny. "Our Pacesetter routine was outta sight. The high kicks definitely distracted the other team. I think I'll tell Johnny he can thank our fab dancing skills for the Cardinal victory."

"You're so lucky," Cindy whispered. "Johnny's such a hunk."

I smiled as Johnny walked through the gate, toward me and his truck. "Hey, Cindy," Johnny greeted Cindy as he pulled me into his arms. "Give me a little sugar, sugar." He grinned as he kissed me.

"We're gonna meet the guys at Midtown Cafe. Do you want to change out of your uniform?" Johnny asked as he opened my door and I slid into the seat.

Before he pulled away from the curb, he paused and stared at the field. "You know what I love?" he asked, looking at the bleachers, not at me.

I followed his gaze. "Football… You love football."

"Nah, babe, I like football." He paused, then turned toward me with a smile, his blue eyes sparkling under the dim interior lights of the truck. "You. I love you."

*****

Present day

"Hey, Ivy."

Jack's voice brought me back to the present. *Could he be any hotter?* The answer was no, absolutely not. His black hair was glistening from his shower, his skin was lightly tanned, and his T-shirt emphasized his broad shoulders. He glanced around and caught my eye, then he smiled. Nope, I was wrong. Jack smiling was super-hot. He had dimples, really white teeth, and his blue eyes sparkled.

Jack stood in front of me, looking down. We stood there, staring at each other for what seemed like forever. It was awkward but not uncomfortable. My heart raced as I thought about kissing Jack again. I wasn't sure, but it looked like he maybe wanted to kiss me, too. "*You. I love you.*" The last words spoken from the boy in my awake-dream crashed into my head. I was overcome with—I don't know, longing?—but longing for who?

"Dude," Collin called. "Bri's going to give us a ride back to school."

Jack reached up and tucked a loose strand of my hair behind my ear. "Okay, so I just realized my truck is at the high school."

"No problem. I can call my mom." I hoped he couldn't hear the disappointment in my voice as I pulled out my cell to call her. Jack clasped my hand to stop me.

"I was hoping you would ride with me back to the high school to get my truck. Bri's good with it," Jack said, gesturing toward Bri and Collin. I wasn't confident that Bri was ready to be my new BFF or even want me in her car.

"I don't mind," Bri said, reading my mind. "I have to drive Collin back too. It'll be my official apology for being a bitch. I really am sorry," she continued as we walked toward her car. When we reached it, Jack opened the door for me. I looked up at him and smiled.

Jack clasped my chin. My mind kind of stopped processing and my heart started to race. He held me firmly in place and kissed me. *Well, crap.* We needed to talk and stuff.

This was going too fast.

"Just checking," he said as he kind of helped and kind of pushed me into the car then quickly climbed in behind me. "Just checking to make sure it was as epic as I remembered it," he said as he casually placed his arm around my shoulders, pulling me into his side. "It was even better."

I tried to scoot away. I didn't want Bri, Collin, and Jack to get the impression I was easy or something. Though, if I were easy, it would be easy to be easy with Jack. Now I was totally losing it.

"Don't fight the inevitable." Jack laughed. "It's in the stars. We are destined to be together. Why fight it?"

"Okay," I said. "I don't even know how to respond to that, but I really like your use of the word *inevitable*." *Jeez, I just complimented the hottest guy I'd ever met on his word usage. I am so basic.*

Jack was undaunted by my...um, compliment. "It's inevitable that you're going to be my girlfriend. This is not ephemeral, and I'm not being impetuous."

"Well, hot damn," Collin declared from the front seat. "I'm not sure about all the other shit Jack said, but Jack just declared Ivy was his girlfriend." He turned in the passenger seat so he could really look at me. "After a whole what? Five minutes? You must be one helluva kisser, girl."

Bri laughed. "Collin, have I introduced you to my new friend Ivy. She pissed off half of the cheer squad. I really like that about her. Here's the high school." Bri continued, "The guys are parked in the back by the gym entrance. You're really going to like it here. Sorry if we gave a bad first impression. Lucky for us, it appears Jack made a really good first impression."

Bri really does ramble. I smiled at the back of my new

friend's head.

The car came to halt beside a red Ford truck. "Thanks for the ride," Jack and I said at the same time. We looked at each other and smiled.

Seventeen would say it's just infatuation, and it will fade quickly. As Jack helped me into his truck, I thought *Seventeen* might be wrong. After all, Jack said the attraction wasn't fleeting, and he wasn't being impulsive. I, for some reason, felt the same way. He had a sick vocabulary and a real truck. I didn't know any guys who drove trucks. Dizzy, I closed my eyes. Not now…

*****

Summer, 1969

"I can't believe you traded in your truck and purchased a sports car," I said to Johnny. "Your dad was okay with this?"

"Sure. All farm boys need a sports car," Johnny said as he opened the car door. "Your chariot, madam," he announced as he held my hand, assisting me into his 1969 Camaro. He walked around the car to climb into the driver's seat. He grabbed my hand then kissed my knuckles. "Since I'm staying home to help on the farm while my brothers finish school, Dad helped me pay for it."

I looked out the window and decided to share my biggest fear. "Johnny, you won't be eligible for deferment if you don't go to college."

"Christine, look at me," Johnny said as he gently clasped my chin and turned my face toward him. "The war in Vietnam has been going on for a long time. It's got to be coming to an end soon. The chances of me being drafted get smaller every day. I'll be home with you. We'll be able to go to University of Iowa or Iowa State together after you graduate. It's gonna be fine."

Taking a deep breath, I looked into Johnny's handsome face. "If you get drafted and die, I'm going to kill you."

"What?" Johnny said with a grin. "If I die, you're going to kill me? Seriously, Christine?"

"I love you, you big dummy," I said as I pulled his head down for a kiss.

*****

Present day

"Ivy. Hello, Ivy. Anyone in there?" Jack asked as he waved his hand in front of my face.

I was startled back to the present from wherever the heck I'd been. "Sorry. I just kind of zoned out. I love your truck, by the way, even if it's kind of big."

Jack turned on the ignition. "Hey, Ivy, when you looked at me after you kinda knocked me to the ground, it was like you recognized me or something." He glanced at me and grinned. He paused then said, "It was a pretty amazing way to meet, though a simple 'hello' would have sufficed. Maybe it is the traditional greeting where you come from."

I punched him on the arm. *Dumb move*, I decided as I massaged my knuckles. His arm was rock solid. "Ha ha," I said, shaking my head and smiling. It was going to be a great story to tell our children. *Okay, that came out of nowhere. Did he just say* suffice?

"It'll be a great story to tell our children," Jack said with a laugh. "Don't deny it. You were thinking it too."

"You are cray cray," I said, not denying his words.

"Cray cray?" He shook his head and lifted his eyebrows, obviously questioning my use of *cray cray*.

"Would you prefer insane, certifiable, or possibly *non compos mentis*?" I asked, trying to remember all of the words I knew that actually meant crazy.

"*Non compos mentis*, of course," he replied, after pretending to think about it for a minute. "So," he continued, "what did you mean when you said, 'It's you. It's really you,' while you were lying on top of me in front of God and everyone."

I punched him again. *Dumb again*, I thought, rubbing my knuckles a second time. *Okay, what to tell him? I'm not going to tell him about dream Johnny. That's just weird. I guess I'll have to go with Flashback Jack, my Internet crush, who he resembles but who no longer seems nearly as attractive.* "Promise not to laugh?" I asked.

Jack was silent. I glanced at him with a questioning look and nudged his arm.

"Hey, I told you on the track that I'm not gonna lie. That's a good trait in a boyfriend, by the way," he concluded as he took a drink out of his water bottle.

"I thought you were this guy I watch on the Internet. His name is Flashback Jack, and I've been crushing on him for a year," I said.

Jack spit his water all over the steering wheel and windshield.

"Holy crap," I exclaimed. "I know it's silly, but not choke-worthy."

Jack pulled into the driveway of my grandparents' house while he tried to recover from his choking ordeal. "You have a crush on Flashback Jack? Well, I'll be damned."

Chapter 8

Jack

Shit. Ivy had a crush on Flashback Jack. I kind of hoped she had dreams about me—or a 1960s version of me—like I had dreams about her or a 1960s version of her. She patted my back as I kind of wiped the water off my windshield and dashboard with a T-shirt I pulled out of my gym bag.

"Do you watch him too?" she asked as she moved across the seat toward the door.

"Ivy," I said, not responding to her question, "I need you to come to my house so I can show you something. Can you come now? I'm not working at my uncle's implement store today, so I've got about five hours before we start our second practice. I've been helping him some this week because his regular guy is on vacation."

"You want me to go home with you now? Are your parents going to be there? I don't think my mom will let me go home with a boy I just met if your house is empty. *I* don't think I should go home with a boy I just met if his house is empty," she said, giving me a look I could only describe as perplexed. "Did you say you work at an implement store? What is that?"

"Well, pretty city girl, we sell farm equipment and supplies at an implement store. Don't say it. I know what you're thinking. You think that's hot." I caught her eye and gave her a wink. "My mom and the twins should be home. My mom works at the elementary school, so she doesn't start work till next week and the twins take their naps around"—I glanced at the clock on the dashboard—"now," I explained with a grin. "So, your virtue is safe with me.

Ivy shook her head and kinda laughed, "Virtue? Jeez,

Jack. Okay. Well, since I've been in town for...oh, about twenty-four hours, my social calendar is pretty empty. Are you comfortable coming in and meeting my mom? You might also be meeting my grandparents too."

She studied my reaction as she started to get out of the cab of my truck.

"Ivy," I said gently, grabbing her arm before she leaped to the ground, "you don't seem to fully comprehend the situation. I am going to be your boyfriend, so I sure as shit...I mean, I sure as heck"—I felt my neck get hot. I really shouldn't swear in front of my girl—"want to meet your mom, your grandparents, whomever."

"Jack, I have to say it, and I don't want you to think it is—or I am—weird, but you have the most amazing vocabulary." Jack gave me a really strange look. "It's kind of a long story, but when my dad died, I found his collection—and it was a collection—of Word of the Day calendars. Since then, I've been kind of obsessed with learning new words. I just tell everyone I'm getting ready for college entrance exams. Anyway, I think you have mad vocabulary skills."

I clasped Ivy's hand. "I'm sorry about your dad," I said. She nodded in response.

I wanted to comfort her, but I didn't know how. Maybe sharing something about me would kind of help. "My vocabulary studies are connected to really bad nightmares. I've had these nightmares for a long time—years actually. I'd wake up and be afraid to go back to sleep. I wanted to do something productive while I was awake, so I started playing vocabulary games on my computer then on my phone. Productive 'cause I need to get some scholarship money, and a good score on the college entrance exam will help."

"I'm sorry you have nightmares."

We stared at each other, not knowing what to say or maybe just enjoying the connection. Before it became awkward, I wanted to say something profound.

"When you said *fortuitous* at the field today, the way it rolled off your tongue, I thought I might be sapiosexual. But, I realized I wasn't just interested in your mind. I liked the whole package." And, damn, I did like the whole package, all maybe five foot three of her—long brown hair, green eyes, and hot bod. And she was smart. Smart was hot.

Ivy smiled then got out of the truck. I swore she mumbled, "Me too."

Ivy stood waiting for me on the lawn as I got out of the truck. I was overwhelmed by a sense of...I can't describe it. It was like I'd been in this exact same spot, looking at this girl just like this before. Ivy was staring back at me, then she kind of shook her head like she was trying to clear it. Maybe she felt it too.

"How did you know where I lived?" she asked as she waited for me to reach her from around the truck. *Damn, how did I know she lives here?*

"I don't know?" I replied. "Maybe Collin or Bri or somebody told me your grandparents were Mr and Mrs Van den Berg. My head's still a little rattled by our encounter on the track."

"Sorry about your head," Ivy said, apologetically as she reached up and rubbed the back of my head gently. My heart started to race. Any physical contact with this girl made my head spin.

"I'm just messing with you," I replied. "My head's fine. My heart, however, is another matter," I said, placing her hand on my chest. "It hasn't stopped racing since we met."

We stood in silence on the steps leading to her

grandparents' house with my hand covering her hand that I'd pressed to my chest. She stared at me as I stared at her. We didn't speak. Then she smiled, stood on her tiptoes and kissed my cheek.

"You're for real, aren't you, Jack Vander Zee? Well, let's go meet my mom and my grandparents and whoever else might be in the house."

"Mom," Ivy shouted as she opened the door, "Grams, Gramps, anybody?"

I followed Ivy through the house and that crazy, unsettling feeling of having been here before, in this place with this girl, was overwhelming. I knew I'd never been in this house, but I knew Ivy's room would be up the stairs—the last door on the left. I also knew a cookie jar was in the pantry with homemade ice box cookies, whatever the hell they were. I just knew they were there.

"Do you want a cookie?" Ivy asked as we walked through the kitchen. "You must be starving after practice. My grandma makes the best pecan cookie things, ice box cookies."

Well, there you have it, I thought as Ivy stopped at the door leading to the pantry. She pulled out the cookie jar and handed me a couple of cookies. "I think everyone's out back," she said as we walked onto the porch.

"Hey Mom, Grandma, Grandpa," she said as she grabbed my hand. "Look what I found, a boy to show me around Newton." She glanced at me with a mischievous grin. "Which should take us all of about what? Ten minutes? Kidding," she said to the group seated around the table under the fan on the back porch. This I did not recognize, I thought with relief or something like it.

"Mom, Grandma, and Grandpa, this is Jack Vander Zee. I was doing a tumbling pass and Jack saved me from being knocked over or knocked out by a wild throw." She paused. "Jack, this is my mom, Mrs Drake." I walked over to Mrs Drake and shook her hand. Mr Van den Berg stood up. "And my grandpa and grandma, Mr and Mrs Van den Berg."

*****

Fall, 1968

"Mom and Dad," Christine said as she pulled me across the room by my hand. "This is Johnny. Daddy, I know you're going to love him because he's the best football player ever. Mom, you're going to love him because…well, I think he's groovy."

*****

Present day

"Nice to meet you," I said as I shook Mr Van den Berg's hand. *Okay, what the hell was that? A flashback memory? Whatever it was, I think I'm gonna need to go back to the doctor real soon.* Today was one flashback after another, and Ivy was a major player. Well, 1960s Christine, who looked a hell of a lot like Ivy.

"Sorry, sir," I said. *Great. Now Ivy's granddad is going to think I'm rude.*

"No problem, Jack," Mr Van den Berg said. "I'm looking forward to watching you play this season. How's the team look? Hopefully, the quarterback is still Trey and not the kid who almost nailed Ivy with the football."

"It's Trey, sir," I replied. "Though, I wouldn't have met

Ivy if the kid with the bad arm had had a good arm."

"True, true," Mrs Drake chuckled.

"Mom," Ivy said, "I'm going to go over to Jack's house for a little. Yes, his mom is home. I'll be back in an hour or so."

"Nice meeting you." I caught a glimpse of Mrs Drake giving Ivy a thumbs up. I guess she thought I was okay. I was grinning as we walked to the truck. "You know what's strange? I felt like I've been to this house before."

"Did you know what kind of cookies were going to be in the cookie jar?" Ivy asked as I assisted her into my truck.

I gave her a questioning look. Then walked to my side of the truck and got in as I intentionally avoided answering.

"What?" she said. "Did you?"

Well, guess I'm gonna answer the question. "Yeah, I kinda guess I did," I replied.

"Okay, this is crazy," she said as we drove away from the Van den Berg's. "I had never been to my grandparents' house. I know that is strange in itself, but it's kind of complicated. Anyway, I had the same feeling about it. I mean, it could have been photos or something, but knowing the type of cookies in the cookie jar was…well, umm, kind of unsettling." Ivy stopped talking. "Sorry. That was an overshare."

"I like listening to you talk," I said as I reached for her hand. "We'll be at my house in like two minutes. I should have been pointing out the important Newton landmarks, all two of them." Ivy smiled at my remark. "I'll take you on the scenic route on the way back to your place. Are you ready to meet my mom?"

Ivy didn't respond. She just sort of stared straight ahead. "Ivy, you okay?"

She took a deep breath as she got out of the truck. "Yeah, sure. Let's go meet your mom, and maybe the twins will be awake. I like little kids. There's a big gap in age between you guys."

"The twins are from my mom's new marriage. My dad left us about five years ago. He hasn't been back. Anyway, my mom's new husband is pretty cool." I grasped Ivy by the shoulders and turned her to face me. "I'm really sorry about your dad."

"My dad," she said as we walked to the side door of the house. It was the door that took you right into the kitchen, "died in a car accident on the way home from work last year. My mom couldn't stand living in St. Louis anymore, so she decided we should move to Newton. She's a librarian and got hired at the Newton Library. That's why we're here."

I didn't know what to say. "I'm sorry," I said again.

"Thanks. Me too," she said. "We can talk more about it some other time." She put on a big smile. "Now I'm focusing on making a good impression. Oh my God, I haven't looked at myself since cheer practice. Don't open the door." She pulled out her ponytail and ran her fingers through her long, dark hair. "Is that okay?" she asked.

She was so damn pretty that I was speechless.

"Oh crap, you didn't say anything, and you promised you wouldn't lie. We can come back some other time. Sorry, Jack," she said as she ran her fingers through her hair again.

I moved her hands from her hair and clasped them in mine. "Ivy, you are the most beautiful girl I've ever seen. Aren't you glad we've established that I don't prevaricate? Come on, gorgeous. Let's go meet my mom. She's going to be very happy to meet you."

I felt it coming as I clasped the door handle…

*****

Winter, 1968

"Don't worry," I said as I held Christine's hand in mine. "My brothers are going to love you. But Mom? My mom is going to be over the moon to have a girl around."

*****

Present day

"Well, are you going to open the door?" Ivy asked.

I opened the door then walked into the kitchen. "Shh," Mom said, inspecting something in the oven, "the twins are finally asleep."

Mom shut the oven door then turned. "Well, hello," she said, walking toward Ivy with her hand extended and a huge smile on her face. "I'm Jack's mom. You can call me Cathy."

"Mom," I said softly, trying not to laugh, "this is Ivy. She's the new cheerleader—the one you mentioned this morning. I decided to take your advice, and here she is."

"It's nice to meet you, umm, Cathy," Ivy said in a low whisper. "I hope you don't mind Jack inviting me over."

"Oh my goodness, not at all. I was just saying this morning that Jack should find a nice girl. He never takes my advice." She paused and frowned. "You are a nice girl, aren't you?"

Ivy's eyes got real big. She was speechless. I laughed, but not loudly. "My mom's kidding. Great, Mom. The first time I bring a girl home, you try to scare her away. I'm taking her to the basement." Clasping Ivy's hand, I pulled her toward the basement door.

"It was nice meeting you," Ivy said as we started down the steps. "You and Jack have the same sense of humor."

Mom quipped, "Jack has a sense of humor? Who knew?"

"Your mom seems nice," Ivy said, then she stopped abruptly and studied my basement studio. The wall I used as the background for my radio show wasn't a green screen. It was decorated with vintage posters from 1969—Woodstock, Easy Rider, signs of the zodiac, the Who, Chevrolet Camaro Z-28 Emblem Poster, Apollo 11's Buzz Aldrin, and Crosby, Stills, Nash, and Young in San Francisco. If Ivy watched the show, she'd know the wall.

"Oh my God," she said, "you're Flashback Jack. You aren't from California or New York. You're from Newton, Iowa. I can't believe I told you that I totally crush on Flashback Jack. Jeez," she said as she hit herself in the head. "No wonder you spit out your water."

"Listen, Ivy," I said as I clasped her hands. "I didn't want to tell you, because I want you to crush on me, Jack Vander Zee. But I wasn't going to *not* tell you, because that would have been wrong. I'm thinking maybe you are crushing on me, Jack Vander Zee, at least a little?"

"Okay," she said with a smile. "I probably shouldn't tell you this but, yeah, I am totally crushing on Jack Vander Zee. But, I think it's totally awesome that you are Flashback Jack. Wait"—she pressed her hand against her forehead and dramatically flung out her arm—"I'm going to have a fangirl moment. Flashback Jack, oh my God! I'm alone with Flashback Jack in his studio. Can I see your albums? No wait, your forty-fives. I've never actually seen a real forty-five."

"You want to see my forty-fives?" I asked as I took her hand and led her to the bins of records.

"Oh, my gosh, I will be so careful," Ivy said as she looked at the container. "I believe I've died and gone to vintage vinyl heaven." She stood at my work station, carefully going through the stack. "Look. You have Elvis Presley, the Zombies, Three Dog Night and tons more. Where did you get all of these?" She asked as she looked up from the bin.

"Garage sales, online, auctions…I'm kinda obsessed," I replied.

"Look at this…Mama Cass Elliot's, 'It's Getting Better'. I love this song."

I walked over to Ivy and glanced at the forty-five she was holding. "Hmm, I don't remember seeing that one before."

She turned over the record to check out the B-side. "Someone wrote on the jacket, 'Dear Johnny. It just keeps getting better. Happy Graduation! I love you, Christine.'"

Ivy looked at me, looked back at the writing on the jacket, then her eyes rolled back as she crumpled to the floor. I caught her right before she hit the ground, then my head started to pound. I sat down next to her…

*****

Spring, 1969

"Ladies and Gentlemen," said the principal from the podium on the stage of the Maytag Bowl, "I present to you the Newton High School Graduating Class of 1969. Graduates, you may now move your tassel."

I reached up and moved my tassel to the left. I took off my cap and pitched it into the air like the other graduates did. "Pomp and Circumstance" played as we turned to walk up the hill from our seats near the stage of the outdoor amphitheater. I studied the crowd filling Maytag Park, trying to locate Christine and my family. They were here somewhere.

"Johnny, Johnny." I heard Christine calling my name, then I saw her waving from a spot on the hill. Tonight I was going to give her my class ring. If she were graduating with me, it would have been an engagement ring. Since she had one more year left of high school, my class ring was gonna have to do. I tilted my head in her direction, trying to be cool.

"Hey, Johnny," Bill called, "you going to the happening at Joe's farm tonight?"

"Maybe, man. I'm going out with Christine."

"You are such a square. Tonight is the night of your high school graduation and you are going to waste it with a skirt. You have plenty of nights for her." Bill's voice was full of scorn.

"What's your hang-up? I have another type of celebration in mind that does not require a crowd." I kinda intentionally unintentionally made it sound like I had bigger plans for me and Christine.

Bill looked at me intently. "Well, you can bring her with you when you're done. You can't just cop out on all your buddies."

"Congratulations," Christine shouted as I caught her in my arms. I gave her a swift kiss then turned to finish my rap session with Bill, but he'd already split. I shrugged. I'd catch up with him later.

"I got you a present," Christine said as she handed me a small gift-wrapped present. I knew it was a forty-five. "Can you guess what it is?"

Giving her a grin. "Well, my guess is that it's another record for my collection. But, I could be wrong."

"Of course it's a record. But what record is it?" Christine

smiled with delight.

I am never going to guess this one. She wasn't gonna give me any time to think.

"Oh, just open it." My girl was definitely not patient. As I opened it, Christine leaned over my arm, watching carefully. "It's the new single from Mama Cass. Oops. I'm not very good at the present giving. Well, I'm good at giving presents but I'm not good at waiting for the receiver to open the present."

Christine was under my arm with her arms wrapped around my waist. I read the writing on the sleeve—

> Dear Johnny,
> It just keeps getting better. Happy Graduation!
> I love you,
> Christine.

We were standing in the middle of the graduation crowd at the Maytag Bowl. My mom, dad, and four brothers were just a few feet away. My best friend Bill was mad as hell, and none of it mattered. I loved this girl.

"Christine, would you wear my ring?" I asked as I slid the ring off my finger and placed it in the palm of her hand.

*****

Present day

I slowly opened my eyes to find I was on the floor of my basement next to Ivy. Ivy's eyes were closed and her breathing was pretty shallow. "Ivy, Ivy," I said as I gently shook her shoulder. She slowly opened her eyes and looked at me blankly for a moment.

"Oh my God, what the heck happened?" She looked around frantically until she spotted the forty-five on the ground, still in the jacket. "Johnny— I mean, Jack. I'm so sorry. I think I fainted. I've never fainted in my whole life. I think hitting you on the track may have really rattled my brain."

"Did you have a dream or anything while you were out?" I asked cautiously, trying to be nonchalant as I probed to see if she'd had the same experience.

"It was totally weird. I pictured you and me—but we weren't you and me exactly—in the 1960s, I think. The girl who reminded me of me gave the boy who reminded me of you the record with the message that was on the B-side of the forty-five, only I think the A-side was the B-side because the message goes with the song that's on the A side. In other words, I think the record is in the jacket the wrong way." Ivy gestured to the forty-five on the floor as she paused for a breath. "You know what else is weird? I've had a couple other dreams about the same people. Maybe I'm just stressed from the move or something?"

"What were their names?" I asked. "The people in the dream."

Ivy looked at me with a raised brow. "The people in my dream, or whatever... Their names were Johnny and Christine...just like on the record jacket."

"Was that in the dream before now or just in the dream now?" I asked. I knew there was a connection. I could feel it.

Ivy closed her eyes. I guess she was trying to remember. "Yeah, it was Johnny and Christine. I remembered the Christine part because my mom told me that was her missing sister's name and the Johnny part because the name is vintage, like Johnny Cash." She paused for a moment. "I think the name Johnny probably came from a song my mom and I heard on the radio. The singer's name was John. Anyway, like I said, the whole move thing must be messing with my head."

Messing with her head? She was messing with my head and maybe my heart. We were lying face to face on the floor of my basement, and I gazed into her green eyes. My lips were just a few inches from hers. I leaned in to kiss her.

"Jack, Ivy." Mom called from the top of the stairs. I gave Ivy a quick kiss on the lips and pulled her to her feet. "Do you guys want lunch or something?"

"No, thanks," Ivy replied. "Jack's taking me home now." Ivy clasped my hand and started walking toward the stairs. We reached the kitchen quickly, but my mom was nowhere to be found. We walked to the truck in silence. It wasn't awkward. It was just silent. I opened the door to the truck and assisted Ivy into the cab.

I went quickly to my side of the car, got in, started the engine, then backed out of the drive heading in the direction of Ivy's grandparents' house. Reaching across the seat, I picked up Ivy's hand, twining her fingers in mine.

"What's wrong?" I asked. Tension radiated from Ivy. Even a clueless dude like me could tell something was wrong.

"Jack," Ivy said, squeezing my fingers, "I'm scared. The dreams, or whatever they are, are kind of freaking me out." Ivy paused then took a deep breath. "When I fainted, or whatever, in your basement, the dream felt so real. It felt like a memory. So did the other ones—today at the football field, the ones at my grandparents' house, and even during the car ride to Newton." She paused again. "I wish I could figure it out."

"Ivy," I said softly, "I've been having dreams about a girl named Christine and a dude named Johnny too. The dreams are so much better than the dreams I have of Vietnam that I haven't tried to analyze. I think your fortuitous rescue was inevitable. I think we were meant to find each other. And now that I know we have similar dreams, I think maybe we're destined to find out why, together."

Ivy remained quiet as we pulled into her grandparents' driveway.

"I'm glad I told you about my awake-dreams. I'm going to need some time to process the fact that you're having similar dreams about the same people," she said as she grabbed the handle to the door of the truck. "It's a little disquieting."

"I think it's kind of remarkable. But, I really like the way you used *disquieting*," I said as she jumped out of the cab of the truck.

"Wait," I kinda shouted. "Give me your phone so I can put in my number."

She handed me her phone with a smile as she held out her hand for mine. We each added our number and exchanged phones in silence. I wondered what she was thinking.

"Would you go to the drive-in with me on Saturday night?" I asked. "That will be our first official date."

"A drive-in?" Ivy repeated. "I've never been to a drive-in. That will be so fun."

"Okay," I said. "I'll pick you up around seven thirty. Can I drive you home from practice the rest of the week?"

Ivy stared at me for a moment. "Sure, that would be great. A little forward, but great."

I walked her to the stairs at the front of the house. "Thanks for the ride," Ivy said as she stepped on the first step. "See you tomorrow." She walked into the house with a wave.

I started to walk away, but it just didn't feel right. The door flew open and Ivy rushed down the steps. I grabbed her waist as she threw her arms around my neck and pulled down my head and kissed me as we stood on the front lawn in front of her grandparents' house on the busiest street in town.

A car horn honked. "Get a room!"

Ivy broke the kiss and looked up at me with a shy smile as a blush stained her cheeks. "See you tomorrow." She ran to the steps, turned, then waved as she walked in the front door, closing it solidly behind her.

Why were we having similar dreams? Was it a coincidence? Was it fate? Was it nothing? It was disquieting, like Ivy said, but it was kinda comforting. It was comforting to know I wasn't alone. I'd found someone special. I'd found Ivy. Hopefully the week would pass quickly 'cause right now, Saturday seemed really far away.

Chapter 9

Ivy

What do you wear to a drive-in movie? I scanned the clothes in my closet, in the drawers, and on the floor of my room. It was so hard trying to look like I wasn't trying to look cute. Sighing, I thought about Jack. He had been so great this week. I was kind of sad that he hadn't kissed me since Monday. Though, after re-reading the article from *Seventeen* on knowing if your guy is into you, I think we're good. And we'd started to get to know each other. In addition to being a logophile… *Why does* logophile *sound kind of dirty, even though it means* lover of words*? I don't think I'll call Jack a logophile.* He was funny and sweet.

Found it! I pulled a pair of jean shorts out from under the bed. It was so hot out that a tank top would be perfect—not too skimpy. I studied my reflection to determine cute or slut. A cute slut? No, just cute. I put on a little make up, brushed my hair, then slid a headband on.

"Ivy," Mom shouted from the bottom of the stairs, "Jack's here."

I slipped on my flip flops then I stopped to put on some perfume. This entire experience had a surreal feel to it, like I'd done this hundreds of times before, yet it still felt like the first time.

"I'll have her home after the last show," I heard Jack say to my mom from the sitting room. "It's the first part of the *Hunger Games* marathon, so it's going to be around one, one thirty." Jack stood up when I walked into the room. He didn't say anything. He just kind of stared. *Crap, what's wrong with Jack?*

"Uh, you look great." Jack kind of stuttered. "Really great."

"At a loss for words… That's pretty unusual for you, Jack," I joked. "You look pretty good yourself," I said as I admired how good he looked in khaki shorts and a T-shirt. Jack was so damned hot, and he actually liked me.

Jack grabbed my hand as we walked toward the truck. He opened the door then assisted me inside. I wasn't very tall, and the cab to the truck was pretty far off the ground. Though I could do it myself, I liked that Jack helped me. It was kind of sweet and definitely old school.

Jack was opening the door to the cab of his truck when Gramps pulled up to the curb. "Have fun at the passion pit," he called. *Strange…that sounds oddly familiar.*

"Passion pit," I repeated, when I waved at Gramps as Jack backed out of the driveway. "That sounds like something from the 1950s or maybe the 1960s. Maybe you could use it on Flashback Jack," I said as I squeezed Jack's hand.

"Hey"—Jack held my hand then tugged me over to his side—"the first rule of the drive-in movie is the girl has to sit right next to her guy for the duration."

"Really," I replied as I reached for the hand he had slung over my shoulder. "I thought you didn't lie, Jack Vander Zee."

"I wouldn't lie to you, Ivy," Jack said as he removed his arm long enough to hand me his phone. "It's on the Internet. The Internet never lies." He kissed the top of my head. Just a brush of his lips, but I felt it all the way to my toes. *How is that even possible?*

I looked at Jack's phone. "Five Rules for a Drive-in Movie," I read aloud as Jack pulled the truck into the line of cars waiting for entrance to the Valle Drive-In. "Rule Number Five: Sit as close to your date as possible; people expect young people to make out at a drive-in. Don't let them down." I laughed as I continued to the next rule. "Rule Number Four: Leave the windows down a crack; a crack in the window will reduce the chance of the window's fogging up when a couple is making out. Rule Number Three: The importance of watching the movie is minimal; if you haven't seen it before, you can look it up on your phone on the way home to explain the movie to your parents so you can spend more time making out. Rule Number Two: Public Demonstration of Affection; making out at a drive-in is not considered PDA. You're in a *private* vehicle even if it is in a *public* place. Rule Number One: Refer back to Rule Number Five." I looked at Jack and started to laugh. "What the heck? Where did you find this?" I looked at the URL and laughed harder. "You posted this on the *Flashback 1969* page. You totally made these up."

"I don't make the rules." He grinned. "I just enforce them." He tilted my face toward his. "You don't want to violate the rules of the drive-in."

"The family in the minivan"—I gestured to the car in front of us—"they expect us to make out?" Jack nodded in agreement. "The couple behind us"—I looked in the rearview mirror at a couple around my grandparents' age—"they will be disappointed if we don't?"

"Absolutely," Jack confirmed. "It's our civic responsibility."

"Civic responsibility? Seriously?" I asked as I looked up into Jack's blue eyes. He had the most beautiful blue eyes I'd ever seen. "Do we do it for the entire five hours, or do we take breaks?"

"Ivy," Jack said keeping his eyes straight ahead as he maneuvered around the parking lot, looking for the perfect spot—not for viewing the movie, I decided, but for making out.

"Since Monday, all I've been thinking about is tonight and being with you for five hours alone in my truck. Five hours seems like nothing."

He turned off the engine then placed both of his hands on the steering wheel. "Here's what we're gonna do. I'm going to give you some cash so you can go buy some pop and some popcorn. While you're gone, I'm going to adjust the speaker on the car window. Then we're not leaving the car for the duration of the movies, both of them."

"Jack," I said, touching one of his hands. "I'm in. I'm in because you used the word *duration* in a sentence—smart and athletic." I paused. "But what the heck is pop?"

Jack shook his head, laughing while opening his car door. He clasped my hand as he tugged me out of the driver's side. He put his hands on my hips then pulled me against his body. "Pop is Coke or Sprite. What do they call it in St. Louis?"

"Soda, Jack. We call it soda. The language barrier is much bigger than I thought," I said with a laugh as I disengaged from his embrace. "I'll be right back." I glanced back at Jack. He was watching me. He waved and kind of shook his head like he was embarrassed that I'd caught him staring. I walked away with an exaggerated swing of my hips.

"Nice," I heard him say. I waved without turning around.

The concession stand was a small building. As I walked toward it, I looked around at all the cars in the parking area. It was really crowded. There was a playground in front of the screen where people were playing catch football, just like in the movies. I took a selfie with the big screen as the background then sent it to the girls in St. Louis. I really needed to send them a picture of Jack.

*****

Summer, 1969

"Hey, Johnny," I called as I raised my new Polaroid Swinger up to take a photo of Johnny as he walked across the beach then into the water. I was so glad we'd decided to spend the last day of summer at Rock Creek. It was a blast. The word *yes* finally appeared in the viewfinder of the camera.

"Don't move." I snapped a picture.

Johnny ran across the beach, grabbing the photo from my hand.

"Hey," I said as Johnny waved the picture back and forth while we waited for it to develop.

"Not bad," Johnny said, holding the developed photo just out of my reach. "You want the picture, babe? I wanna see you walk across the beach in your bikini like Ali McGraw, then I'll give you the Polaroid."

Johnny started humming the tune to the Polaroid Swinger commercial. I shook my head then smiled. I sauntered across the sand with an exaggerated swing of my hips. Johnny let out a wolf whistle as I slowly strolled down the beach.

*****

Present day

"Excuse me," a man bumped into me, jolting me back to reality as I entered through the screen door leading to the sales counter in the concession stand.

"No problem," I replied. The man looked familiar. "Aren't you Will from the football stadium? I'm sorry. I don't know your last name."

He turned and looked at me strangely. "You're not supposed to be here," he muttered. "You're not supposed to be here." Shaking his head back and forth in denial, he walked away. That was odd. I examined the menu.

"What can I get you?" the girl working the concession stand was Katie from the cheer squad—one of the girls interested in Jack. *Great.*

"Hi, Katie, could I please have a large"—I paused, thinking of the word for soda—"pop—a Coke—and a large tub of popcorn, and"—I examined the candy—"Jujubes."

"Oh, hi, Ivy," Katie started filling a cup with soda. She turned suddenly with a big smile. "Buyer beware" was the first thought popping into my head as she gave me the ultimate fake smile. "We're going snipe hunting next Saturday night and would love for you to come. You can meet Becca and a couple of my other friends. Snipe hunting is an Iowa thing. It'll be sick. I'll pick you up around eight."

"Sure," I replied. Well, it would be nice to have some girlfriends, though I wasn't so sure about snipe hunting, whatever that was.

I handed her the money then walked out of the concession stand. *Why did I buy Jujubes? Hmm... Maybe Jack likes Jujubes...*

✳✳✳✳✳

Summer, 1969

"Give me a kiss, beautiful," Johnny whispered as he pulled me over to his side of the car. The Camaro was nice, but the console between the two seats made it hard to make out. I missed his truck—well, at least here at the drive-in.

"You taste like Jujubes," I said against his lips.

"You taste like heaven," he said as he kissed me again.

*****

Present day

"Ivy! Ivy!" Bri and Collin were walking toward me. *Whoa, what a weird dream moment.* I shook my head to clear my thoughts.

"We saw Jack's truck. Are you guys staying for both movies? My mom gave me permission to stay out until they were over," Bri said with a grin. "We're probably going to cut out early and go to a party at Chloe's farm. It's supposed to be a kegger. Maybe you and Jack will come too?"

"I'll ask Jack. I've never been to a party on a farm. Thanks for the invite. Maybe we'll see you later." I waved, then walked slowly away from the couple. I sure hope they didn't think I was being rude. Abrupt maybe? That felt a little abrupt.

"Hey, what took you so long?" Jack was leaning against the truck bed.

I handed him his change and the Jujubes. "No way," he said with a big smile that emphasized his incredibly sexy dimples. "Jujubes are my all-time favorite candy."

Jack opened the door on the driver's side and helped me into the cab. He climbed in after me and pulled me into his side. Grinning he said, "Rule number one."

I placed the popcorn on the floor and handed Jack the drink to put in the cup-holder on his side of the car. "Oh," I said, "I ran into Collin and Bri. They told me about a party at Chloe's, if you're interested."

Jack shook his head. "You know I'm very focused. The

only thing I'm focused on is you." He leaned down and kissed me. The kiss was long and mind-numbing in a good way. The movie progressed as I tried to remember that good girls don't...well, at least not on the first date. The scene from the selection process and the odds being forever in my favor was one of my favorite parts of the *Hunger Games*. I clearly missed it, because when we paused for a breath, Katnis was in a tree in the arena.

"Ivy," Jack whispered into my ear, sending shivers down my body, "lay down with me."

"I don't remember that being in the rules," I whispered back, kissing Jack's neck. "I'm okay if you want to make new rules."

Jack was panting. "Don't think of them as rules. Think of them more as guidelines."

"Guidelines...I like guidelines."

Jack gently pushed me down on the front seat. "What's the name of the second movie?" he asked, his breathing was pretty ragged, just like mine.

"Who cares," I replied, turning my head to find his lips. Jack's hands roamed my body, my tank and shorts left a lot skin exposed for his exploring hands. My hands slid inside his shirt. He felt warm and solid and familiar. *Familiar? That's weird.*

*****

"Mm," Jack murmured, "this is the best movie I've ever seen."

"Seen, Jack?" I asked with a smile. "Sit up. I want some popcorn. I'm really hungry."

Jack's face was right next to mine. I watched him grin as he leaned over to kiss me again. "I'm hungry for you. You taste like heaven." Music was pouring out of the speaker. It was the end of the first movie.

Jack stroked my hair. His breathing was labored and his heart was racing. "I think we should go to the party. I, uh, want to go a lot further but I promised you that your virtue was safe with me. I always keep my promises."

I stroked his smooth cheek, and he turned his head and kissed the palm of my hand. Would it be bad to give it up at the drive-in? *Seventeen* did not have advice about sex at the drive-in. *I guess I'll have to write that one in.*

Jack's cell phone buzzed. "Saved by the bell," I whispered.

We sat up. I looked out the front window of the truck. Very few cars remained.

"Hey, Collin," Jack said into his cell. "What's up? You didn't knock on the side of the truck. We would've heard ya," Jack said.

"Maybe not," I whispered to Jack. He grinned into the phone.

"Are you guys going to Chloe's?" Jack asked. There was a long pause as Jack listened to Collin. "No shit. Good thing we were here and not there. Coach is going to be so pissed. Trey wasn't there, was he?" Another pause as Jack listened to Collin. "Well, that's good. Thanks for giving me the heads up." He nodded, which was pretty cute 'cause Collin couldn't see him. "I'll ask Ivy. Yeah, see you tomorrow." Jack put his phone on the dashboard.

"Well, pretty girl," Jack said as he put his arm around me and pulled me into his side, "we're stuck here at the drive-in."

"What happened?" I asked.

"The police busted Chloe's party. A bunch of kids ran

into the fields, trying not to be caught by Newton's finest. About half of the football team and a bunch of cheerleaders were at the party. If they get caught, they'll be suspended for the first two weeks of the season."

"Wait," I said. "Did you say they were running in the fields—like corn fields— in the middle of the night?"

An image flashed in my mind, an image of me running through a corn field. The emotion I was feeling…it was fear.

I snuggled under Jack's arm. I did not want to go to a party in a corn field.

"Hey." A shout from beside the truck had us scrambling to adjust our clothes and our seating arrangement. Collin pounded on the window as Bri laughed in the background.

"Open up, loser," Collin said as he continued to pound on the side of the truck.

Jack unlocked the door. Collin pushed Bri inside then climbed in behind her. "If we can't go to the party, we thought we'd hang here with you two."

"You've had way too much alone time," Bri continued. "We wouldn't want you to be bored. Also, I had a talk with Katie at the concession stand. She told me about the snipe hunting expedition."

"Snipe hunting?" Jack said with a question in his voice. "Well, that can't be good."

"No, it's not good." Bri agreed. "I, however, have a great plan."

I leaned into Jack and got comfortable by snuggling under his arm and tugging it around me. Bri described her great plan. The girl was devious and I liked it. I closed my eyes and listened.

Chapter 10

Jack

I glanced at the clock on the dashboard. It was one thirty am, exactly when I'd told Ivy's mom we would be home from the drive-in. I'm nothing if not punctual.

"Ivy," I whispered, "we're here, sleepyhead."

"Oh, hey," she said softly, kinda into my armpit. She pushed up from my side. "Oh, I'm so sorry. I slept through most of the second movie." She bolted upright and slapped her hand to her forehead. "Bri and Collin are going to think I'm rude."

"It's fine," I said, pulling her back into my arms. "Bri fell asleep too. And, I liked it, having you sleeping by me. Well, except for maybe the snoring."

"Jack," she said, laughing. "I absolutely do not snore." She paused and looked up, "Do I?"

"We'll have to sleep together more often, so I can be sure," I replied slyly.

"Jeez, Jack," she said. "Did I snore, really?"

"No, but you might. So, I need to do my duty and continue to sleep with you to make sure I'm one hundred percent accurate. You know I'm like that…very thorough."

Ivy flipped on the car light then pulled down the visor to look in the mirror. "Wow, my lips are kind of swollen and red. I look like I've been kissed, a lot."

She looked at me, so damned kissable. I pulled her down and pressed my lips to hers. I mumbled, "They don't look like they've been kissed enough."

Somehow she ended up in my lap, trapped between me and the steering wheel. She leaned back then the horn started to blow.

"Oh crap," she said as she opened up the door on the driver's side of the truck and hopped out. I joined her and we watched as the porch light came on in front of her grandparents' house. She started to laugh. "Well, so much for not getting caught coming home late."

"I got you here right on time; you were just slow getting out of the car," I said, grabbing her hand before she could bolt up the stairs. "Ivy, can I call you tomorrow?"

She nodded her head as she tugged on my hand to release hers.

"Not so fast," I said as I leaned down. "I need that goodnight kiss." I meant just to give her a quick peck, but in a second we were locked in a tight embrace.

The porch light flicked on and off.

"Bye, Jack! Thanks for a great night. I believe the flashing light was a not-so-subtle message from Mom to get my butt inside," Ivy said as she bolted up the stairs. "Talk to you later."

After watching Ivy go in the house, I drove through the quiet streets thinking about my night. Tonight was going to be a long one. *Blue balls may be an actual medical condition, not just a line guys used to get chicks to go all the way. Stop thinking in the '60s, dumb ass.*

I parked the truck in front of the house then quietly let myself in the front door. *No flashing porch lights here.*

Sitting down on my bed, I pulled out my cell. I contemplated the blank screen, thinking of the perfect text to send.

JACK: *Sweet Dreams*

My phone buzzed.

IVY: *U 2*

I studied my phone, noticing all of the missed calls and text messages. They were probably from a bunch of the guys trying to get a ride home from Chloe's—or, should I say, the corn fields surrounding Chloe's farm. The last one was at eleven thirty. I'm guessing everyone had been picked up or I'd have more messages. I read them. It looked like most of the guys got out before the cops actually busted anyone at the party.

Stripping out of my jeans and shirt, I tossed them both on the floor near the laundry basket. *Good thing I'm not a basketball player.* I crawled under the covers and closed my eyes, wishing Ivy were here with me. Shaking my head, I tried to think of anything but Ivy and her lips on mine while her leg gently rubbed up and down along my calf and my hands explored her body. *Stop it, dumb ass*, I said to myself, burying my head in the pillow. *Think about football...*

*****

Summer, 1970

"Are you kidding me?" I said to Mike. "Bob Kalsu from the Buffalo Bills is here, in this hellhole?" As the words left my mouth, I smiled. We were actually on a hill not in a hole.

"What do you know about Kalsu?" One of the guys—I thought his name was Al—who was hauling ammo, asked as he walked by the howitzer Mike and I were manning.

Mike responded with a grin. "Johnny's a walking encyclopedia on college and professional football. He was All-State in 1968. Iowa farm boy that he is, he stayed on the farm instead of attending Moo U, and he ended up here." Mike spread out his arms, indicating the dirt pile that was Ripcord. "He can tell you about Kalsu."

"Moo U," Al quipped. "Isn't that Iowa State?"

I nodded at Al, ignored Mike, and answered the original question. "Bob Kalsu was an All-American from Oklahoma and an eighth-round draft pick for the Buffalo Bills. He was the Bill's Rookie of the Year in '68."

"Why didn't he seek deferment like other pros?" Al asked. "I heard most professional athletes who were drafted opted to serve as Reserves. That would have been my choice, for damn sure." Al put down the ammo then wiped the sweat from his brow.

"Have you met him?" Mike asked. "If you'd met the man, you would understand why he didn't seek deferment. He understands obligation. Kalsu was in the ROTC in college and made a commitment to the army."

"I think he has a wife and a kid," I said. "It was hard enough leaving my girl. It would be a real bitch to leave a wife and kid. Well, if I meet him, I'm gonna get his autograph."

"Who says dreams don't come true?" Mike said, pointing me toward the guy on his other side. "Johnny, I'd like you to meet First Lieutenant Bob Kalsu."

"Incoming," a soldier shouted before I could shake Kalsu's hand. We dove for cover, regrouped, then started firing. We turned our gun toward the west. It appeared the fire was coming from the high ground, maybe hill 1000.

*****

Present day

"Jack. Wake up, Jack." Mom was shaking my shoulder. I was crouched in a ball on the floor of my bedroom. Well, I sure as shit hadn't been dreaming about Ivy or the '60s chick either. I was back to dreaming about Nam. I was soaked in sweat. It had been a bad one.

"Are you okay? Listen," she said, like I was doing something else, "you *will* call the doctor tomorrow. Do you understand?"

"Yes, sir." I saluted from my position on the floor.

"Not funny," Mom replied. "Get moving. It's Sunday morning; well, very late Sunday morning. How was your date with Ivy?"

"Honestly?" I asked as I stood up and stretched.

"No, son," Mom replied, "I was thinking you should lie."

"If you keep up that attitude young lady," I said in a stern voice, using her tone when she was scolding me, "you'll never know."

"Sorry." Mom grinned. "You know I can't help it when you leave the door wide open for a little mother and son sarcasm. Seriously, how was it?"

"Best night ever," I replied. "Honestly. I'm inviting her to come over tonight and watch me do the show. Did I mention she's a fangirl? And you thought my show only attracted a bunch of hippies. Mom," I said as I watched her pick up my clothes and other crap off the floor. "I really appreciate the maid service, which I know is a ploy to get me to tell you more details about my date. I'm not one to kiss and tell."

"So, there was kissing," she said as she tossed a dirty shirt into the laundry basket.

"Mom… Out, woman," I said loudly, directing her to the door.

I shut the door behind her, still trying not to laugh.

"What, Stan?" I heard Mom say. She must be right outside my door. "You need to talk to him about safe sex and condoms and STDs. I mean, the girl is from St. Louis, after all."

"Mom"—I stuck my head out the door—"Ivy is *not* that kind of girl." I glanced at Stan then winked. "Pencil me in for the sex talk, boss. Obviously you must be good at it." I pointed to the twins, who were attached to his leg like little monkeys.

"Get dressed," Mom said as she pushed me back into my room. "It's not nice to eavesdrop."

I picked up my phone, hoping to see a text from Ivy. Nothing. I wanted to text her, but I didn't want to seem eager. I did it anyway.

JACK: *Want to watch me do* Flashback?

Appealing to her inner fangirl. *That oughta work.* Tossing the phone on my bed, I grabbed my stuff for the shower. I glanced at the phone. No response.

The shower was cold. I still needed a cold shower after last night. I pressed my hands against the walls of the stall and let the icy water pound on my head and back. In the quiet of the shower, I let my mind go. I reflected on the dreams—the dreams of Vietnam and the dreams of Christine.

Ivy is connected to all of this. I just don't know how. I mean, we can't both have Dissociative Identity Disorder. What else is there? I turned the water to hot, then scrubbed. After all, I wanted to smell good if I saw her later today.

I dried off then put on my khakis. I picked up my phone and, yes, a message from Ivy.

IVY: *Fangirl is in! Time?*

Glancing at the clock, I saw that it was only eleven thirty. I couldn't wait till tonight.

"Mom," I shouted, "can I invite Ivy to Sunday lunch?"

"Sure," Mom shouted back. "I'll be serving baked chicken with a side of condoms."

"Cathy," I heard Stan say. I could also hear him laughing.

JACK: One, for lunch?

I walked out to the kitchen. "I'll take the truck and pick Ivy up after church."

It was a great day, I noticed, as I walked to the truck. It would probably get to a hundred by this afternoon. Right now it felt really good. *Okay, maybe I'm just feeling really good. Huh?* A piece of notebook paper was shoved under the windshield wiper. I pulled it out before opening the door to the cab of my truck.

Stay away from the new girl.

Seriously? I crumpled the paper into a ball then tossed it into the back seat. The message was like something from a bad detective movie.

Church was gonna last forever, I believed, as I pulled into the parking lot. Then I saw her. She was standing by her mom and her granddad. She was beautiful and she was mine. My heart started to race and my palms got sweaty. I got out of the truck and rubbed my palms on my pants. Seeing her and not kissing her was gonna kill me. She hadn't seen me yet. I walked toward her…

*****

Fall, 1969

She is so beautiful, I thought as I spotted Christine in the group of girls in the Homecoming Court. She hadn't seen me yet, so I could just admire the view. She turned and scanned the crowd. I knew the moment she spotted me. A smile spread across her face as she waved. Christine separated herself from the group then walked toward me. I noticed how the light made her hair shine. Then I noticed her jewelry. She was wearing my ring on a chain around her neck. I got a strange—I don't know, maybe possessive—feeling in my gut. She was beautiful and she was mine.

*****

Present day

"Hey, Jack," Ivy smiled and waved. Suddenly, it hit me. Though it was totally crazy, maybe, just maybe, Ivy and me were Christine and Johnny. *Is it possible we are reincarnated from two kids who'd died? Do I even believe in reincarnation?*

Well, I considered as I stood in front of Ivy, forcing myself to not pull her into my arms and kiss her in the church parking lot, I'm guessing Johnny died in Vietnam, but it was more likely Christine was alive and well with children older than Ivy and me. *Probably not reincarnated.*

"Hey, Ivy," I said as I clasped her hand. She glanced down at our entwined fingers then looked at me and smiled. "I was just telling Mom and Gramps how much I enjoyed the drive-in last night. The *Hunger Games*…it never gets old."

"Which movie did you like the best?" Mrs. Drake asked me as we walked toward the church.

"Mrs Drake," I said, "my mom and stepdad are right over there." I gestured toward the entrance. "I would love for you to meet them. Where is your grandmother?" I asked Ivy as the four of us walked toward my mom and Stan.

"She doesn't go to church," Ivy whispered. "She hasn't stepped foot in a church for years. Nice save, by the way. Which one would you have picked, anyway?"

"The one where I got you to lie on the seat with me," I whispered into her ear.

"Mom," I said, tugging Ivy along, "this is Ivy's mom and her granddad."

I half listened to the introductions as I admired Ivy in her summer dress. What would she think about the whole reincarnation thing? Most likely she'd think I was crazy, then dump me.

"So, Ivy will be going back to your place?" Mrs Drake questioned as we entered the church. "Thanks for inviting her to lunch. Ivy, you can sit with Jack if you'd like."

"Why don't we all sit together?" Ivy suggested.

We sat down in a row. Ivy and I were seated together, hands clasped and arms touching. *Damn, I'm going to have impure thoughts in church. Not good.*

Ivy glanced at me and grinned.

I really hope she can't read my mind.

I stared straight ahead, trying to think about anything but Ivy. Taking a deep breath, I tried to focus on something else. That was a bad idea, I realized too late. I inhaled the warm smell of Ivy. The service went by at an incredibly slow rate, and I didn't hear a thing. All I was focused on was Ivy's neck that was exposed by her hair being in a braid thing. I wanted to kiss her neck.

*****

Summer, 1969

"Hi Johnny," Christine whispered as she settled down next to me in the row at the back of the church.

"What's with the turtleneck," I whispered back. "It's gotta be like a hundred degrees in here."

She glanced at me and blushed.

"What?" I repeated.

"You gave me a hickey," she mumbled.

"I gave you a what?" I replied. She looked at me in a totally disgruntled and still incredibly adorable way.

She pulled my head down then whispered in my ear, "You gave me a hickey last night at the drive-in. You should have focused more on *Midnight Cowboy* and less on trying to get me out of my dress."

"But, I wanted to get you out of your dress," I said into her ear.

"Amen," the congregation said in unison.

I struggled not to laugh as Christine rolled her eyes then smiled at the perfect timing. Well, I thought it was perfect timing. "See? The entire congregation agrees," I whispered

*****

Present day

"Jack, Jack," Ivy elbowed me in the stomach. "Church is

over. We can leave."

"Thank God," I said. Mom looked and me then started to laugh.

"Well, that was a heartfelt prayer. And I thought you weren't listening. Silly me," she said as she clasped the twins' hands and walked toward the parking lot. "See you guys back at the house."

Mom and Mrs Drake talked as they walked together, laughing as the twins tried to escape.

"Come on, beautiful," I said as I put my hand in the small of Ivy's back, guiding her to my truck. I walked her to the passenger's side then opened the door. I assisted her into the cab, accidently on purpose placing a hand on her ass.

"Jack," she said, glancing back at me. She was blushing.

"Sorry." I winked. "Actually, I'm not sorry. I mean, I should be sorry, but I'm not. So if I say I am, that would be lying. I promised I wasn't gonna lie."

I closed her door then walked to my side of the truck, chuckling at the disgruntled look on her face.

Ivy was staring out the window as I closed the door and turned on the engine. Maybe she was really mad. *Damn.* "Ivy, look at me," I said as I tugged on her arm. She turned her startling green eyes in my direction and blinked.

"Sorry," she said as she took hold of my hand. "I was just thinking about the dream I had last night. I know it was totally connected to the movie, but it was still so bizarre." She paused.

"Tell me about it," I said. "It can't be more bizarre then the stuff I dream about."

"Okay," Ivy replied. "So, Johnny and Christine were sitting on a couch with a bunch of other people. I think it was Johnny's family. They were watching people on television draw names for something, maybe the draft. It was so weird. They were pulling blue capsules out of a clear, tub-like thing. But no one said, 'May the odds be in your favor.'" Ivy smiled. "It was like the reaping in the movie, only different." She shook her head like she was trying to unscramble her thoughts.

I pulled out of the church parking lot and turned down a gravel road that would eventually hook up with First Avenue. The only thing I was thinking about was pulling the truck off the road and getting closer to Ivy.

"What the heck, Jack? Are you trying to be in NASCAR? I don't think trucks compete."

I slammed on the brakes and abruptly put the truck in Park. I reached over, unlocked Ivy's seatbelt, then pulled her into my arms. I tilted her face toward mine and whispered, "Give me a little sugar, sugar." I pressed my lips against hers, and it felt so good. I slid my tongue against the seam of her lips, encouraging her to open her mouth. My tongue touched hers, and I was lost. She was kissing me as frantically as I was kissing her. When I realized my hand was on her thigh under her dress, reality came crashing back.

"Damn," I whispered against her lips.

"Damn," she replied, with a smile in her voice.

"Shit." I wrapped my arm around her, put the truck in Drive, then pulled back onto the gravel road. "Any thoughts on how I can explain why a five-minute ride took twenty-five minutes?'

Ivy rubbed her head against my arm. "Not a clue."

We sped down the gravel road then turned onto First Avenue. We arrived at my house in less than five minutes. I parked and pulled Ivy out my side of the truck then kind of pushed her up the driveway. "Sorry it took us so long," I said as I ushered Ivy to the table.

"No problem," Mom said to Ivy. "We are so glad Jack invited you to lunch. I make a big Sunday dinner for the family, then we kind of do nothing for the rest of the day."

"Stan, Stella, Stevie," Mom called out the window. Then she whispered to me, "We put the 'side dish' in your bathroom."

I glanced at Ivy. Mom punched me in the stomach. "Rein in the hormones, dude, I was kidding. Let's eat," Mom said as the rest of the family came to the table.

"Everything looks so good. Thanks for having me," Ivy said as she put a chicken leg on her plate.

The meal passed in a blur of conversation, though I really wasn't listening. I was thinking about Ivy's dream. The reincarnation thing seemed kinda possible and yet totally impossible. "Didn't they do a draft lottery during the Vietnam War?" I asked suddenly.

All conversation stopped and everyone turned and looked at me. "Well, Jack," Mom said, "that was random."

"Sorry." I kind of mumbled. It wasn't just random. It was embarrassing. Ivy was gonna think I'm rude or something.

"Well," Stan said, saving me from my randomness, which actually wasn't random, but no one else knew that. "There was a draft for the Vietnam War."

"By the way," I said to Ivy, "Stan teaches history at DMACC or Des Moines Area Community College," I clarified. "The campus is downtown, kinda near the square."

Ivy nodded and smiled.

"Draft Night 1969 was televised. Families across the country with young men aged nineteen years old and older sat around their TV, waiting for the dates to be announced," Stan paused.

"What dates?" Ivy asked.

"Birth dates. All three-hundred-sixty-six days were

included."

"Three-hundred-sixty-six?" Mom interrupted Stan. "Oh, February twenty-ninth…duh. You may continue."

Stan grinned. "The dates were placed in blue capsules and randomly pulled out of a big tub. The men would be drafted based on the date of their birth. The earlier your birth date was pulled, the greater your chance of going to Vietnam. The poor suckers drawn in the first quarter of the numbers selected were heading for Nam." Stan pulled his cell phone out of his pocket. "There's a video on YouTube from CBS Evening News that covers Lottery Night." Stan tapped his phone then handed it to me. Everyone gathered around the phone to watch.

The words Special Report appeared on the small screen of Stan's phone. The broadcast was replacing *Mayberry RFD*. A guy by the name of Mudd was doing the commentary. In the background, dates were being read by the people running the lottery. The first date was September fourteenth. The third date popped out at me, December thirtieth. *Damn, my birthday*.

"Wow, Jack," Mom said, "did you see your birthday? This was one lottery no one would want to win."

I glanced at Ivy. She was in a daze. *Damn.* "Thanks for showing me the video," I said. "It was way more powerful to watch it than just to hear about it."

"Weird," Ivy whispered, "totally weird."

"We're going to go to the basement and work on the show. Ivy's my latest fangirl," I said as I pulled Ivy to her feet.

"Do you need help, Cathy?" Ivy said as she grabbed a stack of dishes. "Jack and I can bus the table."

Mom laughed as Ivy handed me a bunch of dishes. "Stella made a really interesting design in the mashed potatoes with her green beans."

"I believe she suffers from lachanophopia," I said as I

walked to the sink.

"Stella does not have a fear of vegetables," Ivy replied, then hit me with a dishcloth.

Mom look dumbfounded. "You know what lachnophobia is? Stan, did you hear that? Ivy understands Word Boy."

The last dish was in the sink. Ignoring my mom, I grabbed Ivy's hand then led her to the basement door. "Thanks again," Ivy said. "It was really good."

"Come on, Ivy. Good? You can do better than that."

Ivy stopped, then turned to my mom. "What I meant to say was the meal was superlative, preeminent of other Sunday meals. It was downright sumptuous."

"Jack's dating Word Girl," Mom said to Stan in amazement.

I pulled the door shut then tugged Ivy into my arms, keeping my balance by hanging on to the railing while I kissed her. "That was so good," I murmured against her mouth. "It was superlative, preeminent of any other kiss. It was downright sensuous."

"The word was sumptuous, Jack. Get it right." Ivy laughed against my mouth, and it was sublime. *Sublime… Good word.*

"Come on, Jack. I'm in full fangirl mode. I want to see how you tie the drive-in into the show. You know what? That was so strange. My weird dream was kind of historic. I must have learned about it in American History last year then forgot."

How do you broach the subject of past lives? Reincarnation? I watched as Ivy rummaged through my album collection and I decided that now wasn't the time.

"Sit here, fangirl." I pulled out a chair and held out my hand to Ivy. She clasped my hand and took a seat.

I flipped through the stacks until I found "Everybody's Talkin'" from *Midnight Cowboy*. I held the album up for Ivy to see. "Smooth," she said with a laugh. "I so know where you're going with this." I grinned and jotted down some notes to use with the taping.

I opened one of the drawers in the desk then took out a Camaro muscle car T-shirt, circa 1969.

"A car T-shirt?"

"Work with me, fangirl. To get to the drive-in, you need a car. Now, I think you'll agree that it's easier to make out in truck, but a 1969 Camaro? Now that's a cool car." I pulled off my shirt then glanced at Ivy, who was staring at me. I think she liked what she saw. "What?"

"You have a helluva good body, Jack Vander Zee," Ivy said. "Oh my God, I can't believe I just said that."

"Come here, fangirl," I said holding out my hand. Ivy walked toward me. "I'm gonna kiss you now," I murmured. She reached her bare arms around my naked torso. Damn, it felt so good. "Ivy, you drive me crazy, in a really good way." I moved an arm's length away. "Stand back, girl. I've got a show to do." I tugged my vintage T-shirt over my head then shoved my arms in the sleeves as I sat down in front of the camera and turned it on. "It's Flashback Jack on *Flashback 1969*. If you haven't been to a drive-in, you don't know what you're missing. My hometown has one of the few remaining drive-in movie theaters in the country. If you would've gone to the drive-in in 1969, you might have seen an American classic, *Midnight Cowboy*, starring Jon Voight and Dustin Hoffman. The theme song 'Everybody's Talkin'", performed by Harry Nilsson, made Billboard's Top 100 in 1969, coming in at number forty-three. In the '60s, the drive-in was also called 'the passion pit'. Driving a Camaro, like the one featured on my T-shirt, meant you had one bitchin' ride to get you to the drive-in, but you would have had to fight the console and contend with the birth control seats to pull your girl close. If you don't have a console and bucket seats, grab your girl or your guy and hold 'em close. We're going back to 1969 with 'Everybody's Talkin'', the theme song for *Midnight Cowboy*."

I put on the album then looked at Ivy. She was lying on the floor with her feet on the chair. I wanted to kiss her again. "Stay focused, Jack. The song won't last forever," she said softly.

Holding Ivy close, we listened to Nilsson's song. It felt so right. It felt like we'd done this a million times.

The song came to an end. I shared a clip from the movie and briefly discussed Harry Nilsson's career as a singer and song writer.

"That's it for tonight. This is Flashback Jack. I'll catch you on the flipside."

Ivy smiled at me. I dove onto her, rolling her over so she was lying on me. "I'm so glad you're here." I meant here in my life, not just here as in my house.

She cupped my face in her hands as she stared into my eyes. "I can't believe I'm saying this after only a week, but Jack, there is absolutely no other place I want to be."

Did she mean here in my arms or here in Newton? I think she meant here with me.

Ivy whispered, "If I don't kiss you right now, I think I might die."

I leaned up and met her halfway.

Chapter 11

Ivy

My online journal got an earful tonight. I couldn't seem to verbalize how I felt about Jack. I hoped I wasn't so into him because he was my only friend. After two weeks of being together, I wasn't really interested in being friends with the girls—well, except for Bri. I think she might actually be my friend. Tonight she was working with Jack and Collin to—what's the word I'm looking for? *Surprise*, that'll work—surprise Katie and her friends.

"Ivy," Mom called, "Katie and the other girls are here."

I walked down the steps to discover Chloe and a couple other cheerleaders were in the group. I thought I had been building bridges. I guessed I was wrong.

"This is Becca," Katie said.

"Hi, Becca," I said. "It's nice to meet you."

Becca didn't say anything. *Awkward.* Then I remembered… She was the one I'd bumped of the cheer squad.

"So, I guess we should be going. Mom, I should be home by eleven or maybe earlier." I checked my pocket to make sure my phone was secure. Jack had found an app so he could track my phone by its number. No matter where the girls decided to go, as long as there was a cell signal, Jack would be able to find me.

"Where are we going?" I asked. These girls made me nervous. I felt the way Christine must have felt, running through the cornfield in my dream. I had that one a lot. I hoped it wasn't a warning about tonight. I watched those made-for-TV movies where the girls would take out someone and kill them. *Okay, Ivy. Pull it together, girl.*

"My farm," Chloe said. "We have the best snipe in the area. You are going to love snipe hunting. It's so fun."

Right, bitch. Seriously, did these girls think I was stupid? Collin, Bri, and Jack had explained it to me, then I'd searched "snipe hunt", just to be sure. I liked Wikipedia's definition the best. These girls wanted to make fun of me. I think their plan probably included something on YouTube.

Pulling my phone out of my back pocket, I sent a text to Jack. "Chloe" was the message.

We drove down the country road. Dusk was coming and it gave the landscape an eerie glow…

*****

Summer, 1969

It was Sunday night. Tomorrow was Labor Day, and school started on Tuesday. Johnny and I sat in his Camaro, staring into the night. "School's not going to be the same without you," I said. "I sure wish I'd graduated with you. Then we would both be at college and you would be safe. No, that's not true. You would still be needed on the farm."

Johnny tugged me against his side. "I'm glad I'm home. I know you're worried about the draft, but the chances are slim-to-none I'll be selected to go."

I stared into the dark sky, not wanting to talk about my greatest fear. I wanted Johnny here with me, but if he'd enrolled in college, he'd be in the position for deferment. It was so frustrating. Regardless of how I felt, he wouldn't leave his dad to manage the farm alone.

An unfamiliar sound disturbed the quiet of the night. An airplane appeared to be heading for the airport. It just didn't sound right. The engine sputtered, stopped, sputtered, then a flash of light.

"Oh my God," I whispered, "I think it crashed."

Johnny backed up the Camaro and headed toward the crash site. A bunch of police cars with sirens blasted past us. "I guess they have it covered," Johnny said.

"Whatever it was," I said, "I hope everyone was okay."

*****

Present day

"Hey, we're here," Katie said as she parked the car near the barn.

Whoa, what is wrong with me? "Is there an airport around here?" I asked.

"Yeah. Why?" Chloe asked.

"No reason," I replied. "I was just wondering. Did you guys hear a plane?"

The girls glanced at each other like I was crazy. "I guess not," I mumbled.

"Wow, a real farm," I said as I studied the surroundings that were in sort of a half light. "It's kind of creepy, no offense intended," I said as I studied the cornfield. My heart raced. That dream I kept having about being chased through a cornfield played in my head. I glanced around the dirt road and the field, looking for Jack's truck. I really hoped they were here. I hoped the dream wasn't a premonition about what was happening tonight. *Premonition... Great word.*

"So, how does the snipe hunt work?" I asked in a friendly voice, or at least my attempt at a friendly voice, considering I knew their intent was to make me look like an ass.

I'd rather look like an ass than be chased through a cornfield. Well, at least they didn't want to kill me.

"It's really easy. You take two pieces of wood and bang them together while shouting, 'Here snipe. Here snipe'," Katie said as she handed me a couple of pieces of wood.

"Why don't you demonstrate it for me?" I said, feigning concentration. "I've never hunted anything before. I'm glad we aren't using guns. Once we catch one, what do we do? Knock it out with a club or something?"

"Um, you bag it," Becca said. "Here," she said, grabbing the sticks from my hands.

"Like this… Here snipe. Here snipe."

The corn started to rustle; it was waving back and forth like something was running through it. "Oh my God," I said, staring at the moving corn, "the snipes are coming."

"Get in the car," Chloe yelled. "There are no such things as snipe."

"Actually, there are," I said calmly as the other girls pushed each other into the car. Chloe looked at me then at the waving corn. "They just don't live in Iowa."

Jack, Collin, and Bri stumbled out of the corn. They were laughing so hard they could barely stand up.

"Oh my God," Chloe said as she joined in the laughter. "You totally scared the crap out of me. Sorry, Ivy," Chloe said sincerely. "We deserved the payback."

Katie jumped out of the car, storming over to Bri. "I can't believe you would side with her," she said as she pointed her finger at me. "And you," she said to Jack, "you're just a messed up asshole that's interested in her"—pointing her finger at me again—"because she reminds you of some dead girl, or missing girl, or whatever, you were in love with in another life—which, by the way, is total bullshit. So, don't act like I'm some bad-ass bitch when the only reason you're into her is because you're messed up with Dissociative Identity Disorder—whatever that is—and she's like some kind of anchor for you."

"Whoa, this isn't a shade-throwing contest," Collin interjected.

I looked at Jack, waiting for his words of denial.

Instead, Jack said, "You overheard my conversation with my doctor yesterday? You don't know anything about it—or me."

Jack never lies, and he wasn't denying Katie's accusations.

"Jack, is that true? I remind you of a dead girl?" *I am such an idiot.*

"It's not like that," Jack said, grabbing my hands. "I think you are amazing. *You*, Ivy."

"You never lie, Jack. Remember?" I pulled my hands out of his. It was painful. I felt like I was breaking a physical bond. "Which part of what Katie said is it not like? The part about me reminding you of a dead girl?" I paused. "The reincarnation part?" I took a deep breath. "The part about Dissociative Identity Disorder? And"—I turned to Katie—"I do know about DID. I learned about it in my AP Psych class. It's like multiple personality disorder. Wow," I said to no one in particular, "that probably explains Flashback Jack."

"Ivy," Jack said, "you feel just as connected to me as I do to you. Could those dreams you've been having be memories? Think about it, Ivy."

"What I'm thinking," I replied, "is that I need to go home. I can't deal with you or this right now." I gestured with my arm to Katie and the other girls. "And how in the hell am I supposed to get home? The girls I came with set me up to be humiliated, and the guy I expected to ride home with is…I don't know what he is." I wanted to say something really mean, but I looked at Jack. He looked devastated. I wanted to walk into his arms…not walk away. I was so stupid.

Jack reached for my arm, I jerked away. "Don't touch me," I said between gritted teeth.

The sound of a motorcycle had us all turning toward the barn. Chloe drove toward us on the bike. She shoved a helmet into my hands. "Come on. I'll give you a ride."

"Please, Ivy," Jack said as he grasped my shoulders.

"Not now," I whispered. "Not now, Jack."

I slipped out of Jack's grip then got on the back of Chloe's bike. She revved the engine and we headed down the dirt road, away from Jack. My stomach was in knots. I felt like I was going to throw up.

"Are you okay?" Chloe asked via the speakers in my headset. "Just talk. I'll be able to hear you."

"Not okay."

"I'm really sorry about tonight. Not about the whole Jack thing… Well, I'm sorry about that for you. I'm sorry I agreed to the whole 'be mean to the new girl snipe hunt' thing. We really aren't bad. We just don't get a lot of new girls. And most of the girls who don't have boyfriends have formed a line waiting for Jack to take notice. No excuses. I'm really sorry, Ivy."

"That's okay," I said, and I meant it. I liked Chloe and I needed some friends.

"You and Jack…" she continued. "You guys actually seem made for each other. It's like he's been waiting for you his entire life. The whole thing is kind of cray cray."

"Kind of ?" I couldn't believe I was smiling about the whole incident.

Chloe chuckled, "Okay, totally! See the field over there?" Chloe nodded to the field on our left.

"Chloe, umm, I pretty much see fields everywhere."

"Hey, this is interesting Newton history. In August of 1969 the world famous boxer Rocky Marciano died in a plane crash right over there. You asked about the airport earlier. His small plane was heading for Des Moines. They might have been trying to make an emergency landing at the Newton Airport. No one will ever know what really happened because everyone on board was killed."

"Is that true or is that like the snipe hunt," I asked. Kind of weird that I'd had the dream thing about a plane crash in a field. *Maybe Jack wasn't totally crazy.*

"No, it's completely true," Chloe replied as we crossed the interstate then drove back into town. "My dad graduated from Brockton High School where Marciano was a star athlete. I think they have a huge statue of him at the school." Chloe's laughter echoed in my helmet. "But that's not important right now. My dad knew Marciano died in Newton, and he loved to tell anyone who would listen about Marciano's athletic prowess in high school, even though my dad was born the year Marciano died."

We rode in companionable silence until Chloe pulled into my driveway. I climbed off the back of the bike then handed Chloe my helmet. "Thanks for the ride," I said as I walked toward the porch.

"Ivy," Chloe called, "thanks for forgiving me."

I waved and continued up the steps.

"Give Jack a chance. He's worth it."

I waved again and gave her a thumbs-up. I really did want to give Jack a chance.

"I'm home," I called as I walked into the house. It was only nine o'clock. No one was there.

Pounding on the door caused me to almost have a heart

attack. I could see Jack through the window. His head was pressed to the door and the hand that wasn't knocking was flat against the door, like he wanted to press his palm against mine.

"Ivy… Please, Ivy," Jack repeated as he continued to pound the door. Thank God my mom and grandparents weren't home. They'd think he'd totally lost it.

I placed my palm against the door in the general location of his palm. I swear I could feel the heat from his hand penetrating through the wood, pulling me to him. I placed my other hand on the door knob and slowly turned, pulling the door inward. Jack stumbled into the hallway.

His blue eyes looked kind of crazed. I wasn't sure if I should run up the stairs or run into his arms. Jack pulled me against him, making the decision for me. I was good with that, I decided, as I felt the warmth of his body against mine.

"Ivy," he whispered as he tilted up my face and crushed my lips with his. I hesitated for a moment. Maybe kissing Jack wasn't a good idea. I mean…Jack might be crazy. I mean really crazy, as in multiple personality kind of crazy. Or, he wasn't. I decided I didn't care. I wrapped my arms around his neck and kissed him back.

"Ivy," Jack said through ragged breaths, "I can't lie to you. I don't know what's wrong with me. But you? You make me feel grounded. If you'll listen, I'll tell you everything. I don't have multiple personalities. I don't think I'm crazy, but I do have issues—issues I've never been able to figure out until you." Jack spoke rapidly as he gently stroked my face and hair while staring deeply into my eyes, as if he were willing me to listen…willing me to understand.

"Okay, Jack," I reached up and cupped his face. He turned his head and kissed the palm of my hand. "Okay, I'll listen."

His shoulders sagged with relief as he pulled me tightly against his chest, tucking my head under his chin. Headlights turned into the driveway, casting shadows in the hallway. "I gotta move my truck," Jack said without moving.

"Call me in the morning, and we can figure it out," I said as I disengaged myself from his strong arms.

"Three things," Jack said, placing his hands firmly on my shoulders. "One, I'll see you at church tomorrow. Two, plan on coming to my house for Sunday lunch. Three"—he grinned at me and my heart sort of stuttered in my chest—"watch my channel tonight in half an hour. I'm doing a special broadcast for you." He kissed me swiftly on the lips. "We good?"

I nodded then sort of shoved him out the door. We were *so* good. I ran up the stairs to my room. I really didn't want to talk to Mom tonight, so I turned on the shower and ignored her when she called my name.

After I was cleaned up, I brought my laptop and my phone with me to bed.

JACK: *Are you watching?*

IVY: *Yes*

He appeared on my screen. "It's Flashback Jack with a special Saturday night edition of *Flashback 1969*. Tonight's special broadcast is dedicated to Ivy, the girl I hope will be my—you know what they said in the day—steady. I have three hits from 1969 sure to win her heart. The first song is from the Archies. For your listening and viewing pleasure, I'm bringing you the 1969 broadcast of *The Archie Comedy Hour*, featuring *Billboard* Magazine's number one hit from 1969, 'Sugar, Sugar'."

My phone buzzed. I read the text.

JACK: *You are my candy girl.*

I started to text the lyrics. I deleted the text then replied.

IVY: *Archie turned into a bunny? No, really?*

JACK: *Really*

"Flashback Jack is back with another hit from 1969. Ivy, you are my candy girl. Not only do I want you, I want you to know how you make me feel. To help me do that is a 1969 hit from Tommy Roe, 'Dizzy'—because, girl, you've got my head spinnin'."

    IVY: *I make you dizzy?*

    JACK: *Babe, my head seriously spins when you're around. In a good way, not like when Linda Blair's head spun around in* The Exorcist.

Handsome, smart and funny…works for me.

IVY: The Exorcist. *Nice comparison.*

JACK: *Sorry, not what I meant.*

I could hear his laughter in the tone of the text, even if I couldn't really hear him laughing.

"The final song in this evening's Ivy trilogy is by the Grass Roots. Ivy, I feel like I've been waiting my whole life for you. To be with you, 'I'd Wait a Million Years'. Please don't make me wait that long."

I wasn't sure what to text, how to respond to the final song, so I didn't text anything.

My phone vibrated.

JACK: *You're worth the wait.*

The song ended and Jack was back on my screen. "This is Flashback Jack with a Saturday night tribute to Ivy. Sweet dreams, Ivy, and I'll see *you* on the flipside." I loved the way he emphasized the word *you*.

IVY: *Night, Jack*

I texted, because I didn't know what else to say. It was the nicest thing anyone had ever done for me. Maybe Jack did have multiple personalities, but two of them seemed to like me a lot.

My phone buzzed. It was a group text with a message from Claire.

CLAIRE: *He dedicated his show to you.*

ERICA: *U R his candy girl. How sweet. No really :)*

ALEX: *LOL*

AUDREY: *Steady? Bae!*

IVY: *I miss you*

I really missed my friends. Would they like Jack?

I put my laptop and my phone on the table next to my bed. Snuggling into my pillow, I closed my eyes and thought about Jack…

*****

December, 1969

"Christine, please don't cry," Johnny said as he pulled me into his arms. "I was gonna be called up in early January anyway. Enlisting gave me some choices."

I sniffled as I tried to stop crying. "It's so unfair. You can die for your country, but you can't even vote. Wrong! Wrong! Wrong!" I said as I punched Johnny in the arm to emphasize how wrong this was. "I'm so mad at the president. I want to hit him too."

"The president of the United States of America," Johnny said in a teasing voice. "I'm pretty sure I swore I would protect him today. So, don't threaten President Nixon."

I leaned back in Johnny's arms and stared into his blue eyes. My stomach ached as I thought about him leaving me, me losing him. We had a couple of weeks before he would go to boot camp. I could choose to be miserable or I could choose to make the most of it. I was going to be miserable when he left. I would choose not to be miserable when he was still here.

"Okay, Johnny," I said softly into his neck.

"Okay, what?" he asked.

"Okay, I won't threaten the President," I said as I peeked up at him through my lashes. "Oh, turn up the radio," I said. "It's the song by the Grass Roots. I'd sing it for you, but you know dogs howl in horror when I sing." Johnny chuckled into my ear but didn't respond. I really was a bad singer. "Anyway, just so you know, I will wait for you... I'd wait for a million years."

"Two years," Johnny replied. "I need you to wait for two years."

Chapter 12

Jack—New Year's Eve, 1969

I'm leaving tomorrow. Tomorrow. How do I say goodbye to Christine?

I walked up the steps to her house then knocked on the door. Tonight was New Year's Eve, and tomorrow, January 1, 1970, I departed for basic training in North Carolina. *Happy New Year, Johnny!*

It was pretty damn cold. I stamped my feet and rubbed my hands as I waited for Christine's dad to open the door. I glanced at the Camaro still running in the driveway. The cold night made the smoke from the exhaust pipe look like a fog machine.

The door opened. It was Christine.

"Mom and Dad went to the New Year's Eve party at the Club. I left them a note saying I was going to sleep over at Cindy's after Bill's party ended at one." She closed the door and used the key to lock it. She turned into my arms, and I kissed her. I did not want to go to Bill's party. I did not want Christine to spend the night at Cindy's. I wanted to spend my last night, the entire night, alone with her.

"How would you feel about not going to Bill's?" I asked as I walked her to the car with my arm around her waist. I opened the car door and held her hand, assisting her into the seat. I was still waiting for her answer after walking around the car to my seat behind the steering wheel.

"Johnny, I love that you never lie, not even little white lies. I am not that good of a person. I don't plan to spend the night at Cindy's. I planned to spend the night with you. Bill's your friend. I think he might flip his wig if we don't show up for his party."

I was speechless for a moment. "You're sure?" I asked as I backed the car out of the drive and onto First Avenue, turning the car toward the country rather than toward Bill's house on the other side of town. "Bill might be hacked, but I want to spend my last night with you."

Christine reached down and pulled out a bottle from her purse. "I have a bottle of Ackerman's Concord Grape Wine. Dad got it in an Amana Colonies' gift basket from a client for Christmas. I hid a bottle for tonight. It's sweet and yummy."

"Lucky for me I brought some beer," I said gesturing to the back seat where I had a six-pack.

"Lucky for us, my mom thinks I'm sleeping at Cindy's. I'd hate for you to be a drunk driver like Ted Kennedy at Chappaquiddick and me end up dead in a pond like Mary Jo Kopechne."

"Christine," I said, pulling her over as close to me as possible, "all the ponds are frozen. I think you're safe with me. Besides," I continued, "I love you. I would never drive drunk with you in the car. I am, however, willing to spend the night with you in the freezing cold."

"Where are we heading?" Christine asked as she laid her head on my shoulder.

"A place close to our usual spot," I said as I turned the Camaro down a dirt road that I knew was near an abandoned barn on my dad's property. "I was thinking we could pull the car into the old barn. We'd be more protected from the cold."

"Johnny," Christine said, pushing herself away from me and looking out into the darkness, "did you come out here and plow the snow off this road?"

I grinned into the darkness. "I'm not gonna lie."

"Good plan," she said as she settled back down in my

arms.

The Camaro fit through the door of the old barn. It was a challenge, 'cause the barn door was half on and half off. The barn was pitch-black except for the areas illuminated by my headlights. No people or animals were inside. I wasn't worried about people. I *was* a little concerned about animals.

"Do you have any blankets?" Christine asked as she turned up the radio. Then she climbed between the two front seats to the back of the car, taking the wine with her.

I opened the car door, walked to the trunk, then popped it open. I pulled out a couple of blankets, slammed the lid shut, then pushed the front seat down and climbed into the back seat, pulling the door closed behind me. Then I slid across the seat to be close to Christine.

Christine opened the bottle of wine, took a swig, then handed the bottle to me. I shook my head, but took a drink to make my girl happy. I handed the bottle back to Christine. She took one small sip, capped the bottle, and then placed it on the floor of the car. "I want to remember everything," she said as she opened her arms and pulled me down against her. I pressed my lips to hers in a deep kiss.

"Johnny," she whispered, "I love you with all my heart. We're promised to each other, and, when you come home from your tour of duty, we're going to get married. But—"

Damn, is she gonna break up with me before I go? This cannot be happening.

"Christine," I whispered into her neck, interrupting her, "we can make this work. I know it's gonna be tough, but it won't be forever." She tugged on my hair so I was looking into her incredible eyes, though the color was impossible to see in the dim interior of the car. I knew the color by heart.

"I think we might have our signals crossed," she said

softly. "Johnny, I don't want to break up with you. I want to go all the way, tonight, before you leave me. I want to make a commitment with my body, along with my heart and my mind."

"Are you sure?" I whispered, kissing her neck, her cheek, and her lips. "I thought we were gonna wait 'til we got married."

"I want to do it tonight, now. I don't want to wait. I want you to remember this night every night you are away from me. I want you to have all of me. Please, Johnny," she whispered. "I need you so much."

"I need you too," I said as I wrapped my arms around her then kissed her with all of the love in my heart, with all the emotion I'd kept inside me since my number was drawn. "I guess our first time is gonna be in the back seat of my Camaro with the Archic's singing 'Sugar, Sugar' on the radio."

"It's a very nice Camaro," Christine said as she unzipped my coat then misquoted the lyrics to the song: "You are my candy boy, and I'm a wanting you." She looked at me then smiled. I would always remember this song, this night, this girl.

*****

Present day

"Jack! Jack! Wake up! Wake up! You need to get up for school," Stella and Stevie yelled as they jumped on me and my bed.

"Get off me, you wild things," I said as I gently tossed them off the bed so that they landed in a laughing heap on the floor. "You have two seconds to get out of here, or I'm calling Mom."

"Mom sent them in to get you moving," Mom said from

the door. "As much as I like Ivy, you stayed at her house way too late last night. You have school and practice today. It's the first day of your senior year. Get moving, boy."

"Woman," I replied gruffly, "get Thing 1 and Thing 2 out of my room or I'm going to toss them at you." I grasped Stella by the elastic in her pajama bottoms and started to lift her off the ground.

"Me, me," Stevie yelled, pushing on Stella, trying to get me to drop her and pick him instead. I guess my threat was a game to my brother and sister.

"Come on, kids," Mom said. "You need to eat breakfast, then you are going to Aunt Sally's for the day. Mommy's going to work and Jack is going to school." She looked at me, "Move it, Jack. Remember, you're picking up Ivy. You don't want her to be late for her first day at a new school, do you?"

Mom closed the door. I rolled out of bed, rubbing the sleep from my eyes. I was gonna have to take a cold shower, again. Being with Ivy and having dreams about Johnny and Christine was causing me a lot of discomfort. Dreaming about going all the way with Christine was way better than dreaming about me—I mean Johnny—dying in Vietnam.

I turned on the icy shower and let the water revive me. The last two days with Ivy had been kind of tense and intense. She didn't want to talk about the possibility of reincarnation or past lives or anything, but she did like listening to me talk about pretty much everything else. I got out of the shower and dried off. Slinging a towel around my waist in case the twins had found a way to sneak into the bathroom, I looked in the mirror. I really needed a shave. I lathered up then stared at my reflection in the mirror…

*****

Summer, 1970

"Johnny," Mike said as he walked toward where I was hunkered down, trying to shave, "why do you even bother? It's not like we're going to be inspected any time soon. We're kinda out here on a hill in the middle of nowhere."

"Not nowhere, man," I replied. "This is the A Shau Valley, in the middle of Viet f"ing Nam." I continued to shave off several weeks' worth of growth as Mike stood and stared.

"I got it," he said. "You heard the news crew was coming, and you want to look good for your girl if they happen to catch you on camera. You're pathetic," he said with a laugh. "I can't believe a girl who looks like that"—he gestured to Christine's photo in her Pacesetter uniform that was stuck to my mirror—"is waiting around for a grunt like you."

Mike pulled the photo from the mirror and examined it carefully. "Is she a go-go dancer? Black boots, white gloves, short red dress. Is that velvet? Mmm, mmm, mmm!"

Concentrating on my shaving, I continued to ignore Mike. He was my friend and he was an asshole. If the camera crew could catch me on camera and there was a hope Christine would see it, I was gonna look good. "Photo," I said as I extended my hand to Mike for Christine's picture.

*****

Present day

Damn. I nicked my neck. I stuck a piece of toilet paper on it to stop the blood then stared in the mirror. Johnny looked a helluva lot like me. I'd never seen him before. I just seemed to be in his head, or maybe he seemed to be in mine. The photo on Johnny's mirror was the same photograph of the girl in the trophy case at school—the girl who looked a lot like Ivy.

The dreams or memories were getting more intense and more often. *Where is all of this going?*

Shaking my head, I tried to clear my brain from the thoughts of Vietnam. I walked into my bedroom. On my bed were some clothes Mom must have laid out for the last time I'd have a first day of school. I pulled on the freshly pressed polo and shorts, taking one glance in the mirror. I hoped Ivy liked preppy guys, 'cause Mom tended to buy clothes making me look like I should model for Vineyard Vines.

I grabbed a couple of bagels then walked toward the door.

"Jack," Mom yelled, "we need a first-day-of-school photo."

"Meet me at the truck." I picked up my backpack then pulled some pens and stuff out of the junk drawer in the kitchen.

I reached the truck before Mom and the terrible twins.

Another note was under the windshield wiper. I didn't bother to read it. I grabbed it then stuck it in my pocket before my mom reached me. I picked up the twins and put them in the bed.

"That's so cute," Mom said as she took some pictures with her phone. I stood on the ground beside the truck. Their heads were even with mine because they were standing in the bed.

"I gotta go," I said as I plucked the twins out of the back of the truck and placed them on the ground. "You guys be good for Aunt Sally." I nudged Mom with my shoulder. "I've got a girl to get. See you later!"

I made it to Ivy's house in record time. She was standing

outside, getting her picture taken by her mom. "Hey." She waved as I pulled into the driveway.

I got out of the car then walked toward Ivy and her mom. "Good morning, Mrs Drake," I said as I admired Ivy in her Woodstock T-shirt. "Nice shirt."

"You're not the only one with a vintage shirt collection."

Ivy grabbed my hand and tugged me toward the truck. "Bye, Mom. Have fun at the library." Mrs Drake waved as she sauntered back toward the house.

"Wait," Ivy said before I helped her into the passenger side of the truck. She stretched out her arm and took a photo of us. I grinned and pulled out my phone and took another shot. I assisted her into the truck, walked to my side, then got into the cab.

"Come here, beautiful." I extended my hand then she grabbed it. I pulled her over and proceeded to give her a really intense good morning kiss. Every time we touched, it was better.

"Good morning, Jack," she said as she broke the kiss. We sat and kinda stared at each other. I wrapped my arm around her then backed out of the driveway.

Chapter 13

Ivy

I glanced out the side window as we pulled out of the driveway. "Jack!" I shouted, causing Jack to stop abruptly. A horn blasted as a car sped by. "Wow, they sure were in a hurry."

"I guess so." Jack's face was pale as he glanced in the rearview mirror to pull into the road. "You would have been killed. If that car had hit us, you would've been killed."

"Jeez, Jack"—I laughed—"you're worse than my mother."

Jack didn't respond. He drove in silence until we pulled into what I guessed was the senior lot at the high school.

"You don't understand, do you?" Jack said as he tightened his arm around me. "All the stuff I said on Saturday night is true. You are the part of me that's been missing my entire life." He caressed my cheek then I turned my face into his palm.

"That's good, Jack," I whispered.

"I'm scared, Ivy," Jack said. He slapped his palms on the steering wheel then he pulled me into his arms. "I'm scared about my feelings for you. I'm scared you don't feel the same way about me. And the dreams or memories or frickin' flashbacks—whatever you wanna call 'em? I'm scared about them too. I've never been scared about anything, ever."

What do I say to that?

Jack kissed my head then opened the door. "Come on, beautiful. We can worry about my issues another day. Today is your first day at Newton Senior High. And, did I tell you, you look *so* hot."

"I'm glad you like my T-shirt," I replied with a smile as

we walked toward the school from the parking lot. "I wore it in honor of Flashback Jack's Saturday night dedication, just in case his local fan base was wondering if his number one fangirl accepted his proposal."

I wasn't looking at Jack as we strolled up the hill to the high school. "Is that a yes?" he asked, tugging me to a stop.

I stood on the hill looking down into Jack's blue eyes. He looked serious and elated all at once. "Oh yeah," I said. "That's a definite yes."

Jack lifted me then spun me around. I started to laugh really hard. "You are making a spectacle out of me on my first day at my new school. Put me down, Jack."

"Sorry, Ivy." Jack grinned then he leaned down and whispered, "Umm, I'm not sorry."

He kissed me. I felt the familiar, yet unfamiliar warmth spread rapidly through my body. *Would I always feel like this when Jack kissed me?* Then I wasn't thinking anymore.

"Break it up," Collin yelled as he jumped on Jack's back.

Jack was laughing, and he looked way less tense than he had when we'd pulled into the parking lot. I'd evidently made his day.

Jack slipped something small, hard, and warm into my hand then clasped it tightly. He leaned down and whispered into my ear, "It's what ya do when you're going steady."

The dream, or whatever I'd had in Jack's basement, popped into my head—the one when Johnny gave Christine his ring. I took a deep breath and focused on walking into my new school. I didn't want to ruin my first day by thinking about the dreams of Christine and Johnny, or Jack and his theory of reincarnation. This wasn't about them or that time. This was about me and Jack, right here and right now.

We entered the school, and I looked around. I was

strangely relieved that I did not recognize anything. Jack's ideas about reincarnation were starting to make me paranoid—or maybe it was the frequency of the dreams.

Jack let go of my hand and placed his in the small of my back, navigating me through the crowd of students. I held what I assumed was his class ring tightly in my hand as he guided me through the entrance then the foyer by the performing arts theater. This was a nice school, I decided, as we passed through the groups of students standing in the open area by the entrance to the school's theater. Jack seemed to know everyone, and I was happy to fade into the background, taking it all in.

"This is Ivy," Jack said to a group of guys. *So much for staying in the background.* "You might remember her from the first day of practice."

"Hi, guys," I said to the group, whom I assumed were football players. I started to blush when I remembered exactly what they might be remembering.

A chorus of voices said, "Nice to meet you." "If you dump Jack I'm available." "Hey, Ivy!"

"See ya," Jack said to the group. I kind of waved at the guys as Jack walked me through the crowd.

"Lots of camaraderie and quite the benevolent welcome." I kind of whispered as I was a little overwhelmed by the whole meet-the-team experience.

"Nice use of the ACT top one hundred, Word Girl," Jack whispered back.

We walked down the main hallway toward the principal's office. My heart was racing. I closed my eyes for a moment and I was transported to a different time. In my head, I heard voices…

*****

Fall, 1969

"Christine, your dress is groovy."

"Hey Christine! Remember we have Pacesetters tonight."

"Gee, Christine, it's such a bummer that Johnny won't be here this year."

"Christine, meet me by the gym later."

"Christine, the party at Bill's that you and Johnny missed Friday was a gas."

"Miss Van den Berg, have you filled out your college application?"

"Christine, it was bitchin' you went to Woodstock. I can't believe your parents didn't go ape."

"Christine..."

"Christine..."

"Christine..."

*****

Present day

"Ivy? Ivy?" Jack's voice penetrated the haze, bringing me back to the here and now. He looked concerned. "Are you okay?"

"I'm good," I replied, but I wasn't. I was confused and a little scared. I was clenching Jack's ring so tightly that I was sure it was leaving a deep mark in my palm.

Jack gave me a questioning look. I took a deep breath then smiled in return. "I'm fine, Jack," I said. "Let's get my schedule and figure out where I'm supposed to go for my first class."

"Hey, Mrs Smith," Jack said as he held open the door for me to the principal's office. "This is Ivy Drake. She's new and didn't have her access code for her schedule."

"Hello, Ivy," Mrs Smith said as she typed some information on her computer. She spun in her chair then pulled a piece of paper from her printer. "I was friends with your mom in high school. It's nice to have you with us at Newton High."

She handed me the paper, then I glanced at my schedule.

"It was nice meeting you, Mrs Smith. I'll be sure to tell my mom I met you." I turned to leave. "Thanks again for your help."

I was still clutching Jack's ring in my hand. "Mrs Smith, do you have a few rubber bands I could have?"

"Sure, Ivy. Here you go," she replied as she handed me some.

"Thanks. I promise I won't use them as weapons."

Mrs Smith just smiled and shook her head.

Jack laughed. "Why do you need the rubber bands? They can be quite deleterious in the wrong hands."

"*Deleterious*… You are clearly familiar with the top one hundred. I'm not going to use them to cause harm." I rolled my eyes then unclenched my fist, revealing his ring. "Well, the best plan would be to put this on a necklace and wear it around my neck. Plan B would be to give it back to the original owner." I looked at Jack and he shook his head. "So, Plan C is to put some rubber bands around the band of the ring so it won't fall off."

We walked into a kind of open area with trophy display cases on one wall. The opposite wall was all windows. The dizzy feeling I'd experienced when we'd first entered the hallway near the principal's office hit me again. I clutched Jack's hand and breathed deeply. I couldn't make the voices stop…

*****

Fall, 1969

"Christine, hurry up. We're going to be late to class."

"Christine, did you hear Soul Vibrations will be playing at the Homecoming Dance?"

"Christine, remember to wear the Grecian gown for the International Food Fair."

"Hey, Christine, Bill is still ticked off at you and Johnny missed his party."

"Christine, your Cardinal sign is boss. Did you make it for the Pep Club?"

"Christine, is Johnny sitting in the Dirty Corner?"

"The Dirty Corner's such a great name for where the boys sit at the game. Christine, who thought of that anyway?"

"Christine…"

"Christine…"

"Christine…"

*****

Present day

"Ivy! Ivy, can you hear me?" Jack's concerned voice penetrated the haze in my brain, pulling me away from the insidious voices in my head. Insidious, *that's a great word.*

I looked around the foyer to what I knew was the gym. According to Mom, I'd never been to Newton or Newton High

School, and nothing had been familiar at first. But, I knew this place. Sure, the trophy cases were evidence of a gym. It was more than that. I was confident I had been here before. I just hoped it wasn't in a past life like Jack supposed. I hung on to the idea Mom had brought me to Newton, even though she was adamant she had not. The alternatives, reincarnation or Dissociative Identity Disorder, were not okay. I shook my head, trying to clear my brain. This wasn't okay either.

"Ivy, come on, beautiful. I'll get you to your first class. You're going to be okay. It's just a new place and everything," Jack said as he pulled me against his side.

"Jack," I said softly as I looked into his very concerned face, "the thing is, I think I've been here before. It doesn't feel new. It feels familiar."

I placed my class schedule on a radiator and laid the rubber bands next to it. I examined Jack's ring then wrapped a couple of rubber bands around the back to make it small enough for my finger. "Are you sure about this?" I asked Jack as I admired my handiwork.

Jack didn't say anything at first. Then he nodded his head slowly as he grasped my hand and the ring. He slid his ring onto my finger. "Let there be no doubt," he said softly.

"Ivy," Jack said solemnly as he directed me to the trophy case, "do you see the picture up there?" He pointed toward a victory cup.

I saw the picture. My heart started to race. "Holy crap," I stammered, "that's Johnny from my dreams." The photo of Johnny was in black and white; the caption didn't have his name. The caption read, Iowa All-Star 1968. The resemblance between Jack and Johnny was pretty amazing.

"What are you looking at?" Jack asked. "I wanted you to look at the photograph of the girl." He gestured to the victory cup.

Then I saw the picture Jack was referencing. "Wow," I whispered as I examined the photo. "She looks a lot like me. Who is she?" I asked.

"No one seems to know," Jack replied. "It's kind of weird. Ironically, the library has every yearbook except for 1968, 1969, and 1970." He shrugged. "I was trying to figure out if her name was Christine."

"Jack, take a look at the photo of the football player to the right of the cup." I paused as I waited for Jack to respond.

"Well, I'll be damned," Jack responded, dumbfounded. "That dude looks a helluva lot like me."

Jack and I stood in silence, staring at the photos. The shrill alarm of the tardy bell jolted us back to the present. "Come on," Jack said as he grabbed my hand, leading me out of the gym foyer. "You don't want to be late to your first class.

"Listen. I'll be back to get you after first hour." He leaned down and gave me a quick kiss on the lips.

"Jack," I said before I lost my nerve, "I think you might be on to something with the whole"—I stumbled over the word—"reincarnation thing. Either that or I'm possessed. Reincarnation sounds less frightening than being possessed."

Jack grinned as he leaned down and kissed me again. "Okay then, I'm not sure what happened today, but I'm glad you don't think I'm totally crazy, and I'm kind of glad you might be a little bit crazy."

The bell rang and Jack kind of shoved me into my classroom.

"See you after class," he said as he ran down the hall.

Chapter 14

Jack

I waited impatiently for Ivy to finish talking to Bri and the other girls on the cheer squad. After only a week of school, Ivy seemed to have made a bunch of friends, which was good after the snipe incident. I hated to admit it, but I'd kinda liked it when it had been just me and her. Ivy must have felt my stare, because she turned in my direction. She smiled and waved. She pointed toward me then said goodbye to the other girls.

"Oh my God, Jack," Ivy said as she ran to my side and grabbed my arm. "You were amazing. The interception you made was crazy. Then you ran it in for a touchdown. Seriously, my gramps wasn't kidding. You have some mad football skills."

"Hi," I said as I leaned down, aiming for her smiling lips.

Her hand slid up my shoulder and she grinned. "You're going to kiss me right here in front of God and everyone, aren't you?"

Pressing my lips against hers, I decided the best answer was just to do it.

"Jack," Trey yelled before I had the opportunity to really kiss Ivy, "are you going to McDonald's?"

I glanced at Ivy.

"Whatever you want. If that's where you guys go to celebrate a victory, I'm in," she said.

"It was such a big win," Trey replied enthusiastically. "We annihilated them. I bet they cried all the way back to Marshalltown."

"Like little babies," Collin replied as he and Bri joined our group.

"We'll meet you at the Big M Supper Club in like…fifteen minutes," I said as I grabbed Ivy's hand. "Ivy, do you need to change?" I asked. "Personally, I think you should stay in your uniform. I really like a girl in a short skirt."

Ivy stared at me for a moment. She had the blank expression she got when the past collided with the present.

"Ivy," I repeated softly.

She blinked as she tightened the grip on my hand. As much as Ivy did not want to address the issues we had, we needed to talk about them…the sooner the better. "Change of plans… I'm going to skip Mickcy D's tonight. Ivy's had a crazy hectic week and we need some, uhm, down time. Are you guys cool?" I asked.

"No worries, dude," Trey quickly responded. "I remember when I was the new kid straight from the south side of Chicago. All this community bonding stuff can be overwhelming."

"Hey," Trey's girlfriend said as she punched him the arm.

"I said the community, not you, babe," Trey replied as he wrapped his arm around her.

"No problem, bro," Collin added. "We have next weekend and the one after that. We have the whole damn season ahead of us! Woohoo! We were *sick!*"

"Sick?" I shook my head as I gave Collin a fist bump. "I was thinking our offense was tenacious, our defense was intrepid, and our special teams were exemplary."

"What?" Collin replied.

"Jeez, Jack"—Trey shoulder bumped me—"enough with the ACT review."

I knocked Trey back then grabbed Ivy's hand, leading her toward the exit of HA Lynn Stadium. "Let's go, Ivy."

"Sick," Collin repeated. "Not sure what Jack said, but we were totally sick."

"We can go with your friends," Ivy said as I dropped my arm over her shoulder then pulled her into my side.

"Ivy, we need to talk." She tried to interrupt, but I continued. "You had another memory that can't be yours just now, didn't you?"

She didn't say anything for a moment, then she shook her head. "Yeah, I did. Another time, yet it was the same place and almost the same conversation."

"Damn," I said as we approached my truck. Another note was on the windshield. It was the third one this week. I pulled the note off the windshield, intending to crumple it up and throw it with the other ones in the backseat of the truck.

"What is it, Jack?" Ivy asked, tugging the piece of paper out of my hand.

"Just something stupid," I replied as I grabbed it back.

"You don't tell lies Jack, ever. What is it? A note from one of your fangirls?" Ivy smiled when she looked at me. "I might be a little jealous, but I think you kind of like me."

"Am I so obvious?"

She pulled a chain from around her neck. My class ring dangled from it. "Pretty obvious." Much to my surprise, she stood on her tiptoes and gave me a kiss. It started to heat up. "Hah, I got it." Ivy opened up the crinkled up piece of paper and read, "Stay away from the girl. She is poison." Ivy glanced at the paper and glanced at me. "Get it? Poison...poison Ivy." She paused as she looked at the note again. "This isn't the first note, is it? You don't seem surprised, just annoyed."

"I've gotten a few. I just toss 'em in the back of the truck. I haven't read any of them since the first one. I figured it was one of those disgruntled girls being stupid or something."

"You and your disgruntled girls. I love that you used the word *disgruntled.* You are so going to nail the entrance exam." Ivy shoved the note at my chest. I took the note and tossed it in the back as I assisted Ivy into the cab of my truck.

Walking around the front of the truck, I looked for anyone or anything that seemed suspicious. I didn't see a thing except Willie getting into his car and I gave him a quick wave as I climbed into the driver's side.

"Where do you want to go?" I asked Ivy as I pulled her across the seat to sit next to me. "My house, your house, or somewhere else?"

"Do all girls ride shotgun in Iowa?" Ivy asked as she pulled my arm across her shoulder and over her chest so we were holding hands.

"Well, I can't speak for all girls," I replied, "but all girls named Ivy who are going steady with a guy named Jack ride shotgun. I'm sure we can find the rules on the Internet."

"Got it," Ivy replied. "Kind of like the rules for the drive-in."

"Exactly," I said as I kissed the top of her head and pulled the truck onto the street. "I'm thinking I'm going to take you to my favorite place I go to when I want to be alone. I found it a couple of years ago when I was working for my uncle." I drove down the road, remembering why I'd needed to find someplace, "I'd kinda hit an all-time, lifetime low point. The place we're going—I don't know if I can explain it— brought me solace."

"Thanks for taking me to your special place." Ivy's voice was so sincere. We drove in silence, the kind of silence where you know you are together, not apart. I turned onto the dirt road leading to a field Uncle Joe never farmed. I pulled the truck a little off to the side, then turned off the engine.

I didn't see her smile, but I could tell her face had shifted into a grin by the sound of her voice. "I just have to say it. Your use of ACT vocabulary is so hot. I don't know why, but an intellectual jock, is, well…just hot. *Solace...* That is such a great word."

"Ivy," I said softly in a kinda menacing voice, "you shouldn't tell a guy you think he's hot when he drives down a dark, deserted road. He might think his advances won't be thwarted." It took me a moment to come up with the word *thwarted*. I mean, if *solace* made her hot, *thwarted* should catch her on fire.

"*Thwarted?* Oh my God." Ivy laughed. "I *so* need a piece of that."

"It's all about being sapiosexual," I replied.

Much to my surprise, she wedged herself between me and the steering wheel then straddled my hips. "Are we parking?"

I nodded in response. It was too hard to talk with Ivy's pelvis pressed against mine.

"I think I'm going to like parking," she said as she leaned down and licked the seam of my lips with her tongue. I held her head steady as I took control of the kiss. She squirmed closer. I groaned. The girl was definitely gonna kill me.

I slowly moved my hand under her cheer shirt. She jerked back in surprise. I wasn't sure who was more startled when the horn blasted, me or her. She looked at me and started to laugh. "Once again we were saved by the horn. At least this time we're not in front of my house."

"I don't think 'saved' is the word I would use. More like 'interrupted'." I leaned in to kiss her again.

"Jack, I think we need to talk. My little episodes are starting to be kind of frightening. I really feel like I might be possessed or something."

Pulling Ivy against my chest, I reached over and opened the vehicle door. "Let's go lie down in the bed of my truck."

"I'm not sure lying down in the back of your truck is conducive to a good conversation," Ivy said as she shifted position on my lap, unintentionally causing me some serious pain—pain that made me want to forget about talking and focus on action.

"Ivy," I groaned, "you can't move like that."

"Oh, sorry," she replied as she realized the problem.

"No worries," I said as I brushed her hair out of her face. "It's such a great night. We can stretch out in the bed of the truck and stare at the stars." I paused. "And we can talk."

"Okay, Jack," Ivy replied as she leaned over and grasped the door handle then pushed it open. I slid off the seat, pulling Ivy with me. We kinda stumbled out of the truck. I cradled her in my arms.

"Wow," Ivy exclaimed. "The stars are so bright. I never really noticed the stars back in St. Louis." Ivy leaned back in my arms, tilting her head back and spreading her arms wide. "It's perfect. Hey!" Ivy shouted as she laughed and grabbed my shoulders. "You almost dropped me."

We started to laugh and I spun Ivy around really fast. At that moment I realized I felt…well, good. I didn't have that ache in my stomach or the tightness in my chest. I stopped spinning and stared into Ivy's clear green gaze. It hit me, a realization about love. You know you've found it because it just feels right. Me and Ivy, we felt right.

"What?" Ivy asked looking into my face as I put her feet on the ground.

"I like being with you," I blurted out.

"I like being with you too," Ivy replied. She pulled out

her phone. Holding it up, she snapped our picture. Then, much to my surprise, she tossed her phone into the cab of the truck. I pulled my cell out of my back pocket, pulled her into my arms, took a picture then put my phone on the front seat. *No distractions.*

"No distractions." She winked.

Damn, I sure like a girl who winks, especially a slow, sexy wink like Ivy's.

"How do I get in the back of this thing, anyway?" Ivy gave my truck a disgruntled look and kicked a tire.

"Hey, don't hate on my truck." I grasped her by the waist and lifted her up so she could climb into the truck bed. I pushed myself up on the side of the bed and swung my legs over so I could join Ivy.

I opened up the container in the back of the truck and pulled out a blanket. I spread out the blanket, lay down, then pulled Ivy into my side so she was lying mostly on me. She snuggled into my arms and sighed.

Chapter 15

Ivy

Jack and I stared at the stars. It was so beautiful and peaceful here. It was hard to discern much of anything in the dark. A warm breeze brushed over us as I snuggled into Jack's arms. I'm not sure what Jack was thinking about, but I was trying to remember all of the memories or whatever I've had since arriving in Newton.

Jack took a deep breath. I knew he was going to start talking. I wasn't sure if I was ready to hear what he had to say.

"Okay, you start," I said.

"What happened to *ladies first*?" Jack asked. I could hear the smile in his voice. "It's probably better if I go first, anyway." He paused and took another breath. I liked how I could feel his breathing from my location on his chest.

"I've had one reoccurring dream about the Vietnam War, since...I don't know, maybe since I was five. It's always the same, I'm with a guy named Mike. We're on a hill and we're surrounded by the NVA."

I wanted to ask who or what was the NVA, but I didn't want to interrupt Jack's story. Then I remembered... The NVA was the North Vietnamese Army.

"We're trapped on the hill and Hueys—helicopters—are flying in to pull us out. Not many guys are left. Johnny, whose eyes I look through during the battle, and Mike are waiting to go while they're holding off the attackers." Jack's voice changed. It was kind of eerie, but I didn't interrupt. "The NVA streamed up the hill like a swarm of ants. We kept firing, but we couldn't stem the tide. It was only a matter of time before they breached our defenses. I felt a sting and realized I'd been shot.

Mike pulled me toward the line of guys waiting to board the Huey. We kept firing." Jack shook his head like he was trying to break out of a trance. "I wake up right around then in a sweat. Sometimes I fall to the floor and curl up in a ball. It's not pretty. That's for sure."

He paused and sighed. "My dad, he couldn't deal with it, so he left. My mom thinks I blame her. I don't. I blame me. So, yeah, just so you know, I would never abandon my kid."

I was holding Jack's hand tightly as I tried to keep him connected to the here and now.

"I go to a shrink like Katie said. Dr Marx diagnosed me with Dissociative Identity Disorder, but I really don't fit the profile."

"The first day of football practice, the day we met"—Jack paused and squeezed me affectionately—"I woke up from the usual dream. The rest of the day was unusual. I had a series of memories or flashbacks or something that led me to you. Wait, that's not right. When I was doing *Flashback 1969*, I played a song by the Foundations."

"'Build Me Up Buttercup'," I interjected. "I was listening."

"That's the first time I dreamed about Christine. Only it wasn't a dream, because I wasn't asleep. I didn't know what it was. That night I had the dream where I was trapped on the hill in Vietnam. When I got to school for football practice, I started to zone in and out."

Jack stopped talking and I pushed up from his chest so I could look at him. "You okay?" I asked as I pushed his hair off his forehead. He grabbed my hand and kissed my palm, then he smiled at me.

"Yeah, I'm good. I'm just trying to remember the sequence." He closed his eyes then took a deep breath. I resumed my position on his chest and waited for him to collect his thoughts. "I'm going to call it a flashback, okay?"

I nodded in agreement.

"The first flashback happened after Coach welcomed us to practice. The flashback was a sergeant welcoming a group of recruits to Fort Collins. And when I say 'welcome', I mean 'insult'. Then, I glanced up and saw the picture of the girl in the trophy case. I decided the reason I dreamed about her was 'cause I saw her photo every day. When Collin and I ran to practice, I had another flashback of running during training with Mike, the guy I'm with during the battle." Jack paused and tugged on my hair so I would look at him, "Then the most beautiful girl in the world literally knocked me on my ass. When we were on the ground, after our first kiss, I had a memory of being at a bus stop with a girl and needing to kiss her one more time. I think I—I mean Johnny—was going to basic training."

Jack paused again. "The flashback or memories or disorder don't seem to be following any kind of sequence. They do seem to be occurring in 1968, 1969, and 1970." Jack rubbed circles on my back, waiting for me to talk.

I began. "So, I had my first dream on my way to Newton. The dream was about a guy named Johnny and a girl named Christine making out in a Camaro—a 1969 Camaro, like the one on your vintage T-shirt. When my mom dropped me at cheer practice, I had another one, only I was awake. Johnny and Christine were at a football game and they had a conversation pretty much like the one we had tonight. That was the whole staring off into space thing. I also had a... What are we calling these?" I asked.

"Flashbacks," Jack replied.

"Nice, Flashback Jack," I said, then continued in a more

serious tone. "My flashbacks have been overwhelming. When I arrived at my grandparents' house I had a"—I paused then, looking at Jack—"flashback of coming home late from a date with Johnny, then I remembered things about the house I shouldn't know. After we met, I remembered—or whatever— Johnny getting the new car because he wasn't going to college and Christine being upset because Johnny could be drafted. I also had a memory of Christine and Johnny being at a place called Rock Creek and Christine with a camera called a Swinger and Jujubes…something about Jujubes."

"I love Jujubes." Jack interrupted as I paused for a moment. "I remember Johnny giving Christine his ring, and I remember Johnny seeing Christine wearing his ring on a chain around her neck." Jack's hand moved up to his ring that was on a chain around my neck. "Just like this." Jack rolled the ring between his fingers. "The funniest one was at church…I was thinking about being with you at the movies and a conversation between Johnny and Christine materialized in my head. Johnny had given Christine a hickey at the drive-in." Jack let go of the ring and wrapped his arm tightly around me. "I can't believe I find any of this funny."

Jack rubbed my arms as he stared quietly into the night. I continued, "On the way to the snipe hunt, I had a flashback— or whatever—of a plane crash Johnny and Christine observed. The crazy part—I know it all sounds crazy—is that in the summer of 1969, a famous boxer died in a plane crash in the place I remembered. Oh yeah, and when I had a memory of the draft lottery, your stepdad confirmed it was real."

Then it was Jack's turn again. "I've had new dreams and more flashbacks. I dreamed about a guy named Bob Kalsu and waiting for photographers to visit the outpost. The photographer dream included a photograph of Christine. She was wearing a

Pacesetter uniform in the photo. It was the same photo that's in the trophy case at school," Jack added.

My head started to spin as all of the memories from the past couple of weeks came crashing back. "The very worst," I concluded, "was school. I really heard voices inside of my head. All of the voices were calling me Christine, and they were all talking like they were from the '60s. Oh my God"—I sat up and hit my hand on my forehead—"I am so stupid. Christine… Jack, that's my mom's sister's name—the one who went missing in 1970."

Jack sat up behind me. "Well, if this is really about reincarnation, Christine isn't missing. She's dead."

The hair on the back of my neck literally stood up as a chill raced down my spine. *Could this really be happening? Could I really be the reincarnation of my mom's sister? Do I actually believe in reincarnation?*

Jack pulled me tightly against his chest. "I'm pretty sure Johnny died in Vietnam."

I didn't say anything just reached up and hugged Jack's arm tighter to my chest. "We need to find out what happened to Christine." I took a deep breath. "Maybe that's what this is all about."

Jack didn't say anything for a few moments. "I don't know, Ivy; maybe we were supposed to find each other." Jack paused again. "Maybe we were supposed to find each other so we could find out what happened to Christine, so we—me and you—have a chance at the future Johnny and Christine never had."

I turned into Jack's arms. I didn't want to talk. I didn't want to think; I just wanted Jack to hold me. I pressed my face into his chest then wrapped my arms tightly around him. We didn't speak. We held each other as Jack stroked my hair.

Chapter 16

Jack—Summer, 1969

The smell of pot filled the air. I held Christine protectively in my arms. *What was I thinking?* We were crashed on a sleeping bag in the back of my friend's truck somewhere in upstate New York with every hippie in the country. Bill had left the truck to get stoned and the rest of our group were scoping out a bathroom.

"Hey," Christine whispered, "no one's back yet?"

"No," I replied. "I'm sure they'll be back soon." I really wasn't sure if Anne, Carol, and Rick would ever find the truck, but I didn't want Christine to worry.

"I wonder if my mom and dad will ever forgive me," Christine said. "I can't believe I left a note saying I was going to a concert in New York and I'd be back in a week. They must have gone ape."

"This was a candyass idea. I'm really sorry," I replied.

"Johnny, are you trippin'? This has been rad! Of course, my eyes burned a couple of times with so many naked people doing things a girl like me never imagined. Good thing I promised my mom and dad there wouldn't be any drugs or sex, just rock and roll."

"And here I was wishing you just would have promised no drugs." I said it as a joke, but I was kind of serious.

Christine looked into my eyes and smiled. Her smile was devilish. "If we don't go all the way, I won't be breaking my promise."

I didn't have time to process her remark. She rolled on top of me and made a curtain around my head with her hair. "How do you feel about free love?" she asked as she leaned down to kiss me…

*****

Present day

"Jack! Jack! Oh my God, Jack! Wake Up!" Ivy's distress penetrated my dream.

I slowly opened my eyes. "Holy shit!" I exclaimed. "It's morning."

"I am going to be *so* dead. My mom is going to be freaking out. Oh my God, Jack, your mom's going to think the city girl did something bad to you. We are going to be in so much trouble."

I jumped over the side of the truck bed and held up my arms to Ivy. She jumped over the side. I knew I should have put her down quickly then driven like a maniac back into town. Instead I leaned down and kissed her. "Jack," she murmured against my mouth, then she kissed me back.

The sound of police sirens cut through the tranquil morning. *Damn.* We were in for it now. I wrapped my arm around Ivy and waited for the police car to come to a halt.

"We are in so much trouble," she whispered as the officer got out of his car. When I saw who it was, I sighed with relief. It was Stan's buddy from high school, Joe Clement.

"Well, Jack," Officer Clement said grimly, "Ivy's grandparents had the entire force out looking for her. You are Ivy, aren't you?" He tilted his head in Ivy's direction.

Ivy nodded slowly.

"It looks like you are safe and sound. Well, that is until your parents get ahold of you. I'm just going to call in that I found you and that you're on your way to Ivy's house now.

141

What the hell did you guys do with your phones, anyway? You do have phones, don't you?"

Damn. "Umm, I think our phones are in the cab. We were just staring at the stars in the bed of the truck. I guess we fell asleep."

Officer Clement got in his car and spoke quickly into his phone. "Save it for your folks," he said as he slammed the door shut, but his window was down. He muttered, "Dumb ass kids. Why the hell do their parents buy 'em phones when they don't even turn 'em the hell on."

I opened the door to my side of the truck and helped Ivy climb in. She picked up her phone and glanced at it. "Yep, I have a few messages," she said as she looked out the windshield. She took a deep breath and looked at me closely. "Johnny and Christine used to come here."

"Yeah, I figured," I replied. "I think it was why I was drawn to the place. I found it when I was around twelve. I used to ride my bike all over Newton and the country roads around town. Trying to escape my demons, I guess."

Ivy glanced around, "This place gives me conflicting feelings…good and bad, but mostly good. Johnny and Christine probably had a fight here or something."

I pulled the truck onto the main road then grabbed Ivy's hand. She smiled at me, shaking her head as she leaned into my shoulder. "We are going to be in so much trouble."

"I know," I replied with a grin. "Damn," I said as I realized I was grinning. "I don't care, as long as you're not grounded from me."

"Me neither," Ivy replied. "Is that bad? I mean, I feel bad they were worried and everything. Oh, and I feel super bad they called the police. But, I loved being with you. And, we have a mission."

"Mission?" I asked.

"We are going to find out what happened to Johnny and Christine." Ivy seemed confident. "Then we can be Jack and Ivy, two Iowan kids growing up in Newtonland."

I smiled ruefully. "That is a really bad version of John Mellencamp's song about 'Jack and Diane'. But I like Jack and Ivy." Then I glanced at her as I turned on to First Avenue. "I really like Ivy."

"And I like Jack," Ivy whispered. "Oh crap, there are at least four cop cars in front of the house. Everyone in the entire town is going to know we were out all night."

"Maybe not the entire town," I said as I pulled to a stop and parked the truck on the street, since the drive was occupied by vehicles from Newton's finest and my Mom's SUV.

"Jack, don't lie to me now," Ivy said as she looked at the chaos on the front lawn.

Her mom, my mom, her grandparents, several police officers, and a bunch of people I did not know were standing in large groups or small clusters.

"I said *entire* Ivy, the entire town, every eleven thousand or so citizens who live here... They all won't know"—I paused—"or, maybe they will."

"Jack." Ivy was clearly exasperated. "Well, let's get this over with."

Ivy opened the door and jumped out of the cab. Before her feet touched the ground, her mom hugged her. "Oh my God," Mrs Drake exclaimed, "we were so worried."

"Sorry, Mom," Ivy replied, "we were looking at the stars and fell asleep in the bed of Jack's truck. We left our phones in the cab. I am so sorry I worried you."

I walked to Ivy's side and my mom came running across the lawn. "You are in so much trouble. Do you realize how much angst you caused Ivy's grandparents?"

"Mom," I said, "it wasn't intentional. We were in my truck bed staring at the stars. We fell asleep. It was dumb, but it was an accident. Mom, I'm really sorry, but it's not a big deal."

"Not a big deal? Not a big deal?" Mr Van den Berg exclaimed as he stormed over to where we were standing with a police officer in tow. I recognized the police officer with Ivy's grandfather—Chief Rhodes. He'd been on the force for at least forty years. He was a huge Cardinals football fan. "You had my granddaughter out all night. We thought she was dead or lost or abducted. Hundreds of horrible things could happen to a young girl."

"Sir," I replied, "please forgive me for causing you and your family worry. As I was telling my mom and Mrs Drake, we made an innocent mistake. We fell asleep in the back of my truck. I am very sorry."

I grabbed Ivy's hand and gave it a squeeze. She didn't pull away. She took a step closer so her arm was touching my arm. I realized at that moment that we were a team.

"Gramps," Ivy said softly, "I am so sorry. It was an honest mistake. I don't know what else to say. I'm really sorry."

Ivy's grandfather glared at me then looked at Ivy. His face softened. "I love you, Ivy Godivy." He held out his arms. Ivy let go of my hand and gave him a hug.

"You..." he said as he looked at me. "Ivy will not be seeing you anymore."

"Gramps," Ivy said as she took a step back from him and a step closer to me, "this was not Jack's fault. We"—she gestured at me then at herself—"fell asleep. It was a simple mistake. I promise it won't happen again."

"Dad"—Mrs Drake interrupted the conversation—"it was a mistake. Ivy's my daughter, Dad," she added softly.

"Mr Van den Berg," Chief Rhodes added, "I've known Jack his whole life. He's a good kid. He's also the captain of the football team. You know Coach would not assign that role to a young man who did not have integrity."

Mr Van den Berg looked at Ivy's mom. He looked at Ivy. He looked at Officer Rhodes, then finally he looked at me. Before he could speak, Mrs Van den Berg put her hand on his arm. "This is not like Christine," she said in a strong, yet quiet, voice. "Christine was alone. Ivy was with Jack. Nothing bad will happen to Ivy when she's with Jack. This is *not* like Christine," she repeated.

I glanced around at the scene on the lawn. *Damn.* I bet this scene was like when their daughter disappeared all those years ago. *Damn.* Ivy squeezed my hand. I knew she was thinking the same thing.

"Thanks, Chief," Mr Van den Berg said as he extended his hand to the chief of police. "Sorry I called the force out for nothing."

"No problem," Chief Rhodes replied. "I was a brand new officer when Christine vanished. I remember it like it happened yesterday." Chief Rhodes scanned the people and officers crowded on the lawn, "Let's go, people. Mystery solved."

A chorus of farewells followed the announcement. Several people stopped by to say goodbye to the Van den Bergs. It was kinda awkward, 'cause her grandparents were introducing Ivy to their neighbors for the first time. I'm thinking this was not the way Ivy wanted to meet them. But she managed to look confident and beautiful after sleeping on the bed of a truck all night with a guy—the guy who was standing by her side, holding her hand.

"That's right, Mr Boff," Ivy said. "Jack's the one who

caught the interception and ran it in for a touchdown. Jack"—Ivy nudged my arm—"I'd like you to meet my backyard neighbors, Mr and Mrs Boff."

We stood on the sidewalk, shaking hands and making small talk for maybe thirty minutes. Only Ivy, me, Mom, Mrs Drake, and Mr and Mrs Van den Berg remained in the yard.

"I'm so sorry, Suzie," Mom said to Mrs Drake. "Jack's usually entirely too responsible. This is the first time in his life he has ever acted so irresponsibly. I'm sorry it happened with your daughter."

"Cathy," Mrs Drake replied, "trust me. Ivy is equally responsible for being irresponsible."

"Let's go," Mom said sternly as she pointed to my truck.

"Ivy, are you okay?" I asked.

She looked up at me with brilliant green eyes. "I'm fine. Despite all of this"—she gestured to the now empty lawn—"last night was awesome."

"Just awesome?" I asked. "I would say the night was phenomenal, legendary, maybe even splendiferous."

"*Splendiferous*, Jack?" Ivy questioned with a huge smile.

"I'll call you later," I said as I walked toward my truck. "Definitely splendiferous."

Mom whispered, "I've scheduled 'the talk' with Stan."

"Jeez, Mom," I said as I opened the door to my truck.

"Jack," Ivy called, rushing to my side of the truck, "I forgot something." She leaned in and grabbed her cheer bag out of the truck. Then she dropped it at my feet.

I gave her a questioning glance while bending down to pick it up. As I grabbed the handle, Ivy said, "Jack." I looked up, then she leaned down and kissed me. Just as it started to heat up, Ivy murmured against my lips, "Thanks for picking up my bag." Ivy rushed around the truck, toting it. She waved as she ran up the steps to her house.

What a night. Me and Ivy, we had a mystery to solve.

Honk! Honk! Mom's horn startled me out of my stupor. Mom put her window down, "Seriously, dude, you need to keep your hands to yourself." She put the window back up as she drove away.

Chapter 17

Ivy

IVY: *Almost ungrounded.*

The last two weeks had kind of flown by, even though I was technically grounded. I did a lot of Facetime with Claire, Audrey, Alex, and Erica. I also spent a lot of time with Jack on the phone. It could have been worse.

My phone buzzed.

JACK: *Are we good?*

IVY: *Yep, see you in thirty.*

"Ivy," Mom called up the steps, "we'll be home around eleven. Be good."

What exactly did she mean by "be good"? She probably didn't mean having Jack come over and break into Christine's room.

"I'll try," I replied. Well, that was kind of honest. Jack's never-tell-a-lie policy was starting to rub off on me.

I looked at my phone. It was seven fifteen. *Jack should be here in fifteen minutes.* Before going downstairs, I looked in the mirror, making sure my "I'm not leaving the house" look was cute. We hadn't been alone in two weeks…well, except for when Jack had given me a ride home from school a couple of times. I waited impatiently by the back door. He was going to park in the neighborhood behind the house and sneak in through the back.

I realized I should feel guilty, but I didn't. About half of my thoughts over the past couple of weeks hadn't been my own. They'd been Christine's. Jack was having the same issue. Luckily, his memories or whatever weren't primarily focused on Vietnam. We needed to find some evidence that we weren't crazy. I thought the evidence would be in Christine's room.

Sitting on the porch, I waited for Jack. I closed my eyes…

*****

Spring, 1969

Johnny would be here at any moment. I examined my reflection in the full-length mirror hanging on the back of my bedroom door. Johnny was going to love my dress; actually, he was going to love me in this dress.

I spun one more time, admiring my ice-pink dress with the white lace overlay. My pink satin shoes peeked out from under the skirt. I loved the pink ribbon that went around my waist. Mom had tied it in a perfect bow in the back, and I could just about see it when I turned my head over my shoulder as far as it would go. Maybe I should have put my hair up? I thought for a moment, then I shrugged. Johnny liked my hair down.

I tried to picture Johnny and me twirling around the Maytag Ballroom, but that wasn't going to happen. I wasn't going as Johnny's date. He was technically giving me a ride so I could do my part as a member of the Junior Class Prom Committee. It was such a drag that Seniors couldn't bring a Junior as their date. I pondered the inequity as I applied a little lipstick. Going to a ballroom for prom was really groovy… Too bad Johnny was going stag and I was sitting at the reception table.

"Christine," Mom called from the bottom of the stairs. "Your date has arrived."

I closed the door to my room, butterflies fluttering in my stomach. I didn't know why I was so nervous. It's not like it was our first date or anything, and it wasn't really a date.

Johnny looked up then smiled. He was gorgeous in his white dinner jacket and bow tie. He extended his hand to take mine. I was the luckiest girl alive…

*****

Present day

"Ivy," Jack whispered as he tapped my shoulder abruptly, bringing me back to the present. He wrapped his arms tightly around me and sighed.

I smiled up at him then he kissed me gently on the lips. "Jack, we need to get to work. We have maybe two hours to get into Christine's room and determine what's real and what's not."

"This is so real, Ivy," Jack whispered into my ear, sending chills down my spine—the good kind. "Okay, commander," Jack said a moment later, pulling me to a standing position, "let's do this thing."

Jack clasped my hand and we walked from the porch to the kitchen. I stopped at the pantry and located the coffee canister with random keys.

"I found the key canister when I was helping Grams organize the pantry during my house arrest," I explained to Jack as I dumped the keys on the counter. There were four keys that looked like they might be for a bedroom; one of them was hopefully the key to Christine's room.

I handed Jack the four keys then dumped the rest back in

the canister. We didn't say anything. We walked quietly up the stairs and down the hall. "I'm nervous," I said as I watched Jack insert the first key into the lock. I stared in stunned disbelief as Jack turned the handle on the door. It had worked. We were in.

Jack slowly opened the door and entered the room. Taking a deep breath, I followed him inside. Just like at school, the voices inside of my head started calling...

*****

1970

"Christine, is your homework done?"
"Christine, time to wake up, sleepy head."
"Christine, come downstairs. It's time for Laugh-In."
"Christine, supper's ready."
"Christine, Johnny's here."
"Christine, Johnny's waiting."
"Christine, honey, we are so sorry about Johnny."
"Christine..."
"Christine..."
"Christine..."

*****

Present day

"Ivy! Ivy!" Jack's frantic call broke through my stupor. I was surprised to find I was sitting on the floor of Christine's bedroom, crying. Jack had his arms wrapped around me.

"How long?" I asked as I rubbed the tears from my face.

"Not long," Jack replied. "Maybe five minutes."

He studied the interior of the room. "It's like being in a time warp or something."

I nodded in agreement. My stomach tightened as I looked around the room. The floor was covered with dark green shag carpeting. Three walls had black and white wallpaper with an alternating circle pattern. The third wall was covered with posters of bands from the 1960s. A black director's chair was in the corner of the room with a magazine rack overflowing with *Seventeen* magazines. The bedspread was black with white and lime-green flowers, and two lime-green furry throw pillows were arranged at the head of the bed. A small TV was on one of the shelves above the desk, facing it. The closet didn't have a door; a curtain of multi-colored beads concealed its contents.

"Damn," Jack exclaimed as he examined the posters, "the Monkees, the Beach Boys, the Archies, Davy Jones, the Beatles' *Abbey Road*, Led Zeppelin." I was more interested in the contents of the closet.

I pushed aside the beads and found Christine's clothes. I saw a long bag at the back of the closet. I knew what was inside. "Jack," I said, "I'm going to bring out a bag from the closet. I believe the bag holds a long pink evening gown"—I closed my eyes and thought for a moment—"covered in lace." I laid the bag on the bed. Jack was standing at my shoulder as I pulled down the zipper. My heart was pounding as I separated the sides of the bag. I stared at the dress in stunned disbelief. "When I was sitting on the porch waiting for you, I had a memory of Johnny and Christine going to the prom. She was wearing this dress." My heart was racing, and I felt light-headed. "I think I am going to faint." My breathing was so fast it felt like I was hyperventilating or something. Jack pushed me to a seated position.

"Put your head between your legs and take some deep

breaths."

I breathed deeply, trying to regain my composure. "I'm good," I said as I zipped up the bag then placed it back in the closet. I was swamped by emotions as I stood there...

*****

Summer, 1970

What should I wear to the funeral? I gazed into my closet without really seeing my clothes. The red leather of Johnny's lettermen's jacket was like a beacon. I reached out and touched it. My fingers clutched the sleeve. I sobbed.

*****

Present day

"I remembered something. I—I mean Christine—was looking in the closet to find something to wear to Johnny's funeral," I said as tears rolled down my cheeks. "It was so horrible. She was in such pain."

Jack wrapped his arms around me. "We don't have to do this now. We can come back another time."

Without much thought, I turned in Jack's arms, pulled his head down to mine, then kissed him. I'd known Jack for maybe a month, but I knew, without a doubt, that he was my future. If anything would happen to Jack, I would feel the unimaginable pain Christine felt about Johnny. Jack crushed me to him as he pushed his fingers in my hair.

"I'm not gonna die, Ivy," Jack whispered into my hair.

I didn't reply. I just held him closer.

"I think we might be able to confirm our memories with the scrapbook." Stepping out of Jack's embrace, I gestured to the table next to the bed. A scrapbook was centered on the black and white checkerboard painted bedside table. Opening the scrapbook would be so easy…but it was also scary…an actual confirmation of something…crazy?

Jack walked away, maybe he was scared too, then he opened the armoire.

"Damn, the mystery girl in the trophy case at school is none other than Christine Van den Berg, and the football player, as we thought, is her boyfriend Johnny." I looked up at the open armoire. It held a collection of framed photographs of Christine, including the photo of her in the Pacesetter uniform and several photos of her with Johnny.

"If those photos used to be all over the house, no wonder my mom didn't want to visit. It would be kind of creepy," I said as I examined the photographs. I could feel Christine's memories trying to take over my head. I took several deep breaths in order to push the memories back. I closed the armoire.

"Okay," I said, "let's see what we can discover from the scrapbook." I picked it up and Jack and I sat down on the floor with our backs propped up against the bed.

I opened the scrapbook. Inside the cover was Christine's name with hearts dotting the letter *I*. The first few pages were class pictures from elementary school. Each page had two class photos from kindergarten through sixth grade.

"I got nothing," I said softly as we scanned the pages. The next few pages had photos and stuff from Christine's life in seventh and eighth grade at Central Junior High.

"Anything?"

"Nope, nothing." No Christine memories were trying to

take over my brain as I studied her photos from Junior High.

"Oh, she was a cheerleader in the ninth grade," Jack said as we turned to the next page. "Looks like she ran track too." He pointed at a yellowed newspaper article about a track meet where her name was underlined.

Newton Cardinals was written in big letters on the next page. Pictures of footballs, basketballs, pompoms, a muscled arm, a gavel, and a bunch of other stuff surrounded the words. The cover from high school was followed by a class schedule and some flyers for different high school events.

"It looks like someone pulled almost everything out of the scrapbook from here on," Jack said as he started to flip through the pages. "You can see where tape held stuff down, but there's really nothing here...well, except for some newspaper articles about what was happening in the world." Jack flipped through the pages, looking at the articles. "The articles all seem to be from 1969 and 1970. Look at this," Jack said, "a page dedicated to the moon landing, another one covering the murder of Sharon Tate, and a bunch of articles about Charles Manson." Jack paused then asked, "Did you ever read *Helter Skelter*? That was one scary story."

I nodded in agreement.

Jack turned to the next page. "Look at this. Two entire pages dedicated to Woodstock, and there's even a ticket." Jack sat back and stopped looking at the articles. "The night we fell asleep in the back of the truck, I dreamed that we—I mean Johnny, Christine, and some of their friends—were at Woodstock." Johnny pulled out a piece of yellowed notebook paper that was stuck in the page. He opened it then started reading, "Dear Mom and Pops—"

I closed my eyes. I could see the note in my head and I read aloud, "Johnny and a bunch of his friends are going to a concert in New York. I know you are going to be mad, but I'm going too. I left you this note so you wouldn't worry. You guys might be square, but I love you anyway. Peace, love, and rock and roll. Christine. PS I promise no sex or drugs…just rock and roll."

Jack stared at me in kind of stunned disbelief. "That's exactly what it says."

"Reincarnated or possessed?" I asked in a shaky voice.

"You are not possessed!" Jack said vehemently. "Reincarnated…maybe," he said softly.

Taking a deep breath, I decided not to waste time thinking about being reincarnated. "What else?"

"There's a bunch of articles about Vietnam. A picture and article of the 1969 Draft Lottery, US invades Cambodia, stuff about the National Guard killing four students at Kent State in May of 1970." Jack paused as he studied the scrapbook.

"The articles make a timeline, but photos, announcements, and other personal stuff about Christine were—like I said—removed. It doesn't look like they were ripped out or anything, just removed with a lot of care. I mean, not one page was torn, but you can see the outline of where other pictures and stuff were."

I leaned back, sliding my hands under the bed skirt as I rested my head awkwardly on the edge of the bed. The only connection we'd made from the scrapbook was Woodstock. We still didn't have a clue about what happened to Christine.

"We still don't have a clue about Christine," Jack said, effectively reading my thoughts.

I felt something under the bed. I pulled out a book. "Okay, random," I said to Jack. "It's *Harold and the Purple Crayon*." I opened the front cover. *Johnny* was printed on the inside.

Jack stared transfixed at the book. "Johnny loved this book when he was little. It was about a boy who went exploring and found his way home by remembering the moon." Jack sounded kind of dazed as he held the book in his hands. "Not possessed… Is reincarnation even possible?"

I wrapped my arms around Jack and stared at the book. "The first page was torn out," I said.

We sat in silence. I was trying to make meaning of all of this. I think Jack was too.

"Oh, crap," I said, jumping to my feet and putting the scrapbook back on the table. Jack shoved the book under the bed and turned off the lights. We had both heard the car pull into the driveway. "I don't think I put the canister away," I said as Jack turned the key in the lock. "Jack, they're on the front porch. Go up to my room." I flew down the steps and into the kitchen. The canister was sitting on the table. I tossed the keys in the canister and put it on the shelf in the pantry.

"We're home," Mom called out as they entered through the front door.

I casually walked out of the kitchen to the front door as I bit into a cookie. My heart was racing, but I tried to sound normal. "Hey, how was dinner?"

"It was great," Mom replied. "I saw a couple of people I knew from high school, including the football coach. He told me all about your first encounter with Jack. I bet you can't wait until tomorrow night when you can actually go out again."

"Grams and Gramps, how was dinner," I said, ignoring Mom's comment about Jack. *How in the heck am I going to get him out of my bedroom?*

"It was really good," Gramps said, smiling broadly, "it was great having two of my best girls with me. You should have joined us."

"I'm glad you had fun," I replied, ignoring the part about me going with them. "Well, I'm going to bed now. Night everyone!" I called as I started up the stairs. Luckily no one asked me any more questions.

"Ivy," Mom called, "I saw Cathy at the restaurant. She thought Jack was coming over here. I told her that couldn't possibly be the case because you were grounded from going out and having visitors until tomorrow."

"I don't know." I shrugged, trying to be as noncommittal as possible. "Good night."

I walked up the stairs into my loft bedroom. Jack had his shoes off and was stretched out on my bed, examining the poster my friends in St. Louis had given me. Obviously, he wasn't worried about getting caught.

Chapter 18

Jack

Ivy's bed looked really comfortable. I kicked off my shoes to lie down. Just as I was gonna lie on the bed, I noticed a poster with lots of photographs. I carefully removed the poster from the wall then propped myself up on her pillows. I'm sure she's gonna be thrilled to find me in her bed. Well, I wasn't actually in her bed. I was on it.

I got on my phone and texted Mom.

JACK: *I'll be home late.*

"Jeez, Jack"— Ivy tried not to smile when she saw me on her bed—"comfortable?"

Handing Ivy the poster, I said, "You were a really cute little girl The captions were pretty funny. I especially liked the one under the first day of kindergarten. That's such a big word for describing the fear of big words."

I patted the empty space by my side. Ivy shook her head then walked over to the bed. She gave me a shove so I'd scoot over. "If my mom comes up the stairs, you can roll off the bed. Got it?"

I replied with a nod. "While I was grounded," I whispered, "I found some websites about reincarnation. We can take some quizzes to determine if we were reincarnated."

"Yep," she replied, "an online quiz. That will definitely answer all of our questions."

"I'm hearing tone," I replied as I tried not to laugh. "I mean, this stuff is great. This afternoon I took a quiz and found out that in my next life, I'm going to be a horse."

Ivy punched me in the arm. "A horse, Jack? Seriously?"

I wrapped my arm around her as she rested her head on my chest. She stared at the wall. "Why do you think Christine removed all of the personal stuff from her scrapbook? It doesn't make any sense. I'm guessing it's connected to Johnny, but I would want to keep the reminders, not get rid of them."

"I don't know," I replied. I couldn't figure out the mind of a girl today. It wasn't likely I'd be able to figure out the mind of a girl from the 1960s. I took a shot at it anyway. "I guess it might depend on when she did it. I mean, did she do it right when he died, or maybe she made him a scrapbook from her scrapbook when he went to Vietnam?" I paused and thought about that idea for a moment. "Ivy," I whispered, "are you sleeping?"

"I'm hoping if I fall asleep, I'll remember something that will help us figure this out. I'm not sleeping. I'm just really comfortable. I like laying on you."

"I like you laying on me too. How am I gonna get out of here, by the way?"

"I set my alarm for three am," she replied as she adjusted herself more comfortably on my chest. The more comfortable she got, the more uncomfortable I got. I adjusted my position, trying to ease my, umm, discomfort without Ivy noticing.

She sat up abruptly. "I need a cover." She reached down and pulled a blanket over us. She seemed to want to go to sleep. I wanted to kiss her.

"Ivy," I said tugging on her hair, "I'm not tired."

She pushed off my chest. "What do you want to do? Whatever it is, it's got to be quiet."

"It'll be quiet," I said as I flipped her over onto her back. I had her trapped underneath me and I grinned.

"Oh, you want to do that," she replied as she reached up toward my head. "Me too," she said as she pulled my head toward hers. It was crazy intimate as I pulled her covers over us then kissed her lips. It was hard to think when I was kissing Ivy. Well, I was thinking but not thoughts I should be thinking...like how I could get her out of her shirt before she had time to notice.

"Ivy," Mrs Drake called up the stairs.

"Shit," I mumbled as I rolled off Ivy and onto the floor.

"What?" Ivy replied as she kind of smoothed out the covers. Then, much to my surprise, she dangled her hand over the edge of the bed like she was searching for me. She found my face and started to trace my lips with her fingers.

"Tease," I whispered. I knew she heard me because she gave a muffled laugh. My heart was still racing from the hot kiss and from her mom walking up the stairs. We were going to be in so much trouble if I got caught in her room.

"Are you doing something with Jack tomorrow?"

I tugged her hand to my face and nodded yes so she could feel it.

"Yes," she replied quickly. Then she abruptly pulled her hand from mine and practically leaped out of the bed. I couldn't see what was going on, then I remembered. *Damn.* My shoes were on the floor in front of her bed. Her mom was going step on them if she walked into the room.

Ivy kicked the shoes under the bed. I hated that I couldn't see what was happening except my under-the-bed view. I could hear a drawer open.

"I was so tired I went to bed with my clothes on. I'm glad you woke me up so I could put on something more comfortable."

"I can't believe you fell asleep in your clothes," Mrs

Drake replied.

Damn. Ivy was changing right now. I wasn't listening to their conversation 'cause I was concentrating on the sounds of clothing removal. *Don't think about it,* I said to myself. Something hit me, then something else. I was holding Ivy's shirt and shorts. I tried not to laugh. This was exactly what I wanted, but not even close to the way I wanted it.

"Mom," Ivy said, "do you know anything about the day Aunt Christine disappeared? I saw her picture in the trophy case at school. It just seems so strange that she just vanished."

"The night you and Jack didn't come home, Mom and Dad shared some information that I didn't know. Well, I really didn't know anything at all. I'd never asked, and they'd never said." Mom paused as she appeared to be reflecting on her lack of knowledge or something before she continued. "I learned her boyfriend was killed in Vietnam. She disappeared the day of his funeral. There were some leads the first year she was gone, but after that, nothing."

She smiled at me and gave me a hug. "It was a long time ago. There's nothing we can do about it now. I feel bad for Mom and Dad. Most of my life I resented their commitment to finding Christine. The night you didn't come home, I finally understood. If you had disappeared, I would never stop looking. Never."

"I love you too," Ivy said. "Thanks for the information, Mom. Do you know her boyfriend's name?" she asked.

There was a pause. "Hmm, I think his name was John or Johnny. You know what's kind of strange? There are still people living here who knew her, like the school secretary and one of the guys who does maintenance around the school. I even think there's a connection between Jack's family and Christine."

I could hear a chair being moved. "Have you talked to

Alex, Erica, Claire, and Audrey?" *Who are they? Oh yeah, they are Ivy's friends from St. Louis.*

"Yes, Mother," Ivy replied, "lots of Facetime while I was in solitary confinement."

I heard a loud yawn. "Goodnight, Mom."

"'Night, honey," Mrs Drake replied. I didn't move as I listened to her walk down the stairs and heard the door click closed behind her.

"That was a close one," Ivy said as she glanced at me over the side of the bed. Her green eyes seemed to sparkle as she noticed her clothes in my arms. "Oops, I meant to hit the laundry basket." She gestured to the basket that was at my feet.

"Sure you did," I said as I tossed her clothes in the basket. Then I pounced on her, but very quietly.

She slid her hand under my shirt and gently stroked my ribcage, my abdomen, and my back. "Did you hear what she said?" she asked.

I was trying to focus, but all I could think about was her random stroking. If she would just move her hand down a little... "Jack," she said as she slapped my side, "you aren't even listening."

"Sorry for not listening, beautiful," I replied. "If you recall, we were kissing, then you tossed your clothes at me, and now you're stroking my bare skin. I'm a seventeen-year-old guy. Give me a second"—I paused—"or maybe a good fifteen minutes to cool down."

"I'm sorry, Jack," she replied, trying to move out from under me.

"Don't move," I said. "I like you right where you are. Seriously, just give me a second." I took a few deep breaths. Big mistake; I inhaled Ivy's warm, sexy smell. I forced myself off Ivy and to her side. "I guess I need the distance."

She studied me intently. I couldn't help it. I leaned over and kissed her. I broke away then rolled quietly back to the floor.

"Okay," I said, "I'm ready to listen."

Ivy leaned over the edge of the bed. "What were we talking about?" She started to follow me to the floor, but I pushed her back up.

"Your mom had some information about the day Christine disappeared," I said with reluctance as I looked into Ivy's flushed face. *Damn.* She was so beautiful. I was so glad I'd found her.

"You heard her…Johnny was killed in Vietnam." Ivy's voice shook and tears glistened in her eyes.

"It's okay," I replied. "I've been having dreams about it pretty much my whole life. I figured he died at the part of the dream when I wake up. He was shot in the neck while providing backup fire during an evacuation. Your mom's intel confirms the flashback you had when you looked in Christine's closet."

"Do you know where?" Ivy asked. "You know, from your dreams, where Johnny died."

I closed my eyes and forced myself to remember. "I—I mean Johnny—was in the 506th Infantry of the 101st Airborne at Fire Support Base Ripcord in the A Shau Valley."

"That will be easy enough to research," Ivy said. "Can I come down there and lay on you now?" Ivy asked softly.

Shaking my head in the negative, I stood up. "Scoot over," I said. "Just saying Ripcord was like taking a cold shower."

Ivy scooted over. "My mom said Christine disappeared on the day of Johnny's funeral. My guess is he's buried in Newton. We could go to the cemetery and find the grave. It will have a date on it. It won't be the exact date, but it will be close.

Was that weird, talking about the grave?"

"Nah," I replied. "I like that you have a plan."

"Let's see. She also mentioned there were a couple of sightings of Christine during the first year she disappeared. I bet that was covered in the local newspaper." Ivy paused then hit herself in the head. She pulled her phone off the table next to her bed. She started texting, "Darn it," she said. "I thought if I typed in Christine Van den Berg, there would be an article or something on the web. I guess the local paper doesn't have an online archive. Or, if it does, it probably doesn't go back to 1970."

"I think we should go to the cemetery tomorrow. Then we can check out the *Newton Daily News*. If it's not online, I bet they have it on microfilm. I'm guessing the disappearance of Christine Van den Berg was front page news."

I wrapped my arms around Ivy, holding her close. "You're sure the alarm is set?" I asked as I closed my eyes. All of a sudden, I was so tired I couldn't keep them open...

*****

Summer, 1970

The smooth, repetitive, whirring sound of the rotor blades was kinda lulling me to sleep. Good thing we were going to a mission, not engaged in a mission. I closed my eyes and thought about home...

I glanced down at Christine. She was sleeping soundly in my arms. I hoped she wouldn't have regrets when she woke up.

"Hey," she said, smiling up into my face. "The Camaro's actually pretty comfortable."

"Are you okay?" I asked as I pushed her hair out of her face. "Are you warm enough?" We were naked, and it was January. She was probably freezing.

"I'm a little chilly." She smiled again and rubbed my cheek. "I think you could make me a lot warmer."

"Are you sure?" I asked. She answered with a kiss.

"Wake up, Johnny," Mike shouted in my ear. The noise from the helicopter made normal conversation pretty challenging, even though Mike was sitting right next to me. "What were you dreaming about, anyway? Wait. Don't tell me, man. I do *not* want to know."

I laughed as I nudged him with my shoulder.

"We're getting ready to jump," Mike said with a grin. "I think your ass is going to make a real pretty target for the NVA."

"We're jumping?" I asked as I started to grab my gear so I could check out my parachute.

"Nah, we're not jumping, but I wish we were," Mike replied with a sly smile. "We're getting ready to land on the hill that's gonna be our new home. When you were getting your beauty sleep, I learned all about it." Mike suddenly looked serious.

I didn't think I was gonna like our new home…

*****

Present day

"Time to get up." A soft, sexy voice whispered in my ear.

I pulled her over then kissed her. "Can we do it one more time before I go?" I mumbled against her lips. "I want this night to last forever." I hoped she wasn't regretting going all the way. I deepened the kiss, trying to get her to focus on how good it felt so she'd want to do it again.

"Jack, Jack, I think you might be dreaming. Look at me, Jack. It's me…Ivy."

Damn.

"Sorry, Ivy. I was dreaming about Johnny and Christine's last night. It was strange, even stranger than usual," I added. "It was like a dream within a dream. Johnny was dreaming about his last night with Christine when his friend Mike woke him up. Way too confusing for three am."

I was looking into Ivy's green eyes. I wanted to make love to her—me and Ivy, not Johnny and Christine. I wasn't going to say anything, 'cause it would scare the shit out of her.

"You know, Jack," Ivy said, leaning over to brush her lips against mine, "you and me, we will—you know—sometime, just not tonight."

I kissed her deeply. My tongue rubbed against hers. She moaned into my mouth as I slid my hand under her T-shirt. Her warm skin felt incredible.

"Jack," she murmured as my fingers grazed the underside of her breast for the first time. "I want you to touch me." She was panting as she unconsciously rubbed her body against mine. The last time I'd felt like this was at the drive-in. My body was on fire. My mind filled with thoughts about how good it would feel to bury myself inside her.

"Damn," I said, calling on all of the willpower I had—willpower I didn't know I had. I slid my hand out of her T-shirt then gave her a quick kiss on the lips. We were both panting. I ached. *Is she aching too?*

"Thanks," she whispered.

"What?"

"I wouldn't have been able to stop."

"Now you tell me." I leaned over then kissed her again.

Ivy wrapped her arms around me, pulling me back down to the bed. "Ivy, I won't be able to stop again." She must have heard the sincerity—or maybe the desperation—in my voice.

"Okay, okay, we are stopping. Thanks for stopping." She paused. "Really, Jack, thanks for stopping." She breathed deeply then pushed me off her as she quietly rolled out of bed.

She took another deep breath. "Okay, so here's the plan. We'll go down the stairs together. I'll let you out the back door. If anyone wakes up, I'll explain I was getting some aspirin or something." She pulled my shoes out from under her bed then handed them to me. "Don't put them on until you're at your car."

I nodded as I accepted my shoes before leaving her bedroom.

"That was as close to hedonistic as I've ever been," Ivy said softly.

"You can seek pleasure with me anytime," I murmured in her ear. "If you use any more big words, I am going to drag you back to your bed."

She laughed softly then she shushed me.

We crept down the stairs from her bedroom then quietly opened the door to the second floor. We silently walked down the hallway. "Step where I step," Ivy whispered in my ear.

We made it down the steps and to the back door.

"I'll pick you up tomorrow around ten thirty. Is that okay?"

"Perfect," she whispered back. "Be careful."

Be careful. I laughed on the inside. Newton was probably the safest city in the country. The screen door opened without a creak. I leaped off the porch in case any of the steps squeaked. I waved at Ivy, who was silhouetted in the door.

Dashing through the bushes, I sprinted to my truck.

I glanced back at Ivy's house. It was dark. Then a light flashed in the upstairs window. She'd made it. We'd done it. I sighed with relief. I opened the door to the cab. On the seat of my truck was a note.

If you know what's good for you, stay away from the new girl. She's poison.

"Damn," I said. No one was around, but I had a bad feeling about this. Were they following me? Did they just see the truck and leave a note? If it was Katie and her friends, they were taking this too far. I tossed the note on the seat behind me. I had other things to think about besides the notes. Tomorrow we were going to the cemetery.

Chapter 19

Ivy

We turned onto the narrow road leading to the cemetery. It looked familiar, yet different, just like the high school and the football stadium. "Jack," I said as I clasped his hand, "Johnny's grave is in the Veterans' section."

I stared at the pedestals marking the entrance into Union Cemetery. Christine's memories flooded my head. "The entrance is different," I whispered. My voice was choked as I tried not to cry. "The pillars were stone, and they were taller. I—I mean Christine—stopped right here"—I gestured at the pedestals—"waiting as the procession of cars crawled down the lane."

"Are you okay, beautiful?" Jack asked as we slowly drove down the center path of the cemetery. "I was dead. I don't remember any of this." Jack paused. "Damn, did I just say that?"

I kind of laughed. "Well, I'm telling this story like it happened to me. I mean, a small part of me feels like I am Christine, but the rest is all me—all Ivy. Does that make sense?" I asked as I glanced at Jack's profile. I watched as he slowly nodded his head, keeping his eyes on the narrow road as I looked for the section dedicated to the burial of war veterans.

Jack squeezed my hand.

"Turn right here," I said, pointing to an even narrower road on our right.

Jack turned the steering wheel abruptly. He drove the truck slowly down the road. We passed a couple more sections. I studied my surroundings. Christine had been to the cemetery one time, but her memories were crystal clear. The thought reinforced my belief that Christine died the day of Johnny's funeral. She would have come back to visit his grave otherwise.

"Make a left turn," I said, giving Jack a little more notice this time about the need to turn down a different lane.

We turned left, continuing down the narrow road that snaked through the cemetery. A memorial was located near the road of the Veterans' section. That was definitely new, as in not around in 1970 when Johnny died in Vietnam. "They added a war memorial," I said. "That's really nice."

Jack pulled the truck to the side of the road, turned off the engine, then got out of the cab. Everything seemed to be moving in slow motion. I rested my head on the dashboard, afraid to get out of the truck. Jack opened the door. He reached across me to unfasten my seat belt. I was struggling to move. Sorrow so deep lodged into the pit of my stomach. It was Christine's sorrow. It was smothering. "Oh my God," I said as I clasped Jack's strong hand. "Do not die," I said. "If you die, I'll kill you. Don't say anything, Jack. I'm serious. I can feel her pain, the gut wrenching loss." I stumbled out of the car. I would have fallen, but Jack was holding my hand.

Tears streamed down my face as I passed the graves of other soldiers, some who were killed in action and came back to Newton for their final resting place—others who came home to live their lives and were buried here out of respect for their service.

I tilted my head back, allowing Christine's memories to flood my mind.

*****

Summer, 1970

This cannot be happening.

I joined Johnny's mother, father, and four older brothers. Johnny's mom clasped my hand and pulled me tightly against her. "I wish you would have ridden with us," she whispered. "I was worried about you driving."

I'd driven Johnny's Camaro to the service. I knew she was worried about me, not the car. Driving the Camaro to the funeral seemed like the right thing to do.

I fanned myself as we waited. The August heat was sweltering, but I wore Johnny's letterman's jacket over my summer dress. I pretended the arms of his jacket were his arms, and he was standing behind me, holding me, rather than in the casket still secured in the back of the hearse.

The hair on the back of my neck tingled. I could feel someone staring at me. I glanced around and noticed Johnny's friend Bill, who was in full dress uniform, staring at me. *That's right. Bill joined the service because Johnny did.* I kind of shivered under his intense gaze. For some reason Bill didn't like me. Frankly, whether Bill liked me or didn't like me did not matter. *Nothing matters.* Ignoring Bill's stare, I waited for Johnny.

Six soldiers stood at attention when the driver opened the door at the back of the hearse. The soldiers stepped forward in formation—two rows of three—as a seventh soldier gave the commands. The small area designated for the graves of soldiers and veterans was nearly filled by the seven members of the Honor Guard and everyone attending. I'd never been to a military funeral before. Then I realized that I've never been to *any* funerals before.

The soldiers marched slowly to the back of the hearse. I could see the stars and stripes of the flag draped over the casket. It was hard to breathe. I felt like I was choking. I clung to

Johnny's mom's hand as one of the soldiers approached the casket. The soldiers slowly removed it from the hearse then carefully turned toward the waiting grave. I felt like I was watching a movie, not watching the casket holding the remains of my nineteen-year-old boyfriend, the love of my life.

"Present arms," shouted the soldier who appeared to be in command. On his command, the soldiers walked the casket to the gravesite, and the soldiers with guns changed their position. I guess that was our signal to come closer, because everyone moved forward.

The whole event was surreal, a really bad scene. I tried to focus on the precision of the Honor Guard as they lifted the flag, but all I could think of was Johnny. The commanding officer saluted.

"Ready, aim, fire," the soldier commanded. The soldiers holding the guns shot into the air. "Ready, aim, fire." The shots made me cringe. "Ready, aim, fire," and the third round of shots rang out.

The haunting sound of "Taps" filled the air. Swallowing the lump in my throat, I let my tears fall. I wanted to sob, but I controlled myself as best I could. I watched through bleary eyes as the soldiers folded the flag. They handed it to the commanding officer and saluted. The soldiers turned then walked away from Johnny's casket.

The commanding officer marched over to Johnny's mom and knelt on one knee before her. "Ma'am," he said, "on behalf of the President of the United States and the people of a grateful nation, may I present this flag as a token of appreciation for the honorable and faithful service your loved one rendered this nation."

I wasn't sure what was going to happen next, but I had to split. I hugged Johnny's mom and beat it to Johnny's Camaro.

Getting the door open I slid onto the front seat, then, after jamming the key into the ignition, I rolled down the windows. After turning the radio up, slamming on the gas and, unintentionally, spinning the tires, I turned the Camaro around in the narrow space. Someone was running toward the car. Not stopping, I booked it out of the cemetery. There was only one place for me to go.

Turning sharply from the cemetery onto Fourth Avenue I sped down the road. A quick glance in my rearview mirror alerted me to a car following me down the road. The speedometer read seventy-five. I slowed down, hoping it wasn't a cop.

*****

Present day

"Ivy. Beautiful Ivy." Jack's voice cut through Christine's memories, reaching me.

As my consciousness returned, I found myself sobbing on Jack's chest. We were seated on the ground in front of a grave marker, Johnny's grave marker. Scrubbing the tears from eyes, I read the inscription aloud. "Private First Class, Johnathan Richard Ridder, December 30th, 1950 – July 23rd, 1970, 'And the moon went with him'."

"And the moon went with him," Jack repeated. Then a grin spread across his face. "Johnny's mom and dad put in a remembrance from Johnny's favorite book."

"*Harold and the Purple Crayon*," we said in unison.

"That was the book we found under Christine's bed that had Johnny's name in it. I wonder why Johnny gave the book to Christine?" I said, more to myself than to Jack. Jack wasn't listening anyway.

"Johnathan Richard Ridder," Jack repeated slowly. "In all my dreams or memories of Johnny's life, I never thought of my—I mean his—last name." He paused. "Here's the kicker. My mom's sister, my Aunt Sally, is married to a Ridder. I mean Uncle Joe. They're really old, lots older than my mom, maybe in their sixties."

"So, you think maybe your Uncle Joe was Johnny's brother? That would add another layer of crazy. Not really...I mean you're still you, Jack, just like I'm Ivy. We really do have issues," I said as I got more comfortable in his arms. "It's kind of cool in a strange and mystical sort of way."

"Strange and mystical," Jack said as he hugged me against him.

We sat in silence, staring at Johnny's grave. "Christine left the gravesite before the service was over," I said as I tried to remember the details of the memory, vision, whatever. "She had a direction in mind, but I don't where it was. It's so frustrating." An elusive memory flittered in my head, an important piece of knowledge I couldn't place.

"Let's go," Jack said, pulling me to my feet. "No disrespect intended to Johnny or Christine, but I wanna get out of this graveyard."

I looked into Jack's blue eyes and felt Christine kind of fade to the background in my head. "I think that sounds like a plan...getting out of the graveyard."

A chill ran down my spine. In the distance I saw a car. It was the same car that seemed to have been following me, or Jack, or me and Jack. I wasn't sure how long it had been there, but the person from the car was leaning against the hood, staring in our direction. "Jack," I said, keeping my voice low, "don't look yet, but, in a second, look behind you. Who is it? Do you know?"

Jack and I walked toward the truck. As Jack opened the door for me, he turned and looked at the person standing by the car. It was too late. Whoever it was, he or she was already in the car.

"The car looks familiar, like I should know who owns it," Jack said as he got into the truck. "I just can't place it."

"I'm sure it's nothing to worry about," I said as Jack grabbed my hand and tugged me over next to him.

"When are you gonna get used to ridin' shotgun, city girl?" Jack asked as he wrapped his arm around me.

I didn't reply to the question, I just grabbed hold of his hand. "What's next?" I asked.

"Well," Jack replied, "now that we know Johnny's last name, I thought I would call Uncle Joe and see what I can find out. I mean, if they are related...though Uncle Joe never mentioned a brother serving in Vietnam. He'd know a lot about Johnny. Then we could look into the disappearance at the newspaper like we talked about last night."

"That sounds good," I replied.

"I think I'm going to dedicate *Flashback 1969* to the soldiers who served at Ripcord. I know it actually happened in 1970." He paused reflectively. "I think I can make it work."

"I know you can," I replied. "I think it's a groovy idea."

"Groovy, Ivy," Jack replied with a grin.

I smiled as I considered what else we should be doing. "I wonder if we should get the names of any people who knew Christine who are still living in Newton? We could interview them or something."

"Okay," Jack replied. "Let's see what I can find out from Uncle Joe first. I'm hungry. Want to stop by the Maid-Rite?"

I leaned into Jack's side as we drove into town. We

could worry about Christine and Johnny tomorrow.

Chapter 20

Jack

An entire week had passed since our visit to the cemetery. It had flown by.

I ran up the steps to Ivy's front door, rang the doorbell, then waited for someone to answer. We were going to Pella today and the Amana Colonies tomorrow. I hoped Mr Van den Berg wouldn't answer the door. He was still kinda pissed about the whole stayed-out-all-night thing, even though it had happened nearly a month ago.

"Hi," Ivy said as she opened the door. "Hey, nice letterman jacket. Don't take this wrong, but I didn't know people still wore letterman jackets. Though, I have to say, someone with your incredible football skills can rock a jacket like that anytime."

I raised an eyebrow at her and shook my head, "City girls," I said with pretend disdain as I admired my girlfriend. She was wearing jeans and a sweater. She looked hot, but I was concerned she might get cold. "Are you bringing a jacket?"

"No, I'm good," she said, "but thanks for asking. I can't believe we are actually following a lead." She was so excited that it made me excited too.

"Didn't you forget something?" she asked as I opened the door to the truck for her and helped her climb into the cab. She was sitting on the edge of her seat, looking down at me, and she gave me that—I don't know—come-and-get-me grin.

I was gonna mess with her, but I decided to kiss her instead. I loved the feel of her lips against mine.

"Mmm," she murmured against my mouth, "much better. Now, you may drive." She was sitting in the middle by the time I got in the truck.

"Shotgun," she said as I draped my arm over her shoulders.

I put into my phone the address of the bakery in Pella where we were heading, then pulled out of her driveway onto the street.

"I know why you're wearing your jacket," Ivy said. "You want to flaunt last night's victory over all the people of Pella. I mean, I know the Cardinals kicked butt, but do you need to rub it in?"

Actually, I hadn't connected last night's victory to what we were doing today. I was about to tell that to Ivy, but I realized she didn't want a response to her question. She was giving me a hard time. I could tell by her smile. "You really are an amazing football player. I know you are going to get tons of offers to play in college."

I kissed the top of her head in response. I didn't want to think about college unless she was going to go where I was going. I probably shouldn't tell her that. It might freak her out or something.

"Where do you want to go to school?" she asked.

"Wherever you're going," I blurted out. *So much for not freaking her out.*

"That's what I was hoping you were going to say." She sounded really happy, and that made me smile.

Ivy reached down then grabbed her purse. She pulled out the little notebook with all of our information. "You know what." Ivy said it more than asked. "I haven't had a single Christine memory or dream since we went to the cemetery last weekend. I really thought they would overwhelm me."

"You know what?" I replied. "The dreams I've had are all about Christine and Johnny in the back of the Camaro."

"Oh my God," Ivy said, pretending to be shocked, "you are so bad."

I felt my face heat up. I really hadn't meant to say that; kinda like the college thing. My filter was totally gone.

"I'm going to ignore your inappropriate comments and review our notes," Ivy said as she pressed closer to me in the seat. She was such a tease. I had to grin, though. I liked it.

"First, you haven't talked to your Uncle Joe because he's out of town till next week. Second, the lady we are looking for was a teenager in 1970. She reported sighting the Camaro." She glanced up at me. "Don't even think about it." My hand was creeping toward her breast. I wasn't as stealthy as I thought.

"Remember, seventeen-year-old dude here… Can't help it," I replied frankly.

"Whatever," she replied, shaking her head but still smiling.

"From what we deduced, she now owns the bakery where she worked in 1970." I used *deduced* to see how Ivy would respond.

"Jack, can you kiss me and drive? You know what it does to me when you use words like *deduced*. I don't think you can. It's like texting and driving. Just say 'no'."

"I'll take recompense when we stop," I replied.

"*Recompense*…so hot," she replied, grinning. "Back to business… Her married name is Vermeer. She's been the owner of the bakery for several years." Ivy unfolded the paper that we'd printed at the newspaper office. "She reported seeing the Camaro and a girl who resembled Christine two weeks after the funeral. In the article, she mentioned that she recognized the car and the girl because the girl had come to the bakery numerous times—first with a boy, then alone. Hmm…I guess Christine and Johnny went to the bakery, then, when Johnny went to

Vietnam, Christine went alone. That's kind of sad."

I squeezed her hand. "Let's just hope Mrs Vermeer remembers something. It was a long time ago."

"This is so pretty," Ivy exclaimed as we reached the square in downtown Pella. "I love the colorfully painted buildings. It looks like we're in Holland. Of course, I've never to Holland, but I bet it would look like this."

Ivy followed me out my side of the truck, scrambling to get a better view of the town. She glanced up at me. Before I had a clue what she was thinking, she pulled my head down and kissed me. "That's for *deduced*," she said against my lips. She resumed kissing me until I forgot we were standing in the square in downtown Pella. "That's for *recompense*. Nice word."

She stepped away, leaving me breathless.

"Hey, Pella is a family-friendly town, none of that kissing stuff here," I said.

She kissed me again then grabbed my hand. "It's kind of chilly. I probably should have worn a jacket." She shrugged as she pulled me along. "You can bring me back here for another date. Look at this." She pointed to a sign. "They have a tulip festival in the spring. You can bring me to the tulip festival."

I stopped and made Ivy stop too. "I will absolutely bring you to the tulip festival, and we can come here for another date." I looked into her eyes, hoping she could tell how I felt about her without me actually telling her. "Damn," I mumbled, "I want to kiss you so bad. I am practicing restraint. Come on," I said as I tugged her along beside me. "Are you good with finding the bakery and, hopefully, Mrs Vermeer? After that, we can walk around the town then get something to eat."

"Sounds good," Ivy replied as we continued down the brick-paved street toward the bakery.

"Hey," I said, pulling her to a stop. I shrugged out of my

jacket and placed it around her shoulders. The gesture was oddly familiar.

"Thanks," Ivy replied. "You are the best boyfriend ever. Now, if you put your arm around me, I'll be toasty."

Ivy snuggled into my side as we continued down the street. I tried to keep the past—Johnny's past—from crashing into the present, but the surreal feeling was coming fast. Same place but different time... Downtown Pella was different than it had been in 1970, but the bakery where we were heading would be exactly the same.

"Are you okay?" Ivy asked. "I'm getting the feeling again. The memories are trying to flood my head." Ivy took in a deep breath then let it out slowly. We stood silently at the door of the bakery. I opened the door and the bell rang.

"Hi! Can I help you?" asked a girl about our age who was working behind the counter.

"Definitely not Mrs Vermeer," I whispered to Ivy. "We'd like a Dutch Letter."

The girl handed me the flakey pastry, and I handed it to Ivy. "It's a dollar twenty-five," the girl said. I handed her two bucks and waited for the change.

"Is Mrs Vermeer in today?" Ivy asked as she examined the S-shaped Dutch Letter.

"Yes, she's in the back. Would you like me to get her?"

"That would be great," Ivy replied with enthusiasm. Was her heart pounding like mine? She squeezed my hand tightly. I guessed it was.

"Are you okay?" I asked as I turned her toward me by grabbing the top of the jacket.

She nodded, "Yeah, I think I'm okay."

"You gotta try this," I said as I broke off a piece of the pastry. I placed a piece in Ivy's mouth then popped one in mine.

"Damn," I muttered as I looked down at Ivy, "I want to lick the sugar from your lips."

A gasp from the door had us spinning quickly. Standing in the door frame was a tall, slender woman who looked to be in her seventies. "Are you Mrs Vermeer?" Ivy asked as she brushed the crumbs from her lips.

"Yes, I am," Mrs Vermeer replied. "How can I help you?"

"I'm Ivy Drake, and this is Jack Vander Zee. We are researching a mystery and we are hoping you can help us."

"A mystery," Mrs Vermeer replied with a smile. "I do love a good mystery."

"In late July of 1970, my Aunt Christine Van den Berg attended the funeral of her boyfriend, who was killed in Vietnam. Christine left the funeral and was never seen again."

I studied Mrs Vermeer as Ivy talked.

"Last week," Ivy continued, "Jack and I researched her disappearance in the archives at the *Newton Daily News*. On August 15th, 1970, a teenage girl, Lucy Darling, who was employed at this bakery, informed the police that she saw the blue Camaro and a girl, whom she thought was Christine, at the bakery."

Mrs Vermeer remained silent. She gripped the countertop as Ivy resumed the story.

"We used the Internet and found out Lucy Darling married Don Vermeer, a local farmer. After her husband passed, Mrs Vermeer purchased the bakery. Are you Lucy Darling?" Ivy queried.

Mrs Vermeer sighed deeply. "Yes, I'm Lucy Darling. I've been wondering my whole life when that lie would come back to haunt me."

Ivy gripped my arm so tightly that I was sure I would

have bruises.

"Why don't you kids come to my office? My granddaughter will cover the shop." She pointed us toward a door on the side of the bakery. "My office is upstairs. I'll grab a few sweets and a couple of cups of tea. You do drink tea, don't you?"

Ivy and I nodded.

"Go on up. I'll be right behind you," Mrs Vermeer said as she prepared a pot of hot water for tea. "I promise I'm perfectly harmless. Why don't you text your parents and let them know where you are and who you are with?"

Ivy looked at me as she pulled out her cell to send a text message to her "mom". I wasn't surprised when my phone vibrated. I shook my head at her then opened the door so she could walk up the stairs to the office. I read the text as I walked up the stairs.

IVY: *Been thinking about you. It hasn't all been PG :)*

She glanced at me and winked.

That's my girl.

Before we had a chance to say anything, Mrs Vermeer was up the stairs with a tray of food and the hot tea.

"Thanks for the tea and pastries," Ivy said as she accepted a cup.

"When I walked into the bakery and saw Jack... It is Jack, isn't it?"

I nodded in response.

"Jack was feeding you the pastry, and you were wearing his jacket." She nodded in my direction. "It reminded me of them—Christine Van den Berg and Johnny Ridder. They came to the bakery at least once a month. Christine loved Dutch Letters, and Johnny loved her. I would watch them with such envy, wondering if I would ever find someone who would love me like that. I remember the last time they came in together. It was December. She was wearing his letterman jacket, just like you are now." She nodded at Christine.

"Johnny asked to see the owner. I brought out Mr Scholte. Johnny shook his hand, introduced himself, and explained he had enlisted and would most likely be in Vietnam in a couple of months. He handed Mr Scholte a hundred-dollar bill and asked if Mr Scholte could ensure his girl always had a fresh Dutch Letter when she stopped in the bakery. He introduced the young lady to Mr Scholte as Christine Van den Berg, his intended. The tears were running down her face as she shook Mr Scholte's hand."

Mrs Vermeer paused for a moment and dabbed her eyes with a tissue. "I don't think she knew she was crying. Anyway, Mr Scholte told Johnny he would make sure Christine would have any pastry she liked, for as long as he—Johnny—was serving his country. He handed Johnny back his money then wrote a note and taped it to the register. Johnny thanked Mr Scholte profusely then walked with Christine out the door. Johnny never walked into the shop again. Christine, however... She came to the bakery once a month. At each visit she received a Dutch Letter and would stay for about an hour, updating Mr Scholte on Johnny's life. The last time I saw her was mid-July of 1970. I remember it because she told Mr Scholte that Johnny was serving with a famous football player."

"Bob Kalsu," I mumbled.

Cocking her head, Mrs Vermeer replied, "Hmm... Why, I think that is correct. Oh, my dear"—Mrs Vermeer addressed Ivy—"let me give you a tissue. It is such a tragic story."

Ivy wiped her eyes. "Mrs Vermeer, the last time you saw Christine was before Johnny died. I don't understand."

"A couple of weeks after Johnny's burial—which Mr Scholte attended—a young man came into the bakery. He said he was a friend of Johnny and Christine's. He explained Christine was determined to start a new life outside of Newton without the shadow of Johnny's death haunting her. His request was for me to call the police and tell them I thought I saw Christine and the Camaro here, in Pella. I wasn't going to do it. He removed a photo from his pocket. The photo was of him, Johnny, and Christine. They all looked so happy." She paused for a moment, staring at nothing.

"I called the police and reported what I allegedly saw. The story was in the Pella paper, as well as the *Newton Daily News*. I had my fifteen minutes of fame—fame I never wanted." She paused again. "I've thought about this for years. I believe I should have reported the young man who requested I tell a lie to the police, rather than making the false report."

She walked to the file cabinet and opened the bottom drawer. "I saved every article about the Christine Van den Berg disappearance for this very moment." She handed the file to Ivy. "Maybe something in the file will help you find out what happened to Christine."

I pulled Ivy to her feet. "Thank you for your time and for the information, Mrs Vermeer," I said as we headed toward the door leading to the steps.

"It's really quite remarkable, the resemblance—or maybe the passage of time makes it seem like it. For a moment, I was back in 1969 watching the golden couple from Newton sharing a Dutch Letter at the bakery. Good luck," she called as we walked out the door.

"Oh my God," Ivy said, "I remembered the entire bakery

visit before Johnny went to Vietnam. Did you?"

I nodded in response. It felt like I was choking. It was so hard to breathe. The flashback felt real, like it had happened just moments ago, not years ago to someone else.

Pulling Ivy close, I wrapped my arm around her as we walked back to the truck.

"If Lucy Darling did not see Christine after Johnny's funeral, it's even more likely something bad happened to her after she left the funeral," I said.

"Right," Ivy agreed. "The big questions is, who was the guy and why did he want Lucy to lie to the police? I mean, Christine loved Johnny. I don't think she would want to just forget about him."

I thought about it for moment. "I don't know, maybe she did. She removed all evidence of Johnny from her scrapbook. The only things left in her room that would've reminded her of Johnny were a couple of photos and the book we found under the bed. She probably didn't realize the book was there."

Ivy shook her head. "That just doesn't feel right."

We reached the truck. "Lunch?" I asked.

"Sure," Ivy replied with a small smile. "You are always hungry."

"What can I say? A man's gotta eat."

"We can flip through the file at lunch. Maybe we'll find the missing link in the articles," Ivy said as we entered the restaurant.

"Maybe," I replied as I placed my hand in the small of her back and guided her to a table. "You know, Ivy," I said. "This might sound kind of dumb, but I think you are my missing link."

Ivy looked up at me as she slid into the booth at the restaurant. She grabbed my hand and pulled me in next to her.

"That was really sweet, Jack Vander Zee."

She cupped my cheek with her hand and I felt her touch go straight to my heart. I grabbed her hand then pressed a kiss into her palm. I looked into Ivy's green eyes and, for once, I couldn't find the right words.

"Are you ready to order?" the waitress asked as she set a couple of waters on the table.

"Yes, thanks," Ivy replied. "I'll have the pancakes, scrambled eggs, and sausage."

"I'll have the same," I said to the waitress, "but can you add an order of hash browns?" The waitress nodded and wrote it down.

Ivy opened up the folder. "It looks like the articles go in chronological order. It starts with the *Newton Daily News* obituary for Johnny." Ivy stared at the clipping for a few minutes. Then she looked up at me, her eyes glossy with tears. "This is really hard," she whispered, then she inhaled deeply.

"Okay, the next article is from the funeral. Look. There's your Uncle Joe." Ivy read the caption under the photo as she pointed to Uncle Joe. "I guess he is Johnny's brother."

I glanced at the yellowed newspaper and felt sick. I forced myself not to remember memories connected to Johnny's family. It was too weird.

"It's really hard to look at this," Ivy said as she studied the picture. She glanced at me then she flipped through the newspaper articles, including the ones that mentioned the sightings of Christine.

"Here you go," the waitress said as she placed our plates on the table.

"Thanks," we replied in unison.

Ivy put away the articles. She pulled out a fat envelope. "Are you ready for me to open this?"

"Yeah," I replied. "It can't be much worse than seeing my—I mean Johnny's—obituary. This is really good," I said, referring to the food.

Ivy opened the envelope and dumped its contents on the table. It was a bunch of photographs. All of them were from Johnny's funeral.

We passed the pictures back and forth as we ate. One photo caught my attention.

"Hmm," I said, "that's interesting. That guy is in my dreams a lot." I gestured to a young man in uniform who was not in the same uniform as the Honor Guard.

"His name was Bill," Ivy said. I nodded in agreement. "I don't recognize anyone else in the photos."

I studied the photos carefully. The people looked familiar, but I couldn't put names with any of the faces.

Ivy's phone buzzed. She looked at her texts. "Okay, I need to get back to Newton. My mom and I are going shopping in Des Moines.

I laid a couple of bucks on the table, then we went to the counter to pay.

Our walk to the parked truck was pretty quiet. We were both lost in our thoughts. I walked Ivy to my side of the cab and helped her in. She stayed in the middle of the seat. She'd finally gotten the concept of shotgun.

Ivy leaned against me as she carefully read each article out loud. By the time she'd finished the last article, we were in Newton.

"Thanks for being the reader," I said as we pulled into her driveway. I put the truck in Park then pulled her into my arms, giving her a deep kiss.

"That just never gets old," she said, when I finally stopped kissing her.

I walked her to her door, then leaned down and kissed her again. I agreed. It never got old. It just got better. "Call me later," I said as I looked into her eyes with my forehead resting on hers, so we were really close.

Ivy said, "I'll call you when I get home."

"Let's go, Ivy," Mrs Drake called. Ivy gave me a quick kiss then she was gone.

Driving back to my house, my mind was full of thoughts about Ivy. The drive felt like it took less than a minute as I pictured Ivy in my head. I got out of the car and walked into the house. Luckily my mom, Stan, and the twins were gone. I wasn't in the mood for a big discussion.

I texted Collin as I walked into my bedroom,

JACK: *You want to do something tonight?*

Seeing my bed, I decided a nice afternoon nap might be a good idea. For once, I wasn't too worried about falling asleep, because my most recent dreams had been about Christine and Johnny. They were not about fighting and dying in Vietnam. I grinned as I closed my eyes. What was that saying? Oh yeah, make love, not war.

*****

Summer, 1970

"Here, use the C-4 explosive to heat that. It'll burn, not explode, which is a good thing," I said to the new guy sitting next to me. He must have been new to the service too, 'cause he didn't know how to warm up his C-ration. "My name's Johnny," I introduced myself, "and this is Mike."

"I'm Dan," the soldier replied. "Thanks, by the way. I'm not exactly sure how I ended up here." He gestured around Ripcord.

"In the A-shit Valley or in Viet f'ing Nam?" Mike asked.

Dan grinned and kinda laughed. "Maybe all of the above. I'm a radio repairman. I arrived in-country yesterday. Today I boarded a helicopter, and here I am."

"Well, welcome to Fire Support Base Ripcord," Mike said as he opened the cookies from his MRE. "These," Mike said, holding up the cookies, "are called Danish butter cookies. Now, I say 'called' because they taste like soggy cardboard. I can't say I've actually tried soggy cardboard, but if I did, I would say it tastes just like Uncle Sam's Danish butter cookies."

"Come on, soldiers," our commanding officer shouted. "We're surveying the perimeter of old Ripcord."

Mike stood up then grabbed his weapon. I grabbed mine and added some hand grenades to the mix.

"Let's roll," I said to Mike. "See ya later." I waved at Dan as we headed out.

"It's a lovely day for a stroll," Mike said as we started down the hill. "I really enjoy being shooting practice for the NVA."

"How many times do I have to tell ya to quit with the target on your back; it's your own damn fault they're shooting at you," I replied with a grin.

"Well, damn," Mike said as he cranked his head around, trying to see the imaginary target on his back.

The unmistakable sound of an automatic weapon split the air. "Where are they?"

Suddenly we were in the midst of a battle. Mike and I dropped to the ground and started shooting in the direction of the incoming fire.

"I'm hit! I'm hit!" yelled one of the guys.

"Shit," Mike said. "I hate it when they use our captured weapons against us."

The incoming fire stopped. It was eerily quiet. We waited for our commanding officer to tell us to move out. We got the signal and started forward. Only one of our guys had been hit, and it appeared to be more of a flesh wound. He started back up the hill. We watched intently, covering his back as he slithered up the mountain.

"Make it quick, boys," said our commander.

Quick? I studied the terrain around me. *It's gonna take a couple of hours.*

We scoured the area, looking for signs of the NVA. A hand went up. Our commanding office was signaling to halt. We waited with guns ready for whatever caused our little procession to come to a stop. *Nothing, I guess.* We started to move forward.

Stop and start, stop and start—the process continued for hours. As far as I knew, we had found nothing. Finally, as the sun began to set, we crawled back up the side of the mountain into the relative safety of our station on Ripcord.

The wind was ripping through the camp, but being in the wind-buffeted encampment was a helluva lot better than being on open hillside.

"Hey, Ridder! You got a letter," Leroy yelled as he strode toward me across the station. "It smells real pretty," he said with a grin as he handed it to me. "I sure hope it ain't a 'Dear John' letter. Oh wait, every letter you get is a 'Dear John' letter."

"Funny," I said as I smelled the envelope. It smelled like Christine. It smelled like home. I found a spot out of the flow of base activity and opened the letter.

Dear Johnny,

I miss you so much. I can't believe high school graduation is a couple of weeks away, and you won't be here to see me in my cap and gown. I'll be sure to take a Polaroid and send it to you. The Mamas & the Papas are on the radio. The song is on the record I gave you for your graduation. Did I tell you I miss you? I miss you!

Yesterday one of the girls trying out for Pacesetters noticed your ring on my necklace. I pointed out your All-Iowa photograph in the trophy cabinet. She thought you were as fine as wine.

I guess you probably know President Nixon announced we were invading Cambodia. You'll never believe what happened at Kent State—it's in Ohio. Four college students were shot by the National Guard. I put the article in the envelope so you can read the details. For the last couple of days there have been protests at Iowa and Iowa State. Let's see… There was a sleep-in in front of the Old Capitol. Students, I guess, burned down one of the buildings on campus. I was at the Maid-Rite last night and ran into a couple of your friends who went to Iowa—Joe and Cindy. They told me to tell you "Hi!" They came home from college early because they got the option— or something like that. Sorry I didn't get all the intel.

At Iowa State there was a sit-in at the Selective Service Office. I think some of the students were arrested. There was also a March of Concern and a Peace Rally. I'm sure your brothers will tell you all about when they write. Bill will probably write about it too, from the perspective of being in the ROTC. I'm sure that will be interesting. Maybe the anti-war protests will get you home soon.

I saw your mom at the Hy-Vee yesterday, getting groceries for the week. She invited me to Sunday night dinner when your brothers get home from school. Did you know Joe's engaged? I can't believe he finally popped the question. I'm sure Sally flipped out. I took your Camaro to Pella on Saturday. I think it misses you. Can a car miss its owner? I had a Dutch Letter and thought of you. I love you and I am waiting for you!

Your Moon, Christine

I love that girl. I read her letter one more time before I pulled out the article on Kent State. It was clear things were really heating up at home. Somehow, I don't think the protests will get us home sooner.

"Hey, Mike," I called out, "you'll never believe what's going down back home." I handed him the article.

*****

Present day

The sound of the alarm jolted me awake. *Shit*. I'd missed going out with Collin, and I'd missed Ivy's call. I sent a text to

Ivy then sent one to Collin. I must have been really tired. *Damn.* I was covered in sweat. I thought about the dream as I rolled out of bed. Pretty much everything was connected to stuff Ivy and I had been talking about. Maybe it was just a dream and not a memory this time. I got in the shower and tried to sort through the dream so I could tell it to Ivy.

After getting dressed, I jogged to the truck. I was running late. "Damn," I said as I got there. Another note was stuck under the wiper. I grabbed it then tossed it on the passenger seat.

Chapter 21

Ivy

I waited impatiently by the front door. Jack was ten minutes late picking me up for our drive to the Amana Colonies. He also hadn't answered my call last night. Was I feeling a little uncertain about our connection? *Nope*, I thought with a smile as I read the text he'd sent me, apologizing for falling asleep.

I wondered if the girl who had reported seeing Christine in South Amana was still alive. Would her story be similar to Lucy Darling's? If it was, what did it mean? What would we do next?

The doorbell jolted me out my moment of contemplation. "Hey," I said as I opened the door. Jack smiled and my heart raced. *When will the butterflies in my stomach stop when I look at him?* He clasped my hand. *Maybe never*, I decided, as we walked toward the truck.

"Did you miss me?" he asked as he helped me into his side of the truck. "If you're riding shotgun, it's shorter to go this way. And," he said as he grasped me around the waist, "I wanted to kiss you hello." He leaned down and brushed his lips against mine. A car horn honked. Jack didn't break the kiss. He just waved.

"It sure would be better if you didn't live on the busiest street in town," he grinned, then he helped me into the cab. "Hey, I'm really sorry I didn't answer your call last night."

"That's okay,"

A piece of notebook paper was on the seat. I picked it up before I sat down. I opened the note, expecting to see something about our drive to the Amana Colonies. I read the note.

She will ruin you. Stay away from the girl.

Jack hit his hand on the steering wheel. "I didn't want you to see that."

"Well," I replied, "at least this one didn't say I was poison. I seriously don't get it." I gestured to the back seat with the paper. Jack nodded his head, then I tossed the note in the back.

"I've got a plan. I'll take the notes and check handwriting with the cheerleaders. It should be pretty easy to figure out who wrote them. Sound good?" I asked.

"I'm glad they aren't leaving you notes about me," Jack replied, pulling me closer. "And, I like your plan."

"So, what exactly are the Amana Colonies?" I asked Jack, changing the subject. *Who cares about a bunch of dumb girls, anyway?*

"The Amana Colonies are a group of seven villages. They were settled by a group of German Pietists who called themselves the Ebenezer Society or the Community of True Inspiration. They moved to Iowa from New York in 1855. The Amanians achieved and keep their economic independence by doing traditional crafts and farming. Today it's a major tourist attraction," Jack said in a voice sounding like a tour guide.

"Wow, pretty impressive. Your tour guide voice and remarkable knowledge of history are almost as hot as your extensive vocabulary," I said with a laugh.

"I thought you'd like that," Jack said as he tilted my head up and gave me a quick kiss. "Actually, I did a presentation on the Amana Colonies for my fourth grade Iowa history project. I practiced a lot."

"I bet you were so cute when you were in the fourth

grade," I said in response to Jack's story. "Did you think it was kind of odd that Mrs Vermeer had all those newspaper articles? Sort of stalkerish, don't you think? Maybe you think I'm kind of odd the way I keep changing the subject."

"Actually," Jack said, "I think you're kind of perfect. And, yeah, the whole article collection was kind of—what's the word?—stalkerish."

I pulled the folder out of my backpack then opened it, "The file also included lots of articles about Johnny when he was in high school. Stalkerish. Do you think she was telling the truth? I mean, look at these articles." I held up several articles featuring Lucy Darling telling her story about spotting Christine. "She certainly got her fifteen minutes of fame. I love this song," I said as I turned up the volume.

"'Letters from Home'," Jack said. "I didn't know you liked country music, pretty city girl." Jack didn't say anything for a moment, then… "I had a dream last night. In the dream, Johnny got a letter from Christine…the whole letter from home thing." He squeezed me to kinda emphasize the point. "She told him about Kent State and other anti-war protests going on here, in Iowa." He paused again. "When did that happen anyway?"

I grabbed my phone and looked up Kent State. "It happened on May 4th, 1970. Hmm, that was about two months before Johnny was killed. I guess the anti-war protests didn't bring the guys home." I paused. "Where was Johnny?"

"I think he was at Ripcord." Jack stared forward. "He was definitely at Ripcord. I've been putting off researching Ripcord. I need to do it."

"Why don't I research Ripcord while you talk to your Uncle Joe about Johnny and Christine?" I suggested. Jack nodded in agreement.

"So," Jack said as he changed the direction of the

conversation, "let's talk about what we know from our visit to Pella."

The drive to the Amana Colonies went fast as Jack and I discussed what we'd learned—or hadn't learned—on our visit to Pella. "Hey, there's the Visitor's Center sign." I pointed it out, though Jack seemed to know exactly where to go.

"We're going to stop at the Visitor's Center to get a map. Then we need to find the South Amana School. That's where Sarah Hollrah worked in 1970," Jack said as he pulled into the parking lot.

We got out of the truck and walked toward it. I hung on to Jack's hand as I tried to take in all of the sights. Mostly it was shops and a couple of hotels.

"The Visitor's Center isn't the real Amana Colonies," Jack said as we walked to the counter.

"Hi, I'm Jack Vander Zee. We have reservations for the ten am tour." Jack glanced over at me and winked. "I figured if we were coming, we might as well see the village. We have plenty of time to find Sarah Hollrah."

"Excuse me," said the woman behind the counter. "You're looking for Sarah Hollrah?"

"Yes, we are," said Jack.

"I'm Sarah Hollrah," she said with a smile as she pointed at her name tag. "How can I help you?"

I looked at Sarah closely. She was probably the same age as my mom. "The Sarah Hollrah we're looking for is a lot older than you. She was probably sixteen or seventeen in 1970. She helped at the South Amana School."

"Oh," Ms Hollrah replied, "you two go on the tour. I'll see what I can find out. Why are you looking for her?"

"We're researching the disappearance of a girl named Christine Van den Berg. She's Ivy's aunt," Jack said, gesturing toward me so Ms Hollrah would know I was Ivy. I gave her a little wave.

"The tour van is leaving now," she said as she kind of shooed us out of the Visitor's Center.

"We're going on a tour! You are so thoughtful. You are definitely the best boyfriend ever." I gave Jack a quick hug as we climbed into the van.

"I was kinda worried you would just want to look for clues, but it was too good of an opportunity to miss. You, me, and a tour van," Jack said as he placed his arm around my shoulders.

"We will be starting our tour at Amana, then continue through the other villages that make up the Amana Colonies. At each of the sites, we will tour at least one of the buildings," the tour guide announced.

I squeezed Jack's hand. With all the crazy stuff going on, it was fun to be on a real date. I mean, we came here because of our search, but Jack had planned a date. "Thanks," I whispered. Jack grinned down at me then kissed my cheek.

The tour guide pointed out the historic sites as we rode into Amana.

"My favorite place is the Ox Yoke Inn. It had great German food. I remember coming here once before my dad left," Jack told me. He pointed out his favorite places as I listened. I learned more about Jack than I did about the Amana Colonies. I decided that it had been a great tour as the van returned to the front of the Visitor's Center.

"I hope you enjoyed the tour," Ms Hollrah called as we got out of the van. "I called my uncle. He was married to the Sarah Hollrah you were trying to find. She died five years ago. I knew my aunt was the Sarah you were searching for, but I wanted to call my uncle first.

"At the reading of her will, there was an interesting caveat. I never forgot it. The will mentioned a letter in a security box at the bank for anyone who came looking for information regarding Christine Van den Berg. I called my uncle, and he picked up the letter from the box." She handed me the envelope she had been holding in her hand. "I hope it helps you," she said as she turned back toward the doors of the Center.

I handed the envelope to Jack instead of tearing it open. "We can read it at lunch," I said as we walked toward the car. "Do you want to eat at the Ox Yoke Inn?" I asked, thinking Jack might want to eat at the restaurant he'd enjoyed as a kid.

"I was thinking the Millstream Brewing Company. We could grab some meat and cheese then go try some of their pop. They have really good root beer and an outdoor area where we can sit and eat," Jack said.

"You really are the best date planner ever," I said as Jack helped me into the truck.

"You," he said, "are the best date ever."

What could I do except kiss him? I turned toward Jack. His mouth touched mine and it was like I couldn't get enough of him. Was it possible for every kiss to be better than the last?

"Damn, Ivy," Jack said against my throat, "every kiss gets better and better."

I giggled and kind of snorted—not very cool. Sometimes it felt as if he could read my mind. I snorted again.

"What?" Jack asked, looking a little disgruntled.

I kissed him again until we both forgot about whatever it was that had made me laugh.

A car door slammed. "Oh my God, we were totally making out in a parking lot. I don't think that's actually what they mean by going parking."

"Give me a second," Jack said as he took a couple of deep breaths.

"Seventeen-year-old boy hormones on high alert." I laughed, and Jack frowned. He put the truck in gear then, after a short drive, pulled in front of the meat and cheese store.

"Let's be quick. I think that letter is burning a hole in my pocket," Jack said and winked.

We entered the store. Jack picked out the meat and cheese, and I picked out the crackers and some cookies. The clerk rang us out, and we drove to the brewery.

Jack said, "Grab a table, and I'll get us some root beer. Good?"

I nodded my head in agreement and walked to the garden, looking for a table. I found the perfect spot then laid out our picnic lunch. I took a selfie and sent it to Jack with the same message as yesterday. My phone buzzed. It was a picture of Jack holding a root beer with the message, *I like foam.* I don't know why, but that seemed really funny.

Jack spied me and walked to the table. "One root beer and one letter." He placed both in front of me.

"Well, open it up already," Jack demanded.

I opened the letter and began to read aloud.

To whom it may concern.

If you are reading this letter, you must be looking into the disappearance of Christine Van den Berg and discovered that I was one of the people who reported a sighting of Christine. In early August of 1970, a clean-shaven young man approached me while I was working in the garden outside the South Amana School. I was uncomfortable because I'd never talked to a young man outside of the community before. The young man said he had a special request. He explained he was friends with Christine Van den Berg and Johnny Ridder. Then he pulled a photo from his pocket. It was a picture of him and two other young people. One—the girl—was recognizable. I remembered reading about her disappearance and seeing her photograph. The young man explained that the girl was trying to start a new life after the death of her boyfriend. He asked me to contact the police and tell them I'd seen Christine and her car. With minimal persuasion, I did as he asked. I reported a sighting to the police. I have worried about this for years. I've often wondered if I should have reported the young man to the police rather than fabricating the story about spotting Christine Van den Berg. I hope this information was helpful.

Sincerely,

Sarah Hollrah.

"Well," Jack said, "she didn't see her, either. The story sounds very similar to the story we heard in Pella. Whoever the mystery man is, he most likely played a role in Christine's disappearance."

I stared at the letter before responding. "I think the clean-shaven part is important. Remember, it's the seventies, and lots of guys wouldn't be clean-shaven. Now what?" I asked, taking a bite of cheese.

"I'm not sure," Jack replied. "I guess we talk to my uncle, then figure out what to do next."

We finished the cheese and root beer. "We need to get going," I said as I glanced at my phone. "You have a show to put on."

We cleaned up our trash then tossed it into a garbage can near our picnic table. Jack grabbed my hand and kissed my knuckles.

"This was the best date," I said as Jack opened his truck door for me. I looked up as he looked down. He put his hand behind my head then leaned toward him. I was breathless as his lips touched mine. Jack pulled me tightly against him, wrapping me in a tight embrace.

"Hey," he whispered as he gently put my hair behind my ear then cupped the side of my face with his hand. I turned my head and kissed his palm, then I climbed into the cab of the truck. Jack followed me and closed the door.

I wanted to say the *L* word. It was right there on the tip of my tongue, but I was afraid. I was pretty sure Jack felt the same way, but this was hard. Maybe Jack felt like he did about me because he was actually feeling Johnny's feelings for Christine. Maybe I was feeling the way I did about Jack because I was remembering how Christine felt about Johnny. It was so confusing.

Jack wrapped his arm around me and pulled me tightly against his side. I hung on to the arm that was across my chest. I closed my eyes and snuggled into Jack…

*****

Summer, 1970

"Congratulations!" Mr Ridder said as he held up a can of beer in a toast. "Sally, we are pleased that you have decided to take on Joe as your new mission in life."

I looked around the room at the Ridder family. I missed Johnny so much. Sometimes it was hard to be with his family, even though I loved being with them, because they reminded me of him. *I'm such a flake.*

"I'd like to propose a toast to my little brother Johnny," Joe said, lifting his glass to the sky. "To Johnny, our American soldier, and to Christine"—he directed his glass toward me—"Johnny's moon."

Johnny's moon... I loved being Johnny's moon.

"I don't get it," Sally said as she gave me a side-arm hug. "The whole moon thing…"

"It was Johnny's favorite book," Mrs Ridder joined the conversation. "*Harold and the Purple Crayon.* In the book, the moon goes with him and the moon helps Harold find his way home. Christine is Johnny's moon." She gave me an affectionate pat on the back.

"That's so sweet," Sally exclaimed.

The doorbell rang, interrupting the conversation. Sally and I walked with Mrs Ridder to the door.

Standing at the door were two soldiers in dress uniform. Mrs Ridder, Sally, and I stood in silence as we stared at the young men. *This can't be good.* I grabbed Sally's hand for support.

"Mrs Ridder?" the soldier asked. Mrs Ridder nodded her head slowly as she wrapped her arms around her stomach.

"Good afternoon," the soldier continued, "I'm Lieutenant Dressler. This is Chaplain Jones. Mrs Ridder, we have some news for you. Unfortunately, it's not good news."

Johnny's mom put up her hand to stop the Lieutenant from speaking. "Bob," she said softly as she backed into the living room. "Bob," she said louder. "Come here. Come here *now*."

Sally let go of my hand. She opened the door then gestured the two soldiers to enter into the foyer. Mr Ridder placed his arm around Mrs Ridder's shoulders as Joe, Tom, Mike, and Dave stood behind them near the open door.

"Mr and Mrs Ridder," Lieutenant Dressler continued, "Your son was engaged in a combat situation in Vietnam. On July 23rd, he was seriously injured. I'm sorry to report he died as a result of those injuries."

I tried to swallow. It hurt. I tried to breathe. My chest ached. Tears stung behind my eyes. Sally grasped Joe's hand. Mrs Ridder turned into Mr Ridder's chest and began to sob. Tom slung his arm over Dave's shoulders for support, and Mike placed his arm around Dave. And me? I stood alone.

*****

Present day

"Ivy." Jack's voice. I heard Jack. "Beautiful… Please, babe. Open your eyes. Come on, Ivy. Please… Please open your eyes."

Johnny's dead. I'm not ever going to open my eyes. *How could he be dead? He left me alone.*

Warm lips touched mine—not dead, alive, warm and alive. I kissed him back as I somehow pulled him down next to me on the seat of the truck. Jack or Johnny, Johnny or Jack… Did it matter? I slipped my hands under Jack's shirt, eager to touch his warm skin.

"Ivy, damn, you scared the shit out of me," Jack said. He sounded kind of desperate.

I slowly opened my eyes to find my gaze locked on

Jack's blue, blue eyes. He was lying on top of me, and I had him locked in place with my arms secured around his waist and one foot hooked around his calf. I didn't know where we were, and I didn't care. We were together and, right now, that's all that mattered.

"Ivy, look at me," he said. "I love you, Ivy." Jack's words were heartfelt. He gently caressed my cheek and whispered, "Do you understand?"

Saying the words was hard, but Jack deserved to hear them because they were true. "I love you, too," I said as I reached up and pulled his head down to mine.

Jack buried his head in the crook of my neck. "Tears were pouring out of your eyes. I couldn't get you to wake up. It scared the shit out of me." He braced himself on his arms so he wouldn't crush me. "Maybe we should stop trying to figure this out. Let's just pretend Christine ran away to join the peace movement and she is alive, because if she's alive, you can't be carrying around her memories or shit like that."

"It's okay," I replied as I tugged him back down on top of me so I could hug him against my chest. "I remembered the moment when Christine received the news that Johnny was killed in action." I paused. "I know it's scary, but we can't quit."

Chapter 22

Jack

"This is Flashback Jack. We're going to be leaving the '60s and take a trip to 1970 for the next four shows. So, jump in your time machine and travel with me to Kent State University in Ohio. On May 4, 1970, members of the Ohio National Guard fired into a crowd of Kent State University students who were protesting against the invasion of Cambodia. Four students were killed and nine were wounded. The event triggered a nationwide student strike, forcing hundreds of colleges and universities to close. The event also inspired the song 'Ohio' by Crosby, Stills, Nash, and Young. Whether you were a hawk or a dove, the events at Kent State impacted a nation." I put the needle on the record and the lyrics poured out of the speakers. In the background, images of the fateful day at Kent State played on the screen. Ivy smiled at me from the floor; she was sitting on the beanbag chair perusing albums.

"That's it for tonight. If you have comments, leave a message on my page or send it to me at flash1969 hashtag Ohio4. This is Flashback Jack, and I'll see you on the flipside."

I grabbed the album from her hands then dove on top of her. "You need to stop perusing the album and peruse me."

She lifted an eyebrow. "Are you sure you wouldn't prefer something more tactile? Though I have to say I like what I see."

Her small hands slipped under my shirt. "Yeah, tactile is good," I replied as I leaned down to kiss her.

"I like touching your skin. It's so warm," Ivy whispered. She gave me a hard kiss on the lips then she pushed me away.

"What?"

"Jack, you need to take me home," Ivy said, but she didn't move. She stared into my eyes and I stared back. "One more," she said, leaning toward me.

"Hey, Jack," Mom shouted down the steps, "you need to take Ivy home. You're supposed to meet Uncle Joe at the implement store in fifteen minutes. Hope I didn't interrupt"— she paused—"the show."

"One more what?" I asked as I wrapped my arms around Ivy's waist so she couldn't roll away from me.

"Kiss," she said as she leaned down and kissed me. It should have been a quick peck or something, but she whispered, "Mmm." I had one arm holding her securely around the waist and one arm holding her head in position so she couldn't pull away.

"Jack, I'm sending the twins down," Mom yelled from the top of the steps.

"Come on, beautiful," I said. "I think my mom is sending down the twins to be like birth control or something."

As if on cue, Stevie and Stella came sliding down the stairs on their butts.

"Ivy, play wiff me," Stella said, grabbing Ivy's leg.

"No, pway wiff *me*, Ivy," Stevie cried, tugging on Ivy's hand.

"Me, me, me," Stella demanded.

"Me!" Stevie yelled, knocking Stella to the floor.

"Ivy's *my* playmate," I said with a wink at Ivy. "It's time for Ivy to go home."

"Stay, Ivy! Stay, Ivy! Stay, Ivy!" Stevie and Stella chanted.

"This is great birth control," Ivy whispered as she smiled at Stevie and Stella.

"Come on, guys," she said, grabbing each twin by a

hand. "You can escort me to Jack's truck. I'm pretty sure I heard him mention a piggyback ride or something."

I gave the twins a piggyback ride around the kitchen. Ivy and I walked outside, leaving the twins laughing on the kitchen floor. I grinned at Ivy. "Jump on," I said, pointing at my back.

Ivy leaped onto my back. "Yee haw," she said, then she slapped my ass like I was her horse. I spun around then ran with her to the truck. We were both laughing when she slid off my back at the door. I placed my hands on either side of her head and gazed into her laughing green eyes. "I love you, Ivy," I said as I leaned in and kissed her.

"Jack." Mom sounded exasperated as she said my name from the front door.

I looked down at Ivy, who was ten shades of red. "Now that was embarrassing," she said. "Your mom already thinks I'm taking you down the path of corruption, being from the city and all."

"Ivy." I started, then I saw the note on the windshield. "Damn," I said as I reached over and pulled the piece of paper off. Opening the door for Ivy, I pitched the paper in the back.

"I'll get the writing samples tomorrow," Ivy said as we drove to her house. "I'm going to ask them to list the names of three songs they want the deejay to play at the Homecoming dance."

I am such a dumb ass. I hadn't asked Ivy to Homecoming. "Ivy, I have something special for you on Flashback Jack tonight. Can you be online at ten?"

"Sure," Ivy replied as I grabbed her hand to tug her out of the truck. We walked to her front door, holding hands. "Good luck with your uncle," Ivy said as she went to open it.

"One more," I replied, pulling her toward me.

"One more," she whispered against my lips. My heart

was pounding like a sledgehammer. "One more's never enough, is it Jack?" Ivy asked as she pulled away.

I held her hand as long as I could as I backed away. "Remember, tonight at ten pm. Flashback Jack. Got it?"

"Got it," Ivy replied. I stood with the door of my truck open as I watched her walk inside.

"Damn," I said as I pounded the side of my truck. "Damn, I love that girl." I thought about her on the short drive to my uncle's. They were sweet thoughts.

The sun was kinda blinding as I pulled into the parking lot of the store. I jumped out of the cab, looking for Uncle Joe. He was standing by the pumps. I waved as I walked toward him.

"How was your trip with Aunt Sal?" I asked as I approached him. He didn't say anything. He just stared at me, kinda dumbstruck.

"Uncle Joe? Dude?" I said. "Are you okay?"

"Sorry, Jack," Uncle Joe said with a smile. "For a second you reminded me of someone. Anyway, forget about it," he said with an accent that sounded like he was from Jersey. "So, what do you want to talk about?" Uncle Joe asked with a grin. "Your mom told Sally you were dating a hot little number. Do you need some advice about girls from your old Uncle J-Dawg?"

"I'm good," I said as I helped Uncle Joe haul some equipment into the shed.

"The girl I'm dating, her name's Ivy Drake. She's living with her mom and grandparents, Mr and Mrs Van den Berg on First Avenue." I waited, wondering what Uncle Joe would say.

"Van den Berg," Joe repeated. "Hmm, that's a name from the past."

He didn't say anything else. We placed the saw on a

shelf then walked back outside to bring in the next item.

What the hell, I'm going for it. "Ivy and I are trying to figure out what happened to her Aunt Christine. She disappeared in 1970, the day of her boyfriend's funeral. We went to the cemetery and discovered her boyfriend's last name was Ridder. I thought maybe he was your cousin or something."

Uncle Joe put down the saw he was holding and placed his hands in his pockets. "Johnny Ridder wasn't my cousin." He paused for a moment. "He was my kid brother. Come on," he said, gesturing to the store. "I'm gonna need a beer."

We walked into his office. He opened the mini fridge then pulled out a beer for him and tossed me a can of pop. "Sit down, Jack," he said, gesturing to the table.

"Humph," Joe said with a shake of his head as he sat down. "Funny you should mention Johnny." He paused, shaking his head again. "You looked a helluva lot like him when you got out of your truck tonight. It was unsettling. For years I hoped the army had made a mistake and maybe one day Johnny'd just walk out to the field while I was working. He'd say—"

I whispered, "Hey, Joe, what do you know?"

"What did you say, Jack?" Joe asked, staring at me intently.

Looking up at Joe, I felt like I was looking at him through different eyes—Johnny's eyes. It was friggin' freaking me out. "He was your little brother. I figured he'd say something like, 'Hey Joe, what do you know?' or something else that probably bugged the crap out of ya." *Smooth*, I thought.

Uncle Joe laughed. "Yep, it used to bug the crap out of me. After he died, I would've given anything for the smartass to say it again." He took a deep breath and rubbed his eyes. "He was a great kid. I remember the night of the draft lottery," Joe said, staring at the wall above my head. "His birthdate was pulled third, friggin' third. He was still eighteen years old. The rest of us? All of our birthdays were pulled in the last third. He was so cool about it. I remember he looked around the room at all of us, then said, 'We love this country. It's my time to serve.' Then he goes out and enlists, because if he was gonna serve his country, he wanted to be in the 101st Airborne. We had an uncle who'd served in the 101st during World War II. Johnny had always admired him." Joe took a swig of his beer.

"Sorry about that, Jack, I forgot what you asked. I haven't talked about Johnny in a real long time." Taking another drink from his beer, Uncle Joe picked up on my question. "You wanted to know about Christine Van den Berg. Johnny loved her, and she loved him. He met her when she was a sophomore and he was a junior. We'd promised our mom we wouldn't bring a girl home for Sunday supper until we were sure we'd met the one we were gonna marry. She didn't want to waste her time building relationships with girls who were just 'ships that passed in the night'." Joe looked up at me and grinned. "Her words, not mine. Johnny brought Christine to Sunday supper three days after he met her. She was the one, and he never wavered in his devotion or commitment." Joe shook his head.

"Johnny never lied. It just wasn't in him"—Joe messed with his beer can—"except for the big one. His commitment to Christine was how he ended up in Vietnam. It's just so friggin' ironic. I bet Johnny thought God was punishing him for the big lie, and that's how he ended up as a winner in the draft lottery."

"It must've been one helluva lie," I said, wondering what in the hell it could be.

"He told Christine he needed to stay home and help on the farm. The truth was, my dad had planned to hire someone so we could all be in school. Johnny didn't want to leave Christine, so he told her he was staying home to help our dad." Joe took a deep breath. "He was even recruited to play ball for Iowa State, and he never told her. He made it seem like he had to stay home, because he knew Christine would have manipulated him into going to college. Johnny never lied. She believed him. I think she blamed my dad for his death, believing he forced Johnny to stay home."

"The day of Johnny's funeral, she drove Johnny's Camaro to the service. She sat by my mom, wearing Johnny's letterman jacket. It must have been a hundred and two degrees, and she never took the damn thing off. When the commander of the Honor Guard handed Mom the flag, Christine stood up, ran to the car, then peeled out of the cemetery. That was it. No one ever saw her again."

"Did they find the car?" I asked, hoping Uncle Joe had more information.

"Nope, nothing." Joe tossed the beer can in the recycling bin then stood up abruptly. "Thanks for coming by tonight. I'm glad I got to talk about Johnny." He gazed out the window of his office. "You know the memorial by the Jasper County Courthouse, the one that has all of the names of the people who served from the area etched onto bricks?"

I nodded, "Yeah, I know it."

"Sometimes I get a cup of coffee from Uncle Nancy's, sit on the bench, and stare at the red brick with Johnny's name on it. Sally and I went to the Vietnam Memorial in DC a few years ago. I made an etching of his name. Like I said, glad I got to talk about him."

"Next time I'm on the square, I'll look for his name on the memorial," I replied solemnly.

"Good luck helping Ivy out. It would be great for the Van den Bergs to know what happened to their daughter." He opened the door then walked me to the parking lot. "Jack, I'll let you know if I remember anything else."

"Thanks, Uncle Joe." I couldn't believe I was doing this. My family didn't show a lot of emotion. I gave my weathered old Uncle Joe a hug. He hugged me back.

"Be good, kid," he said as I jogged to my truck.

I turned back with a grin and yelled, "Hey, Joe, what do you know?"

"Smartass," he said as he headed into the shop.

I glanced at my phone. I needed to get home and make Ivy's special show. *So Johnny never lied...except for the big one.*

Chapter 23

Ivy

"It's Flashback Jack with another Sunday night edition for my steady, Ivy. This is the second show featuring hits and history from 1970. On July 4th, 1970 *American Top 40* debuted with Casey Kasem. Kasem introduced the program's first broadcast with the now iconic opening, 'Here we go with the top forty hits of the nation this week on *American Top 40*, the best-selling and most-played songs from the Atlantic to the Pacific, from Canada to Mexico.' Coming in at number twenty on the first top forty was Bread, 'Make It With You'. Ivy, if you're listening, babe, this song's for you."

IVY: *I'm listening.*

JACK: *It's not over yet.*

IVY: *I love this song.*

JACK: *I love you.*

"Ivy, you know I want to make it with you. If you want to make it with me, say yes and be my date to Homecoming. Respond at Flash69 hashtag yes exclamation point, yes exclamation point, yes exclamation point. Though the musical dedications on *American Top 40* did not debut till 1978, Ivy baby, this show is dedicated to you. In the words of Casey Kasem, 'Keep your feet on the ground and keep reaching for the stars.' This is Flashback Jack. I'll see you on the flipside."
        I   quickly   tweeted   @Flash69   #Yes!Yes!Yes!

@poisonIvy. Then I sent him a text.

IVY: *You're the best boyfriend ever.*

JACK: *I'll pick you up tomorrow at 7:15, 'k?*

IVY: *'Kk*

My phone started buzzing with texts from my friends. This time the texts were from my friends in St. Louis and my friends in Newton.

CLAIRE: *OMG, so sweet*

ERICA: *I want one of those...*

ALEX: *Flashback Jack is all that*

BRI: *Collin better get his act together*

CHLOE: *Aren't you glad you didn't dump him?*

I quickly replied to all of the girls. Another text popped up. I didn't recognize the number. I read the message.

641-323-1864: *"Bad Moon Rising" CCR 1969.*

Weird. Why would someone send me a text with the title of a song from Credence Clearwater Revival? I sent a text to Jack.

IVY: *Are you a CCR fan?*

JACK: *One of my favs. You?*

IVY: *Not so much... We can't have everything in common.*

I didn't know why I wasn't a fan. For some reason, the song gave me a sick feeling in my stomach. I'd listen to it tomorrow. I needed to get some sleep. Yawning, I sent another text.

IVY: *Night, Jack. See you in the am.*

I closed my eyes. The lyrics from "Bad Moon Rising" started playing in my head...

*****

Summer, 1970

I sped down the dirt road, making a beeline to the barn where Johnny and I had spent our last night together. Driving over the bumpy ground separating the barn from the road made my teeth rattle in my head. The opening to the barn looked really narrow but I knew from experience that the Camaro would fit through the opening—just barely.

I slammed on the brakes, bringing the car to an abrupt stop before I careened into the wall on the opposite side of the entrance. I turned on the radio. It was the end of *America's Top Forty*. Kasey Casem said, "Keep your feet on the ground, and keep reaching for the stars." *Johnny would love this.* When would my heart stop aching?

I took off Johnny's jacket and laid it on the passenger seat. It was so hot. I opened the car doors, hoping a breeze would come into the car. I climbed into the backseat and brought the shoe box full of all the memorabilia documenting me and Johnny. I opened the lid. On top was the page from *Harold and the Purple Crayon* that I had ripped from the book.

Christine, you are my moon. I will always find my way home to you.
I love you,
Johnny

Tears started to drip out of my eyes. *How would he find his way home when he was dead?* I wondered if a heart could actually break. Mine sure felt like it was. Each photo or news clipping in the box told our story. I carefully examined each one, cementing each memory in my mind. Time flew by as I reviewed our well-documented relationship. Maybe someday I would be able to look at the pictures and smile. Today, I looked at them and cried. I knew what I would find at the bottom of the stack. Maybe that's why I was reading each one so slowly. The letter I'd received from a soldier in the 101st yesterday morning was the last one in the pile. I'd heard about those—letters sent to a loved one when a soldier died in combat, pre-written by the soldier for that occasion. I struggled to hold back the tears, but they trickled down my cheeks anyway.

I pulled the letter out of the box and set it next to me on the seat. I carefully placed all of the other items back in the box, ensuring they were in the correct order. Most recent on top through the football game program at the bottom—the program from the football game where Johnny and I had met for the first time. Some people don't believe in love at first sight. I believed.

It had happened to me the night I'd met Johnny. I remembered he told me when he saw me for the first time that it had been like a lightning bolt to the heart. He'd known I was the one. I smiled at the memory and took a deep breath. Now…I was going to read the letter now.

I opened the envelope then pulled out a note.

> Dear Christine,
>
> My name is Mike. Johnny was a great soldier and close friend. He told me to send you this letter if anything happened to him. I'm sorry I had to send it. He always thought he would make it home to you.

Me too.

I studied the envelope enclosed in the one from Mike. My name was written in Johnny's familiar handwriting. I traced the writing with my finger. Underneath my name, he'd written *My moon.* Opening the letter was so hard, but it wasn't as hard as the funeral had been. The nauseous feeling was back. I felt like I was going to puke as I pictured the casket being carried to the grave—Johnny being carried to his final resting place.

I could hear Johnny's voice talking to me as I read the letter.

> Dear Christine,
>
> Well, beautiful, if you're reading this, you know by now that I won't be coming home. I wish I could be there, holding you in my arms to help you through the pain. So, what does a guy say to the girl he left behind? First, my life was complete because of you. I died a happy man,

knowing you loved me. As hard as this is for me to write, I want you to live a great and wonderful life. I need you to be strong, go to college, meet some other guy—who won't be as wonderful as me, but he will be wonderful to you—get married, and have some kids. If you ever feel alone, look at the moon and think of me. Maybe we will meet in another lifetime because a love like ours can't die. I love you, Christine.

    Forever yours,

    Johnny

It was hard to read the letter because tears were blinding me. They dripped on the letter. I waved it so the writing wouldn't smear. I don't know how Johnny thought I was going to pick up the pieces and move on. I would try. I really would, I believed, as I read the words one more time. For being such a jock, he was really romantic.

I'm not sure how long I sat in the Camaro, but the sun had definitely moved in the sky because the barn seemed to be a lot darker. I placed Johnny's letter carefully in the box before I set the box on the floor of the car. I got out then walked outside. It was a beautiful sunset. I stood in silence as I watched the colors change in the sky. It would be dark soon; I'm sure my parents were worried about me. It was probably time to go home. I took a deep breath then turned back to the barn.

A car was bookin' down the dirt road toward me. Dust was billowing up from the road. The windows must have been down because I could hear CCR's "Bad Moon Rising" blaring from the car stereo. The driver spun a brody then slammed on the brakes, bringing the car to a full stop right in front of me. I recognized the car and I knew the driver…

*****

Present day

"Ivy, time to wake up," Mom called from the bottom of the steps. My head ached. I felt like I'd cried all night. The dream—or flashback—had come back with brilliant clarity. Now, if Jack and I could only find the barn.

I pulled on some jeans and a sweater as I tried to remember any important details from the dream. The hardest thing about that was I didn't know what was important and what wasn't. One thing was for sure…I don't know how Christine kept it together for the funeral. The letter from Johnny was so sweet and so sad. I remembered reading somewhere soldiers would write a letter to their loved ones just in case they died. It was just sad.

Trying to figure out who was leaving notes on Jack's car just seemed kind of—I don't know—lame, compared with finding out what happened to Aunt Christine. Oh well, it should be easy to figure out the culprit. *Culprit*…great word.

"Jack's here," Grandma called up to me.

I grabbed my backpack then rushed down the stairs.

"Hi," I said as I almost knocked Jack over when I ran into him at the bottom.

He grabbed my arms to steady me. His blue eyes sparkled. "There you go again, trying to knock me over with the traditional St. Louisian greeting."

"I'll show you the real traditional greeting as soon as we get to the car," I whispered as I tugged Jack into the kitchen. "Do you want a bagel?" I asked as I grabbed one from the fridge.

"Sure," Jack replied with a grin. "I'm a growing boy."

I thrust a bagel at Jack and grabbed his other hand to pull him out the door. "Bye!" I shouted as we left the house.

"Um, what's the real traditional greeting?" Jack asked.

Before he completed his sentence, I grabbed his hair and tugged his head down. Then I wrapped my arms around his neck and kissed him.

"Whoa," said Jack, holding me tightly against his chest. "I really like that greeting."

"That was my, 'Why yes, Jack, I would love to go with you to Homecoming' kiss," I said as Jack helped me into the truck.

Jack wrapped his arm around me and pulled me close to his side. We drove toward school. "Hey," he said, "I think you're gonna like this. Flashback Jack made you a playlist. It's called 'For Ivy'. I know. What can I say? It's a totally original and unique title." He turned up the volume. The lyrics to "Build Me Up, Buttercup" blasted out of the speakers.

"I love this song," I said as I started to sing along.

"I know," Jack replied with a grin. "I did put a couple of songs from CCR on your list. I didn't know you didn't like 'em."

"That's okay. Wait. You know what is so strange?" I didn't wait for Jack to reply. I was going to tell him anyway. "I got a text from a number I didn't know right after the show. All it said was *'Bad Moon Rising' CCR 1969*. Then the song was in my dream last night. Which, oh my God, reminds me. I know where Christine went after the funeral. She went to a dilapidated barn, only I don't know where the barn is actually located."

Jack didn't say anything for a moment as he pulled into his spot in the senior lot. He opened the door then tugged me out behind him. "Was it a tight fit? Umm, was it hard to get the car in the barn?"

I considered Jack's comment as we walked into the school. I tried to remember. "Yeah," I finally replied, "it was hard to fit the car into the barn."

"Hmm"—Jack thought for a moment—"I think it's the same barn that they spent their last night together." Jack kind of blushed. *Oh, that must be the memory that challenges his seventeen-year-old guy hormones.*

"It was on Johnny's dad's farm, which means it is on Uncle Joe's farm," Jack said. "The car was never found. Wouldn't it be crazy if the car was in the barn?"

"We just need to find the barn," I replied as I squeezed Jack's hand. "Today we are going to solve the mystery of the notes on your car. Tomorrow we can worry about the mystery from 1970."

The gym lobby was packed, and it was only seven thirty in the morning. The cheerleaders had a meeting and so did the football team. "I'll find you after the meeting. Okay, beautiful?" Jack asked. He held both of my hands and was kind of swinging them. "I love you, Ivy," he said, looking into my eyes. He raised an eyebrow, grinned—showing off his sexy dimples—then he walked toward the football team.

"Jeez, Jack," I heard someone say. "Way to raise the bar for the Homecoming invitation."

Somebody else said, "You could've just called her."

I was still laughing when I reached the cheerleaders. "Ivy, Jack is so in love with you. That was so cute," Chloe said, giving me a hug.

"Collin's feeling a little pressure," Bri said with a laugh. "I'm sure whatever he does will be equally as impressive." I nodded in agreement. In my heart, I knew no one could compete with Jack.

"Hey, girls," I said, pulling a stack of notecards out of

my bag. "Jack's not only my date for the Homecoming Dance, he's the deejay. I'll be playing the role of fangirl and date," I said with a laugh. "If you guys could write down your top three must play songs for the dance, I would really appreciate it."

Everyone grabbed a notecard and started writing.

"Too bad Jack is the deejay. That'll make for a pretty boring night," Katie said. "I'm going with Evan. He's so good looking. I'm surprised you didn't tumble into him."

Seventeen, *where are you with a really great comeback line when I need one?* I took her notecard and didn't respond. Collecting all of the lists, I put them in a neat stack.

"Remember, everyone. Practice tonight. Next week is going to be so busy," Bri exclaimed. "You are going to love Homecoming week. It is so fun," Bri said as we walked toward the football meeting.

"Hey"—someone grabbed my arm—"you dropped this." He handed me a notecard.

"Oh, thanks," I replied, sticking the card into the stack. I glanced behind me to see if any more cards had fallen to the floor. *Nothing.* I turned quickly and almost knocked Will, the custodian and general fix-it up guy, to the ground.

"I'm so sorry," I said. "It seems like we keep running into each other." He gave me a blank look. "Sorry," I mumbled again. I guess he forgot about me bumping into him at the drive-in.

"Will's not very social," Bri chattered on. "I think he served in Vietnam or something. Come on." She tugged on my arm, dragging me toward the football team.

"That's it, boys," the football coach said. "Be on time for practice. And by 'on time', I mean early."

Trey, Collin, and Jack joined Bri and me as we started to walk to class. "Where's Anna?" I asked Trey.

"Pacesetters," Trey replied. "They practice till the bell."

"You sure you're okay with me being the deejay for the dance?" Jack asked as he draped his arm around my shoulders, pulling me into his side.

"It'll be fun. We can just dance near your turntable." I paused. "You do dance, don't you?"

"Ivy..." Jack lifted an eyebrow and gave me a kind of disgruntled look as he said my name with feigned disgust.

"Sorry, Renaissance Man," I said as we reached the door to English class.

The day went by quickly. I had planned to meet Jack at his truck after our last class. "Here's another one," I said to myself as I pulled the note off the windshield.

"Hey, Ivy," Collin said as he walked toward the truck. I stuck the note in my bag. "Jack's giving me a ride to practice."

Jack came charging up the hill and jumped on Collin's back. "Let's go. We don't want to keep Coach waiting."

When Jack turned on the ignition, "Bad Moon Rising" was playing. Jack reached forward to change the song, but I stopped him. I wanted to hear the lyrics. Maybe they were important. I hadn't thought to pull them up on my phone. Collin and Jack fist bumped in front of my face and started singing really loud. I guess "Bad Moon Rising" was one of their favorites.

I listened to the lyrics. Okay, maybe they were a little creepy. There was stuff about being prepared to die and an eye for an eye. I don't know how it had anything to do with anything except it was the song Christine heard when the other car pulled up to the barn. It was just kind of strange that I got a text with the song title. Of course, the song might have been in the dream because of the text. *Complicated.*

Jack pulled in front of my house then opened the car. He

got out then helped me. "Grab the notes," I said. Jack dug around for them he'd tossed in the backseat over the past month. I waited patiently for Jack to hand me the stack.

"Notes, milady," he said with a grin. "I hand them to you with flourish." Then he winked.

"*Flourish?*" I questioned. "Nice word."

"Remember it," he said.

"Oh, I will," I replied.

"Come on, dude," Collin called out from inside the truck. "We're gonna be late."

Jack gave me a quick peck on the cheek then jumped back in. I waved as he pulled out of the driveway. I could hear CCR's "Fortunate Son" blasting from Jack's speakers as they drove away.

"Hey, I'm home," I called as I entered the house. Nobody answered. I ran up the steps, heading to my room. As I passed Christine's room, I patted the door. I guess I was letting her know we hadn't forgotten about her. Now, however, I was trying to figure out who was trying to break up me and Jack.

I pulled the notes out of my bag then tossed them on the bed. I put the notes from the truck on the bed next to the stack of song suggestions. *I am such an idiot. Jeez, I forgot to have the cheerleaders put their names on their notecards. Wait, not a big deal. When I find the matching writing, I will send a text to everyone asking for the name of the person who created the list. Problem solved.*

Unfolding the notes left on Jack's truck, I smoothed them out and stacked them up. Well, they weren't very original. Basically, they just told Jack to stay away from me.

Now, to match them up with the cheerleaders' song lists. I took the first notecard and placed it next to the notes. Definitely not. One after another I laid the notecard next to the note. Not one matched. *Well, crap.* Maybe it wasn't important, anyway. I collected the notecards and notes and put them on my desk.

I looked at the poster from my friends in St. Louis. The pictures and the multisyllabic words made me smile. *Oh.* That had reminded me that I needed to review my vocab for English. I dumped everything from my backpack on my bed. A notecard fluttered to the floor. I perused it; listed on it were a number of locations: Gym, 1201, Office, Soccer Field, and Announcer Booth. *Hmm.* That must have been the extra notecard someone handed me. I tossed it on my desk. Once again, I looked at the poster of my friends. In one of the photos we stood side by side in our Halloween costumes. The caption used the word *juxtaposition* to describe how we were standing. I looked back down at the notecard and the note from Jack's car. *Oh my God.* I laid them side by side. It was undeniable. The handwriting was the same. The writing on the list of school locations was the same as the notes. *Dang it.* We were no closer now than we had been before we'd done the writing test. But, we did have a match. I'm not sure why the person who wrote the list had something against me and Jack.

Weird.

Chapter 24

Jack

Ivy should be here any minute. I reviewed all the info Ivy had gathered about the Battle of Fire Support Base Ripcord. Dedicating this weekend's show to the dudes who'd served there seemed fitting, and I wanted to be sure I gave them the credit they deserved.

The door to the basement opened.

"Thanks, Cathy," Ivy said. "I'll be sure to keep Jack in line." There was a pause. "So, it's his first dance with a date? I'll be sure to make him dance, even though he's the deejay."

Ivy walked down the steps with her backpack.

"Hi," she said as she walked to my chair. I stood up as she got closer. She gestured with her finger for me to come closer still.

"What?" I asked.

She smiled and continued to gesture. I stood right in front of her.

"*Flourish* is a very good word." She reached up and kissed me.

I'm not sure how long we stood there kissing. I kinda got my head together when I realized where my hands were, and I realized Ivy hadn't noticed.

She looked totally disappointed when I gave her one final brush of the lips. "I have a whole list of words for your listening enjoyment. I mean…an assiduous dude such as me is always working hard to impress his girl." My lips were about an inch from Ivy's when I was talking.

"Jack, are you teasing me?" Ivy asked as she brought her lips closer to mine.

"Never, beautiful," I said then crushed my lips to hers.

"Mmm," Ivy said after a while, "it is just so good." I couldn't speak, but I wholeheartedly agreed. Ivy sighed and tried to push me away.

"We need to concentrate, Jack Vander Zee, and get down to business. I don't know who's leaving the notes, but I know it's not a cheerleader," Ivy said as she slid out of my arms then sat in my chair. I gestured for her to stand. She gave me a questioning look then she grabbed my hand. I pulled her to her feet, sat on the chair, then pulled her into my lap before she had time to protest.

"Concentrate, Jack," Ivy repeated, but she sounded kinda—I don't know—breathless.

"I am concentrating," I replied as I looked up in her eyes then back down at her neck. "I'm concentrating on if I should kiss your neck or maybe your ear. Or maybe someplace I haven't kissed before."

"Jack," she said in a pretend-shocked voice. "Seriously, we need to talk."

"Seriously, Ivy, I would prefer not to talk"—I kinda leered at her—"if you get my meaning."

"Jeez, Jack," Ivy replied, play-punching me on the chest. "Well, I know who's been leaving the notes. Okay, I guess I should phrase that differently. I know none of the cheerleaders are leaving the notes. But, look," she said, handing me a notecard with a list of places around the school. "Whoever dropped the notecard with the school locations on it is the person who left the note. Of course, we still have no idea who dropped the notecard, so we don't know who left the notes."

"Nah, Ivy," I said as I looked at the card. "This is Will's to-do list."

"Will?" Ivy questioned.

"You know...Will, the school's handyman dude. I'm sure you've seen him around," I finished.

"Oh yeah," Ivy replied. "I ran into him at the drive-in, then the other day at school." She blew her hair out of her eyes. "Well, shoot. I guess I just thought the handwriting looked alike...maybe because the cheerleaders' handwriting looked nothing like it."

I was playing with Ivy's hair, listening to her talk about the dumb notes. "You know," I said, "maybe we should just let the notes go. I mean, it's not like they are going to change my feelings about you or our feelings about each other. Forget about it," I said in a Jersey accent. The accent reminded me of my conversation with my Uncle Joe. "Damn," I said, "I forgot to tell you about my conversation with Uncle Joe, who turns out to be Johnny's big brother. He didn't know anything about what happened to Christine or the car after she left the funeral. What I did find out was Johnny, like me, just did not tell lies—except for a lie Uncle Joe referred to as the *big one*."

"The big one," Ivy repeated as she traced around my hands and fingers with her fingers. For some reason, the contact made me sweat. I grabbed her hand to stop her exploration.

"Yeah," I continued. "He lied to Christine about having to stay home and help his dad on the farm. According to Uncle Joe, Johnny wanted to stay home to be near Christine. Johnny knew Christine would use her wiles on him and get him to go to college. She didn't even know he was awarded a football scholarship. Uncle Joe thought Christine blamed their dad for Johnny's death. If Johnny hadn't been forced to work on the farm, he could have gone to college and received a deferment from the draft."

"*Wiles*," Ivy said with a grin. "I'm going to use my wiles on you."

I said, half to myself and half to Ivy, "If Johnny felt about Christine the way I feel about you, I would have stayed home. I might even lie about it." I paused. "Nah, I wouldn't have lied. I would've just told you that I'm staying and there was nothing you could do about it."

"So Christine blamed Johnny's dad for Johnny's death. That's sad, but it still doesn't help us find out what happened to Christine."

"Yeah," I replied, trying to figure out our next steps. "I think we should start looking for the barn. Uncle Joe's got a lot of acreage, but if we start where we know Johnny and Christine used to go parking, maybe we can just start searching one dirt road at a time."

"Okay, Jack," Ivy replied. "I guess we can worry about it after Homecoming. Right now, we need to work on our chemistry."

Ivy got off my lap and picked up her backpack.

"Ivy," I said.

She looked up at me and smiled. My heart raced. "Um, I'm thinking our chemistry is pretty damn good." I smiled as she kind of blushed.

"Jeez, Jack," Ivy said pulling out her chemistry book, "is that all you think about?"

"Pretty much." I nodded, emphasizing my point. "But, for you, I will pretend I'm interested in the chemistry Mr Schwartz is teaching us. Come here, beautiful. You can sit on my lap while we create a video on stoichiometry."

She grinned as she sat on my lap in front of the computer. I kinda moved her to one side so I could see the screen. "So..." I said as I kissed her neck. I felt her shiver. "Do you think that's the kind of reaction Mr S is looking for?"

"Work, Jack," she said, but she pulled one of my arms

around her waist.

Chapter 25

Ivy

The Homecoming parade finally ended. "Bye," I said to the other girls then weaved my way through the crowd, looking for Jack. I looked around the football players and didn't see him in the group.

Oomph. "I am so sorry," I said to the back of the person I'd run into.

Will the handyman turned and glared at me. *Overreaction much?*

"I really am sorry," I repeated. This time I didn't make the joke about running into him. Obviously, he didn't think I was funny.

"Ivy," Jack shouted. I glanced around, trying to find him. I saw him and waved. I turned to apologize one last time, but Will was already gone.

Jack reached me and pulled me into his arms. "Give me a little sugar, sugar," he said as he leaned down to kiss me.

"Damn," Trey said with a pound on Jack's back, "you guys are going end up with your lips fused together or something. It's embarrassing, if you know what I mean."

"Go away," Jack said against my lips, giving Trey a straight arm to the chest.

I was embarrassed. I pulled away from Jack just as Trey planted a big one on his girlfriend.

Jack cleared his throat.

Trey replied, "It's only embarrassing for you. For me, it's all good." Trey stopped kissing Anna and wrapped his arms around her waist from behind.

"What do you think of Newton's Homecoming

traditions?" Anna asked. "My mom told me in the old days they used to have a bonfire with a pep rally around it. During the pep rally, they would throw an effigy into the fire that represented the other team."

"Brutal," Trey said.

"It's busy," I replied. "Friday should be awesome, with the whole-school pep rally and the game. I'm glad we get a break tonight. I'm exhausted."

"We've got to go," Jack said, tugging me away from Trey and Anna. "We'll see ya tomorrow."

"I'm pretty sure I know where we can find Johnny's Camaro," Jack said as he pulled me behind him toward his truck. He opened the truck door then lifted me into the cab. "I love that I can lift you up and put you where I want you to be," Jack said as he climbed in behind me. "It makes me feel all manly."

"You are so manly," I replied, laughing at him. "You know," I said, "you probably would have been Homecoming King if you weren't dating me."

Jack looked at me and rolled his eyes. "And why would you ever imagine I wanted to be Homecoming King?"

"Because Katie told me you did, today, during the parade."

"Katie?" Jack questioned, "You think Katie is an expert on me?"

We were driving down the highway toward the cemetery. I hung on to the arm Jack had hugging me to his side. "Nope. I just wanted to be sure I hadn't dashed your dreams into the sand, or dirt, or whatever."

"I don't think I mentioned that I love you," Jack said into the top of my head.

"Not today, anyway," I replied. "So, where are we

going?"

"Remember where we went parking the night we fell asleep in the back of the truck?" Jack asked.

I nodded. *How could I forget?*

"Well, there's another road back there. It's blocked off by some debris and trees, but it's back there. I was gonna drive out there myself, but I figured you'd want to go. And, if I found anything, I wanted you to be with me." Jack squeezed my hand.

We continued down the highway, passing both the cemetery and the dirt road where we'd gone parking. Several miles down, Jack turned off the highway onto another dirt road. The road came to an end. It was blocked by fallen trees and branches.

"Are you ready for this?" Jack asked as he turned off the engine.

I nodded in response. A chill ran up my spine. The hair on the back of my neck stood up. This was the place. I could feel it. Jack opened the car door. Christine's memory of driving the car down this road assailed my mind.

"We're going to find the car," I said.

"My flashbacks of this place are about Johnny making love to Christine," Jack said as he helped me over a fallen log.

"Well, that's pretty distracting," I said. "The flashbacks I have are of Christine reading the last letter Johnny wrote to her. And the things that were gone from the scrapbook? She had them with her in the car."

Jack and I continued in silence, walking through the trees. Beyond them was a dilapidated barn. Jack squeezed my hand tightly. "Are you okay?" he asked again.

I took a deep breath, trying not to be overwhelmed by the discovery. "Do you think the car is going to be in there?"

"Yeah," Jack said. "I think the Camaro is in the barn."

In and out, in and out; I tried to regulate my breathing. If the car was here, it was pretty likely Christine had died nearby. "Oh my God, Jack. What if her body's in the car?" I stopped walking.

"We'll deal with it," Jack said. He stopped too. "Do you want me to go in alone?"

I wasn't a coward. "Thanks, but I think we should go in together." Jack lifted our clasped hands to kiss my knuckles.

The barn had kind of collapsed in on itself. It certainly didn't look sturdy. We walked around the outside, looking for a place to enter. "It's not exactly a door," Jack said as he gestured to a big gap between boards.

Jack entered first then pulled me in behind him.

We stood in stunned silence as we stared at the 1969 Camaro that was part of both of our flashbacks. Sunlight filtered in through the slats of what remained of the barn, basking the car in an ethereal light.

My heart was pounding.

Jack placed my hand over his heart. It was racing "You ready?" he asked.

In response, I started walking toward the car. "Wait," I said. I pulled out my phone and took a picture of the car and posted it on my Instagram. Then I turned Jack so his back was to the car and took a picture of me and Jack with the car in the background. "Just in case," I said.

Jack nodded in understanding. Christine had disappeared, maybe we'd disappear too.

We took a step toward the car. "Whoa," Jack said, pulling me against his chest. Something flew up at us from the ground.

"What was that?" I asked as I pressed my face against Jack's chest.

"A snipe," Jack replied.

"Ha, ha," I responded smiling into his shirt. "Your mom did tell me you had no sense of humor."

"I thought it was pretty funny and very quick." Jack said. "It was actually a pheasant, pretty city girl."

Jack stepped over a piece of wood that had rusty nails protruding from it, then lifted me over the board. "You look first, okay?" I said.

He didn't let go of my hand as he stepped up to the window of the car. Taking the bottom of his shirt, he cleaned off the grime covering the window. He placed his hand on the roof of the car and peered in the window. Jack stood for what seemed like an eternity. It was probably more like thirty seconds. "Ivy," Jack whispered, "Johnny's letterman's jacket is in the car."

Jack took hold of the door handle and pulled. Nothing happened. "It's not locked. It's just stuck," Jack said as he gave it another tug. "Stand back," he warned, letting go of my hand. He put one foot on the side of the car and used both hands. The door flew open and Jack fell on his butt, just missing the board with the nails sticking out.

I grabbed Jack's hand and pulled him to his feet. We looked in the car. "No body, thank God," I said.

"Look at this," Jack said in awe. "The keys are still in the ignition." Jack pulled the keys out then walked to the back of the car. "This was one sweet ride," Jack said. "Ivy, I'm checking the trunk."

I couldn't watch as Jack turned the key in the lock on the trunk. "You know," I said, "it would smell if there was a body, right?"

"Damn," Jack said. I rushed to the back of the car, expecting the worst. In the trunk was a couple of beers, a bunch of blankets, and a half-full bottle of wine.

"That—" Jack pointed to the stuff in the trunk.

"Is from the last night Johnny and Christine spent together," I finished his sentence.

"You remember?"

"I remember," I replied, smiling. No wonder Jack had hormone overdrive.

"Ivy," Jack said my name softly as he grabbed my waist, "we're here. We're alive." He pressed his lips to mine. I wrapped my arms around his neck. Jack lifted me up and I wrapped my legs around him then he carried me around to the side of the car. My mind was mush. Jack somehow opened the door, pushed the seat up and rolled us into the backseat of the Camaro. *Frantic. I feel frantic.* I started to pull Jack's shirt out of his jeans. Jack continued to kiss me as he started to pull off my top.

"God, Ivy," Jack said against my neck. We were lying kind of side by side in the backseat of the Camaro. Jack was staring into my eyes. He pushed his fingers through my hair. "I don't want to stop. Do you understand?"

I was so mixed up. I didn't want to stop either. "Jack, I'm so confused. I feel the same way."

"But," Jack said as he continued to gaze into my eyes, "you're not sure if the intensity is ours or theirs."

He'd nailed it. "Yeah," I said. "I want it to be about us, not about them."

Jack pulled me in tightly and took several deep breaths. "We have the rest of our lives, Ivy." He paused. "Let's try to solve our mystery."

"One more," I whispered.

"I'll always have one more for you." Jack leaned down and kissed me with passion and…well, love.

"Wow," I said, "I can't believe we are in the Camaro.

Crazy."

I scrambled up from Jack.

"Humph," he groaned.

"Oops, sorry," I replied. I think I accidently hit the family jewels.

Climbing into the front seat, I picked up the letterman jacket. My fingers tingled at the contact. I was surprised it was in such great shape. I placed the jacket on the driver's seat. "Oh my God," I said, "the box from my dream. It's right here, just where I dreamed it would be."

The box was still intact. I guess the closed car and the protection of the barn had kept the sun and stuff from causing the box to disintegrate. I handed it to Jack. "I can't open it," I said. "The last letter Christine got from Johnny is on top," I told him.

Jack lifted the lid of the box. "Ivy," Jack said softly, "the letter on top isn't from Johnny to Christine. It's from Johnny to his friend Bill."

"That can't be right," I muttered.

"The letter from Johnny to Christine is here too," Jack said.

"That's not right," I said again.

"Jack," I said. A feeling of panic was starting to set in. "We need to look around, outside, *now*, before the sun sets."

He covered the box then climbed out of the car from the backseat. I clasped the hand he held out to me to assist me out of the car.

We slid out of a narrow opening really close to the front of the car. When we stumbled outside, we faced a field that didn't have anything in it. "What would have grown here?" I asked.

"Corn or soybeans," Johnny replied. "In 1969 or 1970, it

probably would have been corn."

I started to sway…

*****

Summer, 1970

Run. You need to run faster, I told myself as I ran into the cornfield. Bill was either drunk or high. He'd accused me of being the reason Johnny hadn't gone to college. *It wasn't me.* Johnny told me he had to stay home and help his dad. It was not my fault he was drafted. It was not my fault Johnny was dead.

"Get back here, you bitch," Bill yelled. "I'm not done with you yet. Ask his dad. He didn't need to stay home. Johnny gave up an f'ing college football scholarship because of you. Christine, Christine, Christine… It was all you. You killed my best friend. You may not have held the gun that shot him, but you killed him."

His voice was getting louder. He was getting closer. A ravine was up ahead. If I could make the ravine, I could hide in the ditch. The sun was setting. He wouldn't be able to see me. I glanced behind me. My foot hit a root. I started to fall. Everything moved in slow motion…

*****

Present day

"Ivy, Ivy," Jack's voice was strong. It penetrated the haze that was my brain.

"She died here," I said with conviction. "Christine died here. She was running from Bill. He accused her of being the reason Johnny died." I paused, remembering what Jack's Uncle Joe said to him about Johnny's big lie. "Bill knew about the big lie. Christine blamed Johnny's dad, and Bill blamed Christine."

I looked at the barn, trying to figure out which way Christine ran. "This way," I said to Jack. It was getting dark. I pulled out my phone and turned on the flashlight app as we walked through the field toward a small grove of trees and bushes. I started to shake. It was hard to breathe. Jack held my hand tightly as we moved forward.

We walked through the trees. Directly below us was a ravine with a dried-up creek bed. "She fell around here," I said with certainty. Jack nodded in support. Then we started looking for something—anything that might help us discover what had happened to Christine.

I watched Jack as he scanned the ground with the flashlight from his phone. Jack didn't think I was crazy. He believed. He believed in us…past and present.

Chapter 26

Jack

"You aren't going to find her, at least not without diggin'." A deep voice came from the grove of trees.

I pushed Ivy behind me, attempting to keep her out of harm's way. I scanned the tree with the light from my phone, trying to determine the location of the voice. Ivy tugged on my arm, pointing to a man standing behind a tree.

"I tried to warn you. I told you to stay away from her, but you were just like him. You couldn't see past a pretty face." The voice sounded familiar.

"How'd ya warn me?" I asked.

"I left you notes on your windshield. You just ignored them—just like him. I told him to break up with her. I told him, but he ignored me, too." Now he sounded pissed. I didn't want him mad. "When I saw you that day at the football field—the day she knocked you over—I knew this was going to happen. You looked just like 'em. For a moment, I thought they'd come back to haunt me."

"Who?" I asked. "Who came back to haunt you?"

"Don't play with me, boy," he said. "Johnny and Christine. I know you know all about 'em. I don't know how, but I know you do."

It came together. I knew the voice. "Will, you were his best friend. Why did you hurt his girl?"

"That's right," Will replied. "I was his best friend. We were best friends since grade school, then she came along. Christine..." he said with a sneer. "He loved her above all others. He was willing to risk his life and die for her. She should've died for him, just like the words from 'Bad Moon

Rising'. I didn't kill her, though, 'cause—like you said—he wouldn't have wanted her dead."

Ivy was hugging me tightly. I reached back to give her a reassuring pat.

"What happened, Will? If you didn't kill her, why'd you have to bury her?" I asked in hopes of keeping him talking.

Will walked out from behind the trees. "No one would have believed me. They would have found me guilty, but I didn't kill her."

Will looked down at the ground, taking a deep breath before he continued. "It's time now. It's time to let her rest in peace. I've lived my life with this burden. If they find me guilty of murder, the time I have left to serve will be short."

Ivy stepped out from behind me. I tried to shove her back, but she grabbed my arm. I wrapped it around her, pulling her tightly against my side.

"I don't think you killed her. I think it was accident," Ivy said with sincerity. Was she bluffing? If she was, she was good.

"You showed up here the day of the funeral and found Christine. You were drunk. She ran from you and your accusations that she was the reason Johnny was drafted, the reason why Johnny was dead." Ivy paused, waiting for a response that didn't come. Ivy continued. "She ran to just about here." Ivy gestured to the area in front of our feet. "She tripped and fell down. What happened next?"

Will stared ahead. "I heard her scream, then nothing. Her scream sobered me up real quick. I ran through the trees. There she was, flat on her back. Her head was at an odd angle. And her eyes. Her eyes stared sightlessly into the sky. Christine's neck was broken. I didn't kill her, but it was my fault." Will's shoulders shook with emotion. "In Johnny's last letter to me, he asked me to take care of his girl. He trusted me with the one thing he loved above anything else, and I caused her death."

Will's shoulders continued to shake. Sobs racked his body. I didn't know what to do or to say. Ivy's soft voice floated toward Will. "Why did you ask the girls in Pella and the Amana Colonies to say they saw Christine? Why didn't you just tell the truth?"

"I told ya," Will said as he struggled to pull himself together. "They wouldn't have believed me. I didn't want people looking for her. If they thought she was gone, they'd stop looking. It seemed like an easy plan. They'd stop looking for Christine if they thought she'd run away. No body, no car, no worries."

"Where is she, Will? Where did you bury Christine's body?" I asked.

"The last letter I got from Johnny... I put it with his letters to her in the car. It seemed fitting for them all to be together." Will shook his head. "I didn't mean to hurt her. I should have protected her."

"Where is she, Will?" I asked again.

Will looked down at the ground on which Ivy and I were standing. "Oh my God," Ivy whispered, "we're standing on Christine." Ivy's whole body started to shake.

Suddenly, sirens screamed, cutting through the stillness of the night. The police would be here any moment. Ivy must have notified them with her phone. *Smart girl.* I like smart girls.

"Johnny, Christine," Will said, in an urgent voice that sounded way younger than he'd sounded a moment before, "we need to split. It's the fuzz."

"Will," I said, "we need to stay right here."

"Johnny, you know I hate it when you call me Will. Knock it off. Come on. Get some beat feet. We need to book."

Will looked around anxiously as he tried to get Ivy and me to move, only Will thought Ivy and I were Johnny and Christine.

"Christine, tell him to get going." Will moved quickly and grabbed Ivy by the arm.

"It's okay, Bill," Ivy said, holding her ground as Will tried to drag her along.

"Don't you get it?" Will sounded exasperated. "Coach is gonna go ape if we get caught out here. Tomorrow night's the Homecoming game. We can't be benched. Recruiters from all the top schools in Iowa are gonna be there to watch you play. Come on," he said again.

Flashlights were coming toward us. Newton's finest had arrived.

"It's okay," I said to Will, trying to keep him calm. "We won't be benched from the game."

"Hey, there," Chief Rhodes said as he cautiously approached us. The other officers must have turned off their flashlights because the only light illuminating the area was from the chief's flashlight.

"Will, you doing okay?" Chief Rhodes asked.

"I don't know you," Will said, staring intently at the chief. "You look like an older version of the new guy on the force. What was his name? Rhodes… That's right. His last name was Rhodes."

The Chief sent a questioning look in my direction. I shrugged. I wished I could convey my suspicion that Will was mentally back in the 1960s.

"Kids," the Chief said, looking at me and Ivy, "your folks are worried about you. You need to get in the truck and drive home. We'll see you at the Van den Berg house in an hour." We nodded in response.

Will started to walk with us. Chief Rhodes gently

grabbed his arm. "Will, you need to stay with us. We'll give you a ride into town."

I clasped Ivy's hand and we walked toward the trees. As soon as we'd passed them, I pulled her into my arms and kissed her. "Oh God," Ivy whispered against my chest, "I was so scared."

"I know, beautiful," I replied as we carefully walked through the field back toward the truck, using the flashlight app to guide us. "I was scared too. Mostly I was scared he would try to hurt you."

We got to my truck. Luckily it wasn't blocked in by the police cars. *Where were the police officers?* There were four cars, but we only saw Chief Rhodes.

I opened the door to the truck and boosted Ivy up onto the seat. She was staring out the front window when I climbed in behind her.

"I don't feel her anymore," Ivy said softly. "All the stuff I dreamed, all the flashbacks... They are still in my head. But, Christine... I think she's gone."

Do I still feel a connection to Johnny? I sat perfectly still, trying to connect with a piece of me that had been part of me for most of my life. "It's strange," I replied. "I don't think he's in me either. Come here," I whispered as I wrapped my arms around Ivy and pressed my lips to hers. It was still there— the urgency and the love. Her lips molded to mine and she sighed into the kiss. The kiss changed from sweet to passionate. I had her on her back on the front seat of my truck before my mind registered my intent. It was so intense, maybe even more intense because it was about me and Ivy. I wanted her so badly. I didn't want to stop.

"Ivy," I mumbled, "I want you so bad, beautiful. I need you so bad." I pressed her down, waiting for her to tell me to stop.

Instead of stopping me, she slipped her hands under my shirt, trying to draw me closer.

Bam, bam, bam. Someone was pounding on the side of the truck.

"Damn," I said to Ivy, trying not to groan as I sat up in the seat. I tugged down her shirt and pulled her up next to me.

"How many police officers?" Ivy asked. "Please tell me it is only one, and it's not Chief Rhodes."

I didn't reply for a moment.

"Ja-a-*ck*," Ivy said.

"Remember, Ivy," I said as I pulled her into my arms, "I promised I wouldn't prevaricate."

"It's the entire force, isn't it?"

"Well, I wouldn't say it's the entire force," I replied with a smile.

I rolled down my window, "Sorry, Officers," I said. "Ivy and I got a little carried away."

"Jeez, Jack," Ivy whispered, "filter."

"As long as you're still here, Chief Rhodes has a few questions before you guys head home. The Chief sent Will with another officer to the station. What was he doing out here anyway? He keeps calling you guys Johnny and Christine, and he's talking like he's living in the '60s? What you guys were doing"—he shrugged—"that's pretty obvious. Ivy, by the way, good job with the phone. The 9-1-1 dispatchers were able to find you guys without a hitch."

"Where's the chief?"" I asked as I opened the door, jumped out, and pulled Ivy with me. "We'd be happy to answer a few questions."

"What?" she asked.

"They don't know about Christine or the Camaro. They

came because you called 9-1-1."

"Oh," Ivy replied.

"Here he comes," the officer said, pointing toward Chief Rhodes, who was walking in our direction."

"Glad you're still here," the chief said as he joined us.

"Chief," I said. "Remember the night we were at the Van den Bergs' house and you mentioned how the night reminded them and you of the nights and days following their daughter's disappearance?"

Chief Rhodes nodded. "So? What about it?"

"Ivy and I started investigating it. We discovered a whole bunch of clues that led us here, to the barn over there." I gestured to the barn that was barely visible in the dark.

"Christine was driving a Camaro, the Camaro that belonged to her boyfriend Johnny, the day she disappeared," Ivy continued. "The Camaro is in the barn."

Chief Rhodes said nothing for a few moments. "You're shittin' me," he said. Ivy and I shook our heads. No, we definitely weren't.

"Boys," he called to the officers standing by their cars, "I need a couple of you guys to go check out that barn." He gestured to the barn in the distance.

"Chief," Ivy said softly, "Christine's body is buried in the ravine where you found us, just about where we were standing."

"Well, how in the hell do you know that?" he said in kinda stunned disbelief.

"Will... He told us," Ivy replied. "It was an accident. Christine fell down the hill. When Bill—I mean Will—found her, her neck was broken, apparently from the fall."

He took off his hat and rubbed his head. "Well, I'll be damned. After all these years, the mystery has been solved.

Your grandfather and grandmother will finally have their answers."

"Chief, Chief." One of the officers hollered from the barn. "You're never going to believe this. There's a 1969 Camaro in mint condition in the barn. It's a little dirty, but, man, she's a thing of beauty."

"I need to call Homicide." Chief Rhodes still seemed to be stunned as he went to his patrol car.

I wrapped my arm tightly around Ivy's shoulders and pulled her close. We stood in silence, waiting to see what would happen next.

"Team," he called to his officers, "get out the big lights and grab your shovels. There's a body in the ravine."

The police went into action. Crime scene tape went up over the debris separating the area from the road. Chief Rhodes called Ivy's grandparents and told them to meet him here, at the scene.

"I wonder if my grandparents are going to be okay," Ivy said softly, wrapping her arms tightly around my waist. "I mean, I thought they would want closure, but maybe they like thinking she's alive somewhere."

"Okay, the papers were in the car," one of the officers said to Chief Rhodes. "The car belonged to Johnny Ridder. You think he's related to Joe Ridder? That would make sense, as this land belongs to the Ridder family."

"Johnny Ridder was Joe Ridder's little brother. Johnny Ridder died in Vietnam," I said to the officers.

"Call Joe Ridder," Chief Rhodes told the guy holding the papers. "We can have Joe identify the car."

"Johnny and Christine," Chief Rhodes said. "That's what Will was calling you two. I think he might have had some kinda mental breakdown."

"Wait here," I said to Ivy. I opened the truck and grabbed my jacket.

"Here you go, Ivy," I said as I wrapped the jacket around her shoulders.

"Thanks," she replied with a smile.

We stood around for about fifteen minutes, waiting, at the request of Chief Rhodes. Several cars turned onto the dirt road and came to an abrupt stop at the crime scene line. The cars belonged to Ivy's mom and grandparents, my mom and Stan, and Uncle Joe.

Chaos erupted as our parents verified that we were okay. Mr and Mrs Van den Berg stood with heads bowed, listening to Chief Rhodes. Mr Van den Berg wrapped his arm around his wife as she collapsed into his side.

"Mom," Ivy whispered, "we found Aunt Christine."

Mrs Drake looked around at the scene. Crime tape across the road, several police cars with their red lights blinking and large searchlights out in the field. She pulled Ivy to her tightly and didn't say anything.

"Jack," Mom asked, "are you okay?"

I nodded in affirmation. I walked over to Stan and whispered, "We need to have that talk soon, or I will be going in blind."

Mom must have heard me because she whispered, "Abstinence makes the heart grow fonder."

I watched silently as Ivy and her mom joined Mr and Mrs Van den Berg. They wrapped their arms around each other and waited.

After what felt like eternity, Ivy broke away and ran to my side. "Can you take me home now?"

"Sure, beautiful," I said as pushed some of her hair behind her ear. I helped Ivy into the truck then jogged over to

Chief Rhodes. "Ivy and I have to get up for school tomorrow. Is it okay if we go?"

"Go ahead, Jack," Chief Rhodes replied. "I'm looking forward to watching you play tomorrow night. I heard scouts from the Iowa, Iowa State, and UNI are going to be at the game. You get a good night's sleep so you can impress the shit out of 'em. We'll catch up with you and Ivy on Monday at the station. I know we're going to have a few questions."

"Thanks," I said as I walked backward and waved. "Mom," I said, "I'm taking Ivy home. I'll be at the house soon. I need to get to bed."

Ivy was leaning her head back against the seat with her eyes closed. When she heard the door open, she smiled. I draped my arm over her shoulders then backed the truck onto the highway. We rode in comfortable silence as we drove to her house.

I turned the truck into the driveway. The house was dark except for one light.

"That's weird," Ivy said. "The light is on in Christine's room." Ivy looked at me. "Can you come in for a little? I just want to make sure everything is okay."

We walked in the house and up the stairs. The door to Christine's room was open and the bedroom light was on. A note was propped on the mirror. Ivy picked up the note and read it.

"It says, 'thank you'." I looked at Ivy, and she shook her head.

"Do you believe in ghosts, Jack Vander Zee?" A reply did not seem necessary.

"You're welcome," Ivy whispered as she looked around the room, turned off the light, then closed the door.

We walked down the stairs together. I had her hand

clasped in mine. "We did it. We really did it." Ivy looked up at me, smiling.

"Yeah, and you, my pretty city girl, were intrepid. Together we were anything but prosaic. We were really quite astounding. And even though Will—or shall we call him Bill?—was perfidious, it appears he will be vindicated."

Ivy tugged me into the sitting room. "I thought you needed to go home," she said as she pushed me onto the recliner. She straddled my hips and pressed her body to mine, "Jack," she whispered in my ear. "You've beguiled me with your logomania."

I smiled as I pulled her head down to kiss her. My phone vibrated. I pulled it out of my pocket. *Home* was the message on the text. "I gotta go," I said as I stood up, holding Ivy in my arms. She wrapped her legs around me as I walked to the door.

"One more," she whispered against my lips.

I kissed her again. "I love you, Ivy." She slid her legs down my body so she was standing at the door.

"I love you too, Jack," Ivy replied as she leaned against the wall. "I'll see you tomorrow."

Chapter 27

Ivy

"Ivy, are you ready?" Mom called from the hallway.

I studied myself in the mirror. I was as ready as I'd ever be, I decided, as I put on a little more lip gloss. My short black dress was definitely more of a cocktail dress than a traditional Homecoming dress. I really wished I would have discussed what to wear with Bri. *Oh well, Jack will like me in this dress.* It made me look curvy. Jack liked my curves.

I held up my phone and made a pouty face in my selfie. *Where are you?* was my message to Jack.

"Ivy, Jack's here," Mom called again. *That answer's that.* I grabbed my wristlet from the bed.

My heels were super high, so I held on to the rail to make my descent presentable. Jack was standing at the bottom of the stairs looking so handsome in black dress pants, a blue shirt, and black tie. The blue of the shirt made his eyes even bluer. He smiled at me and my heart raced.

"Hi," I said.

Jack continued to stare. "You leave me speechless."

"You leave me breathless," I replied. He smiled broader.

"Okay," Mom said, "it's picture time."

We took a bunch of pictures on my phone, my mom's phone, and Jack's phone. I sent one to the girls in St. Louis and Jack sent a bunch to his mom.

"Grandma and Grandpa are sorry they aren't here to see you off. They've been at the police station, the funeral home, and the cemetery. They were petitioning to place Christine's headstone next to Johnny's in the plot reserved for members of the military and their spouses. The Ridder family agreed. The story's gotten so much press that I guess the cemetery board will probably allow it." Mom finished the update then looked kind of upset. "I did not mean to ruin your special night with details about the funeral. I have to say that closure has made my mom and dad seem ten years younger. What you guys did was pretty remarkable."

If she only knew.

Jack walked me out to the car. I was surprised to see a black Mercedes instead of his truck.

"Uncle Joe let me borrow it," he said as he escorted me to the passenger side, then held my hand as I sat down on the low seat. I tried to remember *Seventeen's* advice on getting into a car with a short skirt and high heels. I put my legs together then swung both legs in.

"You are so sexy," Jack said, more to himself than to me.

Thank you, Seventeen.

The stick shift separated the two seats. "They called these 'birth control seats' in the 1960s," Jack said. "Maybe the peeps back then thought the back seat was too small." We both chuckled. They were so wrong. "Speaking of small back seats, I'm gonna work with Uncle Joe on fixing up the Camaro. I think I remind him of his brother."

"I'm sure you do," Ivy said softly. "But, you? You're all Jack."

The school parking lot was empty. We were the first ones at the school because Jack was the deejay.

"Wait," Jack said as he got out of the car, came over to my side, then opened the door. "My lady," he said, extending his hand to assist me. I remembered to swing my legs a la *Seventeen* and allowed Jack to bring me to my feet.

"I love that you're wearing my ring," he said as he

clasped it in his fingers. He leaned down and gave me a quick kiss. "If we start, I'm gonna see if the back seats of a Mercedes are as comfortable as the back seat of a Camaro, then we'd miss our first dance."

We walked into the gym foyer and stopped in front of the case that held the photos of Johnny Ridder and Christine Van den Berg. The photos now had a position of honor at the front of the case. In Loving Memory was posted on a sign below the photos. Each one also had a paragraph with information about their contributions to Newton High and Johnny's service during the Vietnam War. "That's really nice," I said to Jack with a catch in my voice.

Jack clasped my hand and led me into the gym. The Homecoming committee had done an incredible job transforming the gym into a tropical paradise.

"Wow, it's really pretty."

"Uh huh," Jack said, nodding his head. He was looking at me, not the decorations.

"Come on, pretty city girl. I gotta check out my equipment."

I sat down next to the deejay table while Jack tested it. "What do you think's going to happen to Will?"

"I don't know," Jack replied as he dug through his stack of albums. He had CDs and albums and some music on his phone. "I think he is going to the hospital first. He still thinks it's 1969. I feel sorry for the guy."

"Me too," I replied. "I really believe it was an accident. The last flashback I had was of Christine tripping and falling into a ravine."

"Okay, I'm doing a Flashback Jack recording from here. I want you to be my background," Jack pulled out a chair near where he was standing.

Jack put up the camera and started talking.

"This is Flashback Jack, and tonight's special edition is being filmed on location at my Homecoming dance. Tonight's show is dedicated to the men who served at the Battle of Fire Support Base Ripcord from March 12th through July 23rd of 1970. During the same time in 1970, the turmoil in the States overshadowed the sacrifice and dedication of our American soldiers in Vietnam. The soldiers at Fire Support Base Ripcord fought for twenty-three days in one of the bloodiest and least-known battles in Vietnam. During the twenty-three-day siege, seventy-five Americans lost their lives. For those who made it home without a homecoming and for those who did not come home, the first song of our Homecoming is dedicated to you and your brotherhood that fought to save the man on your left and the man on your right. The Hollies, 'He Ain't Heavy, He's My Brother', Currahee!"

The song played as Jack continued to set up for the dance. When the song ended, Jack said, "To those who serve, we salute you. This is Flashback Jack, and I'll see you on the flipside."

"Yay." I clapped my hands in appreciation of Flashback Jack. "What's currahee?"

"I was wondering if I should explain it to my audience. Then I decided it sounded way cooler to just end with it. Those who need to know will know and, if they don't, they can look it up."

"Jack, I need to know."

He grinned emphasizing his incredible dimples. "Currahee is the motto of the 2nd Battalion, 506th Infantry Division of the 101st Airborne, Johnny's division. It's a Cherokee word that people believe means *stand alone*. The Stand Alone Battalion."

"Maybe you can add a message on the channel page. It's interesting."

Jack nodded as he put another album on the turntable. He extended his hand and asked, "May I have this dance?"

"Of course," I replied, taking his hand in mine. We were the only two people in the gym. "This Guy's in Love with You" poured out of the speakers.

One of Jack's hands was on my waist and the other had clasped my hand, holding it close to his heart. "You know, Ivy," Jack said as he spun around on the empty dance floor, "Christine and Johnny may have brought us together, but it's up to us to stay that way. I just wanted you to know that I'm all in."

"All in, Jack?" I asked with a grin.

"You know me, Ivy," Jack replied grinning back at me. "I don't prevaricate, *ever*." He kissed me gently as he spun us around the floor. The song came to an end and so did Jack's kiss.

I pulled Jack's head back down to mine and whispered, "One more."

Epilogue

Jack—Five years later

The buzzer blasted and the crowd went crazy. We were the victors in the final Iowa vs Iowa State game of my football career. Trey and Collin jumped on my back, nearly knocking me to the ground.

"We did it, man," Trey shouted, knocking his palm to my helmet.

Collin added, "We demonstrated some badass football skills today."

"Badass," I agreed, pounding Collin on the pads.

I shook hands with a couple of guys on the opposing team. "Good game. Nice job," I said, though I wasn't really thinking about what I was saying. I was thinking about my big plan.

A reporter from the local news station stuck a microphone in my face. "Jack, how would you characterize tonight's victory?" he asked.

"It was a great night for football. We just really came together as a team and pulled out a big win," I replied, pretty much saying what I'd said after every victory since I'd become team captain two years before.

"Tonight's your final regular season game in this uniform," he said, kind of patting me on the back. "What's next for Jack Vander Zee?"

I glanced at the JumboTron. I needed to stall for about thirty more seconds. "I hope to trade this uniform for the uniform of a Navy SEAL."

"So, you're not considering the NFL?"

"No, sir," I replied, trying not to appear rude as I

glanced at the JumboTron again.

"What are you going to say to your teammates in the locker room tonight, after this, the last game of your regular season?" the reporter asked.

I didn't reply. I gestured to the reporter to look at the JumboTron. My previously recorded message was about to play.

"Hey," the reporter said as he gestured at the screen, "isn't that you?"

I nodded in response as I looked at me on the big screen. Would anyone recognize the uniform was vintage 1969?

"This is Flashback Jack with a special edition of *Flashback 1969*. For those of you who don't know me as Flashback Jack, you may know me as Jack Vander Zee, number sixty-nine. I need the camera crew to focus on one of our fine cheerleaders, Ivy Drake."

I watched as the camera crew scanned the line of cheerleaders. The rest of the squad pushed Ivy forward, and she kinda waved at the crowd. Then my pre-recorded show was back on the screen. I was gonna owe the camera crew and the guys in the announcers' box big time.

"Ivy, five years ago I asked you to go steady on a special edition of *Flashback 1969*. The past five years can be summarized by a classic from 1969, a *Billboard* Top 100 tune from Blood, Sweat and Tears, 'You've Made Me So Very Happy'. Tonight, I want to know if you'll go steady for good. Ivy Drake, will you marry me?"

The crowd went wild—nothing like a big show. "You've Made Me So Very Happy" blared across the stadium. I looked at the sports broadcaster and grinned. "Tonight, in the locker room, I'm gonna invite my teammates to my wedding."

As I jogged down the field toward Ivy, the team

manager caught up with me to hand me the box holding Ivy's ring. He gave me a pat on the shoulder—for luck, I guess.

Ivy was standing next to the sideline; she was the most beautiful real-life person I'd ever seen. I dropped to one knee and clasped her hand. "Ivy Drake, will you be my steady for good? Will you be my wife?"

She smiled down at me as tears streamed down her cheeks. She nodded her head then threw her arms around me with so much force that we tumbled to the turf.

"It's very fortuitous I was here to keep you from hitting the ground," I said as I looked into the eyes of the girl of my dreams.

"Fortuitous indeed," she said with a smile.

I reached up, pulled her head down to mine, then kissed her. It was phantasmagorical.

The End

9

About the Author

Liz Costanzo is the author of contemporary/historical young adult fiction featuring "R and R"—"Romance and Reincarnation". Morrison's work is classified as young adult; however, her novels appeal to anyone who loves history, mystery, and romance.

In addition to being a writer, Costanzo is a National Board Certified Social Studies Teacher, a NCSS National History Teacher of the Year, and a former flight attendant for Trans World Airlines. Morrison combines her passion for history and her world travels to create memorable characters and settings, both past and present.

Liz earned her BS from the University of Iowa and her MA Ed from the University of Missouri-Columbia. Liz Costanzo lives in St. Louis, Missouri.

Website:
http://www.lizcostanzoauthor.com/

Facebook:
https://www.facebook.com/lizcostanzoauthor/

Twitter:
@lizwriteon

Instagram:
lizwriteon

Email:
Lizcostanzo2016@gmail.com

Titles by Liz Costanzo

Available from **Fireborn Publishing**:

UNTIL NEXT TIME
The Second Chance
Flashback

Author's Acknowledgements

Historical fiction combines research and fiction. *Flashback* builds on numerous historic and contemporary resources to ensure the story is historically accurate and an interesting read. The following resources were utilized to ensure the historical accuracy and contemporary realism of *Flashback*.

- 101st CAB Prove Valor at Firebase Ripcord – US Army
- 4 Kent State Students Killed by Troops – New York Times
- After Action Report: Firebase Ripcord, 23 July 1970 – Wikisource
- Amana Colonies Official Visitor Website
- 'American Top 40' Flashback: July 4, 1970 – Billboard Articles
- Camaro Research Group
- Campus Life: Grinnell; Class That Missed A Commencement Returns to Campus – New York Times
- Cemetery Superintendent, Parks & City Grounds, City of Newton – Jim Kling
- The Draft Lottery, Dec. 1, 1969 – CBS News Special Report YouTube
- The Famous Boxer Rocky Marciano Was Killed Today In a Plane Crash – Aviation News Online Magazine
- FSB Ripcord Association – Facts About the Battle of Firebase Ripcord
- Incident on Chappaquiddick Island – July 18, 1969, This Day in History
- July 21, 1970: Bob Kalsu killed in Vietnam – Buffalo Rumblings
- Newton, Iowa – Official Website
- Newtonian 1969 – Newton Yearbook borrowed from Kathy Allen Stevens
- Pella, Iowa – Official Website
- The Siege of Firebase Ripcord: War Stories with Oliver North – Fox News
- Student Protests of the 1970s – The University of Iowa

Libraries

- Summer of 1969 – CNN
- Trials and Tribulations – VEISHEA: Iowa State's Right of Spring
- Top 100 Songs – Billboard Chart 1969
- The Vietnam Lotteries – Selective Service
- Vietnam War: Siege of Fire Support Base Ripcord 1970 – YouTube

Trademarks Acknowledgement

The author acknowledges the trademarked status and trademark owners of the following wordmarks mentioned in this work of fiction:

60 Minutes: CBS Broadcasting Inc.
Abbey Road: produced by George Martin for Apple records, The Beatles artists
Ackerman's Concord Grape Wine: Ackerman's Winery, Inc.
American Top 40: Premiere Radio Networks, Inc.
Bad Moon Rising: written by John Fogerty
Billboard: Billboard Holding IP, LLC
Buffalo Bills: Buffalo Bills LLC
Build Me Up Buttercup: written by Mike d'Abo and Tony Macaulay
Buzz Aldrin: Buzz Aldrin Enterprises, Inc.
Camaro: General Motors LLC
CBS News: CBS Broadcasting Inc.
Coke: The Coca-Cola Company Corporation
Des Moines Area Community College / DMACC: Des Moines Area Community College non-profit corporation
Des Moines Register: Des Moines Register and Tribune Company Corporation
Dizzy: written by Tommy Roe and Freddy Weller
Easy Rider: Columbia Pictures
Elvis Presley: ABG EPE IP LLC
Everybody's Talkin': written by Fred Neil
Facetime: Apple Inc.
Ford: Ford Motor Company
Fortunate Son: written by John Fogerty
Google: Google Inc.
Harold and the Purple Crayon: written by Crockett Johnson
He Ain't Heavy, He's My Brother: written by Bobby Scott and Bob Russell
Helter Skelter: written by Vincent Bugliosi and Curt Gentry
Huey: Textron Innovations Inc.
Hy-Vee: Hy-Vee, Inc.
I'd Wait a Million Years: written by Gary Zekley and Mitchell

Bottler
Iowa State University: Iowa State University of Science and Technology
It's Getting Better: written by Barry Mann and Cynthia Weil
Jack & Diane: written by John Mellencamp
Jujubes: Ferrara Candy Company
JumboTron: Sony Corporation
Kent State: Kent State University Instrumentality of the State of Ohio
Leaving on a Jet Plane: written by John Denver
Led Zeppelin: Superhype Tapes Limited
Letters from Home: written by Tony Lane and David Lee
M60: SACO Defense and U.S. Ordnance
Maid-Rite: Maid-Rite Corporation
Make It With You: written by David Gates
Mayberry R.F.D.: Warner Bros. Television Distribution
McDonald's: McDonald's Corporation
Mercedes: Daimler AG Corporation
Midnight Cowboy: United Artists
Millstream Brewing Company: owned by Chris Priebe, Tom and Teresa Albert
NASCAR: National Association for Stock Car Racing, Inc.
Newton Daily News: Shaw Newspapers
NFL: NFL Properties LLC
Ohio: written by Neil Young
Ox Yoke Inn: Ox Yoke Inn, Inc.
Polaroid / Polaroid Swinger: PLR IP Holdings LLC
Pomp and Circumstance: written by Sir Edward Elgar
Rowan & Martin's Laugh-In: SFM Entertainment
SEAL: Department of the Navy
Seventeen: Hearst Communications, Inc.
Small Town: written by John Mellencamp
Sprite: The Coca-Cola Company Corporation
Sugar, Sugar: written by Jeff Barry and Andy Kim
Taps: arranged by Daniel Butterfield (General)
The Archie Comedy Hour: Filmation
The Archies: Archie Comic Publications, Inc. / Kirshner Records
The Beach Boys: Brother Records, Inc.

The Beatles: Apple Corps Limited
The Exorcist: Warner Bros. Entertainment, Inc.
The Hunger Games: Lionsgate Films
The Mamas & the Papas: Denny Doherty Productions, Inc.;
Owen Elliot-Kugell, Individual, US; Michelle Phillips,
Individual, US; The John E.A. Phillips Trust Robert T. Tucker,
US citizen
The Monkees: Rhino Entertainment Company
Thing 1 Thing 2: Dr. Seuss Enterprises, L.P. Geisel-Seuss
Enterprises, Inc.
This Guy's in Love With You: written by Burt Bacharach and
Hal David
Three Dog Night: Three Dog Night Blue Water Music Inc. and
Hutton Music, Inc.
Twitter: Twitter, Inc.
University of Iowa: University of Iowa *(Iowa City, IA)*
University of Northern Iowa: University of Iowa State Agency
Iowa *(Cedar Falls, IA)*
Valle Drive-In: Valle Drive-In
Vineyard Vines: Vineyard Vines, LLC
Walmart: Wal-Mart Stores, Inc.
Wikipedia: Wikimedia Foundation, Inc.
Woodstock: Woodstock Ventures L.C.
YouTube: Google Inc.
You've Made Me So Very Happy: written by Brenda Holloway,
Patrice Holloway, Frank Wilson, and Berry Gordy